THE LITTLE GIRL WITH A SECRET

A Psychological Thriller

C.G. TWILES

Chapter One

"This isn't what you're thinking."

These were her fiancé's first words to her. Interesting. Because what Syra was *thinking* is that her fiancé was having sex with her best friend. After all, the pair of them were currently naked in the bed that she and her fiancé shared.

The whole scene was so shocking, so something-out-of-a-movie, that Syra stood in the doorway with her mouth wide open. Her brain, on the verge of exploding, clicked into something that could be described as calm. If it hadn't... she knew something violent would happen. She'd snatch up that small lamp sitting on the nearby dresser. The lamp was about two feet high and had the perfect base for cracking over someone's head. She could crack one of their skulls, then the other.

It would be him first, no doubt about that. Then her. But Syra would get them both. It wouldn't be a fooling around crack, either.

Her hand still gripped the doorknob. She'd known

something was strange, because why would the bedroom door be closed? Her mouth was still wide open. She could only imagine what she looked like—and, actually, she didn't need to imagine because her eyes flicked to the mirror over the headboard. She kept meaning to move the mirror, because when she and Sam made love, it would rattle against the wall. Had it rattled for him and Catrina? It must have.

While she'd imagined that she looked like the oval-mouthed, hands-on-cheeks shock-emoji, the mirror's surface reflected back a much more mundane image. As if she hadn't just stumbled into the most grotesque scene of her life. The mirror showed her looking as if she was casting around for something she needed—her cell phone, say, or her slippers.

Sure, maybe she was a bit paler than usual. Maybe her black curls were a bit more out of control. Maybe her dark hazel eyes were glassy. Her mouth wasn't even hanging open as she'd felt certain it was. Perhaps, at some point, she'd closed it.

Sam, the man she was going to marry. Catrina, her best friend.

They didn't even *like* each other.

Sam scrambled to the edge of the bed, his hands up in a *relax* gesture, the same gesture he used in arguments to get Syra to stop spewing words. Catrina sat in the bed, breasts exposed, looking as if she didn't know how she found herself in this predicament. Syra noted that Catrina's breasts were long and heavy, with dark brown areolas.

The betrayal was made worse by knowing what her

best friend's boobs looked like, and that the vision of them would be seared into her memory. Really something she could have done without. Thank god the sheet was wrapped around Catrina's hips so Syra didn't have to see what was between her legs.

"She was upset…" Sam stammered. "Crying… I was trying to… console…"

"It was James," Catrina whined. "I checked his texts. I came over to wait for you… then we drank…"

"It's not…" Sam went on. "We didn't…"

"No…" Catrina added. "It wasn't… not like… it wasn't like…"

Syra closed the door and walked back into the living room. Not speaking would have more impact than anything she could think to say.

Just before she left, she removed her engagement ring and plunked it on an end table.

Chapter Two

*O*utside, Syra wandered aimlessly, stepping into the street before the light turned and getting honked at by irritated drivers. She kept walking and walking, with no idea where she was going. The thing she'd witnessed took up her brain space to the extent that she could make no decisions, not even about where to walk. She barely processed that her phone, somewhere inside of her tote bag, was ringing and ringing…

A small portion of her mental faculties returned, and she recognized Catrina's neighborhood. Veering onto a familiar tree-lined street, she walked until she reached a prewar limestone building.

She numbly took her keychain out of a pocket on her tote bag and laboriously hiked up four steep floors. She had Catrina's key for emergencies, as Catrina had hers.

She had no idea if Catrina was here, if she'd wandered long enough to give her (former) best friend time to get dressed, hop on the subway, and return home. But Catrina would be back at her apartment with Sam, soaking up all the drama. Saying things like *What have we done?* while furtively reveling in the excitement of it all.

How many times had Syra seen her friend recount some travail of a mutual acquaintance, eyes sparkling excitedly with the recounting of someone who'd been fired, or who'd had a breakup, or who could no longer tough out the city and had moved to the middle of nowhere.

She couldn't hack it, Catrina would say, self-importantly, shaking her blonde head. *She broke her lease and moved back to Iowa. Can you imagine?*

Sam. He'd be sitting silently, broodingly. Probably still naked. He could be lazy like that, sometimes not dressing for a full day. He'd be hunched over in that ratty futon that their late cat had left claw marks all over. His dick would be hanging low between his hairy thighs, his finger hitting Syra's number over and over.

Or perhaps it was Catrina calling. Syra still wouldn't look at her phone, not even to turn it off. She feared the temptation to answer would be too great. Once she answered and said *You fucker* or *You goddamn whore* (the slurs were interchangeable as far as she was concerned), or she whimpered *How could you do this to me?* then they had the power.

If she didn't speak to them, *she* had the power.

Passing a garbage can—not the stinky, overflowing wire ones of her less affluent neighborhood, buzzing with wasps and picked at by pigeons, but the fat, clean, tall lidded ones provided to Catrina's brownstone-flanked neighborhood—Syra wrapped her palm around her phone.

Before she was conscious of what she was doing, she'd dropped the phone inside the receptacle. The horrid pair of them were now where they belonged: in the trash. Then she registered that a chain locked the lid to the base. She wouldn't be able to retrieve whatever she'd put inside—which, in this case, was her cell phone.

The reality of what she'd done hit her.

You could have changed your number, moron!

But no. She didn't have the brain power to do anything. Certainly not to find her cell provider's nearest store (who *was* her cell provider?), then sit there for an hour or more, answering a dozen questions: ID, password, social security number. She wouldn't be able to answer the secret questions they would ask her. What *was* the first concert she'd ever attended? What *was* the model of her first car? She knew none of it, didn't know her own history.

You could have blocked them. BLOCKED THEM. So easy, just hit the "Block this caller" option. How had that completely slipped her mind?

This was shock, she realized. What do they call it? *Shellshock.*

You're in shellshock, a doctor would have said if this was a television show. She didn't know shellshock was for stuff like this—betrayals of the heart. She'd thought it was only for soldiers who had a hand grenade tossed at them. She had the sudden need to get off the street because this thick mental fog meant she was a danger to herself or others.

Opening Catrina's apartment door, Buster, a saucer-eyed pug of indeterminate age, wiggled over to her, soft folds of fur rippling.

Syra often took him for walks when Catrina was working late (Working late! *Now* she knew what they were *really* doing while Syra made dinner for Sam or walked Catrina's fucking dog), so Buster bobbed up and down in anticipation. She clipped on his leash and grabbed his plush carrier from the top of the shoe rack behind Catrina's front door, where she knew the carrier was kept.

Syra knew where nearly everything in the apartment was kept, as she'd been over here hundreds, maybe thousands, of times. By herself. Then with Sam.

Sam. Whom Catrina didn't even *like*.

You could do better, that's all I'm saying.

Sure. Now she knew why Catrina periodically informed her that *she could do better*.

Syra walked out the door with Buster at the end of the leash, the soft carrier slung over her shoulder. She didn't bother to lock the door and wasn't even sure she'd closed it.

On the sidewalk, she looked around, at a loss. Which way was the subway? She'd have to buy a card as she'd dumped her phone into the trash. Why had she done that? How was she supposed to call a car? Did she have her wallet? Did she have money?

Suddenly, there was a sickening, inescapable surge in her gut. She crouched down by Buster and vomited onto the sidewalk, one palm digging into the dirty, scratchy pavement, the other clutching his leash.

Chapter Three

*I*t was a woman who stopped to help her. Of course. Men generally only stopped to help if you were looking attractive and they thought there was something they could get out of it.

The woman was about her age but had a child with her. The child looked to be five or six, on a kick scooter, her big eyes staring up from under her helmet as her mother said things like, "Can I walk you somewhere? Should I call 911?"

In the end, the woman called a car service and stood with Syra until it showed up a few minutes later. Syra confirmed that the driver would allow Buster (in his carrier) to accompany her. She pressed a twenty-dollar bill into the woman's hands because the woman didn't want to take it.

The woman said that she hoped Syra would realize she was better off without them. Syra didn't remember telling the woman about Sam and Catrina, so it came as a surprise that the woman seemed to know about them.

The helmeted child smiled shyly and said "Mommy?" in a bewildered fashion. Syra wondered if the girl understood what Syra was talking about—if the little girl understood *infidelity*. Had Syra just unwittingly introduced her to this concept?

In the backseat of the car, Syra stared at Catrina's passing neighborhood and thought, *How could they have done this to me—both of them? Both.*

Not one of them, at the moment, had the determination to say, *Let's not do this to Syra. We love her. She loves us. Or, if we're going to do this, let's at least not do it in her bed, where she might come home from work early because the internet was down at her office. Let's not do it on the day we're all supposed to leave on a long weekend trip that she'd planned for us. Let's do it some other time, like never.*

At Penn Station, she waited at the train ticket window, something she hadn't done in ages because she always bought her tickets online. But now, of course, she had no phone, and she didn't know if Buster could get on the train.

Told by the woman at the window that the dog could get on the train so long as he stayed in his carrier, Syra was charged an extra thirty-five dollars. She had to return to the window twice to ask the gate number because it kept slipping right out of her head.

The realization that she was like a helpless infant without her phone began to sink in. How much of our lives are contained in that thin, little piece of technology. But Syra remembered the rental home's address because it was one of those easy-to-remember, quaint addresses.

10 Scenic Way.

Even in her shellshock, she couldn't forget that. The simplicity, the obviousness of the street name is partly what had drawn her to the home. And the name of the home itself: The Hansel and Gretel House. Even if she'd forgotten the address, she probably would find someone who knew the house thanks to its quaint name.

She was betting there'd be taxis at the train station. If there weren't, she'd find a kind stranger (there were bound to be more of them in the country than in Brooklyn, and hadn't she found one in Brooklyn?) who would call her a cab.

She'd tell the driver, 10 Scenic Way. The Hansel and Gretel House.

Staring out the train window, she watched as the graffiti-scarred tunnels, smoke stacks, power stations, and steel grids of the city gave way to the yellow-toned tract homes of suburbia, then to endless rows of bushy pines and tangles of green, green, so much green.

Finally, the train moved into vistas so unlike anything she'd seen before. Long, wide, open space. Green and gold rolling out endlessly.

The brilliant palette began to penetrate her shellshock. The long stalks of emerald-green corn, the plains of yellow-gold wheat, the silver silos, large red and white barns—it all reached in, like a fist, and gave her insides a jolt. A jolt of excitement.

And something like fear.

Chapter Four

*F*or several moments, she remembered none of it, and life was fine. Then it trickled in, behind the reddish hues of her closed eyelids, tones growing brighter as sunrise seeped into the room.

Then all at once, she remembered. Sam and Catrina. In bed together.

A wail of anguish escaped from her mouth. She was overwhelmed with emotional pain of the magnitude she'd never experienced and wasn't sure she could survive.

Then there was an insistent, small-sounding *arf arf arf*. She remembered that she'd stolen Buster, Catrina's dog. The strange, agonized, not-her-at-all sounds coming from her must be upsetting him. She stuffed one palm over her mouth, her cheek squished into pillows she didn't recognize.

This went on until she was able to drag down enough deep breaths that the wailing subsided. She peeled open her eyes and woozily sat up, looking for

Buster, her head raw with a wine hangover. The pug stood at the side of the bed, hopping frantically, unable to get his eggroll body up on the bed, apparently worried for her. Or no. He probably had to pee.

Syra had no idea what time it was, but felt it must be early morning. She pulled on the clothes she'd arrived in —black yoga leggings and a ribbed, royal blue cotton t-shirt—and staggered out of the bedroom, trying to remember where she'd placed Buster's leash. Why hadn't she grabbed a few things before she'd fled Brooklyn? A couple of shirts? A pair of shorts? Fresh underwear? A *toothbrush*?

She wobbled down a staircase that creaked underfoot and came upon a large entryway. Buster's leash was hanging on wall pegs by the front door.

"Come on, Bus," she grumbled, clipping his leash and stepping into a spectacularly green front yard with flagstones in various patterns. Stone steps led up to what she barely remembered was a thin road threading through thick green forest, dripping with pine and willow trees.

The house had two stories, its bottom half stone, its upper half dark wood panels, and a gray-shingled roof. The muntin windows were tiny—six on the first floor, four on the second, with pointed gables. Exactly what you'd expect something called The Hansel and Gretel House to look like.

Yesterday, after arriving at the Lancaster County, Pennsylvania train stop, she'd wandered outside and, sure enough, saw a few taxis. The trip to the cottage took maybe half an hour. Along the way, there were several moments of panic as she tried to recall the message she'd received through the home share app a few days before, telling her the code for the door. She was fairly certain it was the last four digits of her phone number. If worse came to worse, she'd ask the driver to bring her to a hotel—any hotel.

Luckily, the code had worked. The inside of the cottage was so adorable—everything vintage, wooden, and soothingly simple—that her heart began a pleasantly accelerated patter despite being broken in half.

Two bedrooms upstairs, low-ceilinged with carriage beds, antique dressers, and frilly curtains. Downstairs, a large living room, a screened-in porch, and a kitchen with modern appliances. To her unending gratitude, on the counter was a wine-rack holding six bottles of wine. An attached handwritten note read, "Help yourself."

First, she took Buster for a short walk down the street, marveling at the thickness of the woods, almost as if it were a jungle, and let him do his business. With no bags to pick up his waste, she'd kicked brush over it, then returned to the house to settle in and get thoroughly smashed.

After two glasses of rich red, she wished she had her phone so she could call them. First Sam. She'd tell him he was an absolute piece of shit and why couldn't he have chosen a different woman, *any* other woman?

Then Catrina. She'd tell her (former) best friend that Buster wasn't coming back any time soon. After the dog had swallowed a ball of tinfoil in the park, Syra had paid for his emergency room visit—almost one thousand dollars. Presented with the exorbitant bill, Catrina had called Syra blubbering. Dutiful and ignorant friend that she was, Syra had agreed to foot the charges since Catrina had hit all her credit card limits.

You'll get your dog back when you repay me, bitch, she'd say on the phone. If she had one. Well, there *was* a phone. A black, plastic rotary-dial one sitting forlornly on a cherrywood table in the front hallway. But Syra had no idea what Sam's or Catrina's phone numbers were. She remembered that Sam's number had a one and a nine in it, but that's all she could remember. The perils of automated dialing.

The only phone number she had memorized was her mother's, but she couldn't call her. Not yet. It was all too excruciatingly embarrassing. How was she going to tell her mother that the wedding was off?

Syra's parents had one of those strange and rare fairytale marriages. They'd been together since high school and she'd hardly heard them have the slightest tiff about anything. Secretly, she felt this doomed her chances at a great marriage. How was any marriage of hers going to live up to the one her parents had?

She was embarrassed when her friends would come over to her childhood home and say something like, "Wow, your mom bats her eyelashes at your dad like she's just met him" or "Your dad looks at your mom like he's not married to her, like she's a girl he has a crush on." Why couldn't they hate or ignore each other like normal parents?

She'd also always had the dispiriting idea that they'd had her because they felt that's what married people did —have children. They'd always given her everything parents are supposed to—food, clothing, shelter. She'd had a respectable education, grew up in a relatively safe area, had toys, books, spending money.

But she couldn't remember ever having an intimate talk with either one of them. Couldn't remember either one ever showing much interest in anything she was doing. Except for her upcoming wedding. The one she'd have to cancel.

She'd met Sam on a dating app, and found him to be average in the way her father was—not too exciting, not too good-looking, and even, dare she admit it, not too intelligent—but, overall, a good, solid man. And, more importantly, a man willing to commit to her (try finding that in New York City).

He wasn't perfect. He got frustrated easily, and would rail against unseen forces that were apparently conspiring to deprive him of the life he was meant to live—primarily one of financial success. But just when one of these faults of his would begin to convince her they weren't a good match, he'd do something so touching that she would recommit herself.

Like the weekend they'd gone to Boston to meet some of his college buddies and she'd fallen sick with the flu. Despite Sam's buddies urging him to go bar hopping, he'd refused, and spent all weekend tending to Syra, buying her orange juice and vitamins, boiling her tea, until she was well enough to get back on the train.

Eventually, she'd accepted that he was a flawed man —and weren't we *all* flawed?—but one who wouldn't hurt her. Not deliberately.

How could she have been so disastrously *wrong* about him?

She'd wandered around the Hansel and Gretel House, sinking deeper into an inebriated stupor. At some point, she'd undressed and passed out on one of the upstairs carriage beds.

Bringing Buster back into the house, she sat on the screened-in porch for at least an hour, hardly able to move, head throbbing, stomach feeling split in two.

What had she been thinking, running off to Pennsylvania? Stealing Buster? Throwing out her phone? The tossing out of her phone was the worst part. How did she think that would punish *them*?

Now, she was stuck with no food, no transportation, and with a dog who hadn't eaten for a day and must be starving. Hunger was beginning to assail her as well, her sore gut bubbling with growls. If she didn't get food soon, it would be too late, as she assumed most stores in the country closed at an early hour.

With no phone to summon a car lift, the only thing to do was to put Buster on the leash and start walking. On the way to the cottage, the taxi had wended up and up a small mountain. She was deep in the forest, but she recalled that when the taxi had been on a main road, it had passed a small strip of stores. If she walked long enough, she'd find it.

The original plan had been that Catrina's boyfriend, James, who had a car, would drive them all down to Lancaster County—to a rural town called Prairie. Though he didn't know where he'd be driving. This weekend was supposed to be a surprise for everyone except Syra, who had booked their getaway.

James was a busy corporate lawyer (no matter how many times he explained what he did, Syra still couldn't quite grasp the intricacies). Catrina and Sam were (supposedly) working on a start-up that they were set to launch any day. Sam had been a stockbroker for ten years and Catrina a senior editor at a popular financial news site. But both had been laid off last year.

That's when the pair had started working together, using their combined knowledge of the market and their contacts to put together an investment newsletter. This despite them (supposedly) not liking each other. Catrina with her *You could do better, that's all I'm saying*, and Sam with his *It's not that I don't like her, exactly, I just find her irritating sometimes…*

A long weekend getaway was to be a deserved break for the foursome. But after weeks of discussion about where to go—Upstate? Newport? Miami?—they were nowhere closer to making actual plans. Syra had taken charge, offering to plan it all. But she told them the destination had to be a surprise because she was fed up with the debates.

And she'd decided. Prairie, Lancaster County, Pennsylvania. Because it was smack dab in the middle of Amish country.

In her mind, it was perfect. The couples only had Thursday through Monday, so they needed somewhere easy to get to (the area was a three-hour train ride from Manhattan). But she also wanted somewhere that felt removed from the city. Somewhere that felt like another world.

You couldn't get much more "another world" than a place that felt like another century, with a populace that spurned cars and electricity, dressed like pioneers, and spoke their own language, Pennsylvania Dutch. Lancaster was the oldest and largest Amish settlement in the world.

Syra had booked an "Amish Experience" for the group. This entailed a horse and buggy ride, a tour of an Amish dairy farm, and a visit to an Amish one-room schoolhouse. Only, the tour was today. And she wasn't going anywhere today except to a grocery store because starving to death was not on her agenda.

Chapter Five

About twenty minutes into her trek to find a store, Syra had the despairing sensation that her walk was futile. She was too weak, and it was too hot —even here in the dense tree shade—for her to get very far. And poor Buster was panting. She'd not only stolen him from his owner but would kill him with heatstroke.

For the first time, it occurred to her that Catrina might call the police and report Buster being stolen. Catrina's brownstone may have surveillance cameras. For all Syra knew, blurry video of her ferrying the pooch out of the building was circulating the news. The media would love that kind of story.

Spurned Woman Steals Best Friend's Pooch.

But Catrina must know that Syra would never, ever do Buster any harm. Hell, they'd picked him out of the shelter together. He wouldn't have even made it out if Syra hadn't come along, because Catrina had her eye on a pocket pet—one of those ultra-tiny, scrawny breeds with tufts of fur sticking up around the ears and that looked more like a rat.

Syra had even inadvertently named him Buster, as upon seeing him squished in his steel cage, frantic barks echoing all around him, his googly brown eyes begging *Get me out of here*, Syra had said, "Hey there, buster."

Syra plopped to the side of the road. There was no sidewalk, so she sat on the strip of grass and hoped that the cars—there weren't many that had passed her, but there were a few—would see her as they came around a blind bend. She kept Buster behind her so she'd take the brunt of the wheels in case one didn't.

She should have at least brought a container of water with them, but she hadn't realized how hot it would be outside. The temperature had steadily risen all morning, which she hadn't noticed inside the comfortably cool cottage. Built with stone and wood, it sealed out the heat so effectively that she hadn't even turned on the air conditioning.

But now the heat was sticky and brutal, unrelenting. The kind of heat that punched you in the face, made it difficult to breathe, made you feel you were going to burn up and die. If it was this scorching in the country, she couldn't imagine what it was like in the city. She hoped the heat was incinerating Sam and Catrina.

Burying her face in her palms, she tried to breathe deeply through her nose. She had some intuition that if she gave up completely, if she air-dropped into helplessness, something, someone, would come along and save her.

Lalalalaalala

Lalalalala lalaaaaaaa

Syra thought she was hearing someone's radio, so she twisted around and peered into the dense, dripping forest.

Lalalalala laaaaaaa

It sounded like a little girl singing, which was terrifically odd. Syra leaned towards the edge of the woods, squinting into the junglelike vegetation. Buster didn't acknowledge the sound, only sat panting.

If a little girl was nearby, that meant there must be a house nearby, hidden by the tangled forest. Maybe she could ask the girl for help… ask her to go fetch a parent? Could Syra pay someone to bring her to a store?

Then, in a gap between the trees, she spotted a flash of light blue cloth, like a portion of a dress. Then she saw a face. A pale little face with what appeared to be long, dark, somewhat curly hair. Syra and the vision locked eyes for a moment. The girl opened her mouth—and seemed to laugh—then was gone. Syra continued to stare into the woods, not convinced she'd seen what she'd seen.

"You alright there?"

She startled. A maroon SUV was stopped on the street. The driver was a woman. Syra could only determine the fundamentals—long, reddish-blonde hair, possibly in her fifties, a concerned pucker.

"Oh!" the woman exclaimed. "You wouldn't happen to be Syra, would you?"

It took Syra a moment to process that the woman had said her name, as she'd pronounced it incorrectly. *Sigh-rah* instead of what Syra preferred, *Seer-ah*.

She had made up the name. Her birth name was Sarah Jane. But she'd always found that too ordinary, so she'd jazzed it up, using inspiration from the heroine in a fantasy book she'd been reading at the time. When she was 18, she'd changed her name legally via probate court. Having a unique name had its advantages, but it also meant half the time, it was mispronounced.

"Yes," she croaked, not correcting the woman's pronunciation, too grateful that it seemed she was about to be rescued. "That's me."

"I'm Millie. I own the Hansel and Gretel House. Thought I'd stop by to see if you got in alright."

"Oh my God," Syra burst out. "I—I'm so... I brought a dog. Is that okay?"

Millie craned forward, trying to peer over the passenger side door. "Why don't you get in and I'll take you where you're going."

Syra nodded numbly and stood. She opened the passenger door to an exquisite blast of air conditioning. "Should I put him in the back?" she asked, indicating Buster.

"Awwrr, look at that cutie!" Millie yelped in a curiously musical and unusual accent, the consonants curling in on themselves. "Sure, back, or on your lap. Don't matter none to me."

Syra decided to keep Buster with her, and lifted him up. Inside, she was hugely relieved when he ceased panting. On the floor were all kinds of wrappers and a few paper cups. The smell of coffee and grease wafted up to her nostrils.

"You headed somewhere?" Millie asked, the car moving again.

"I didn't have any food. I thought I'd try to find a store, but I got so hot and tired. I didn't realize how hot it was." She failed to mention her pounding hangover.

"I can bring you to the grocery store," Millie said. "Or I was headed to the farmer's market myself. Welcome to come along."

"Great. But I really need to get dog food, too."

"We can do both." Millie side-eyed her. "You didn't think to bring dog food?"

"I didn't know I'd have him. His owner had an emergency."

"Ah," Millie said, sounding like she wasn't going to pry further.

Syra leaned back, gratefully sucking in a lungful of the gloriously chilly air, and stroking Buster, who was busy staring out the window at the passing greenery.

A COUPLE HOURS LATER, Syra and Millie were back at the cottage. At the farmer's market, Syra had let Buster devour a chicken pot pie, while she herself had gone for corn pie and gobbled that down.

At the grocery store, she picked up food for herself and Buster. As much time as she'd spent at Catrina's apartment, she wasn't sure what kind of food the dog ate, so she scooped up a variety of canned food. The store also had limited amounts of clothing so she bought a couple of t-shirts and packages of underwear, though she couldn't find any shorts.

In the cottage's kitchen, Millie sliced lemons for iced tea. It was only now that the woman caught on that Syra was alone instead of with the three other people who'd booked the cottage.

"Just you?" she asked, peering over Syra's shoulder as they sat at the kitchen table, as if expecting the additional guests to momentarily appear.

"Yes, there was an emergency." Syra kept her eyes down. "They couldn't come."

"I see. Well. If you need anything, let me know."

"That's another thing," Syra sighed. "I lost my phone so I can't contact you through the app."

"I'll write down my phone number before I go."

Syra now felt that she was being sized up somewhat suspiciously.

"There's a regular old phone in the hallway," Millie continued. "You know how to use one?"

"To be honest, I never have, but I'm pretty sure I can figure it out."

"You stick your finger in the little hole, like so," Millie said, demonstrating on an invisible rotary dial. "Then you pulllllll your finger round to the little silver ring, like so. I can show you before I go." She shook her head. "Imagine that. Never used a real phone."

Syra glanced at Buster, who seemed perfectly content, sprawled near her feet on the Tuscany beige stone floor. She felt terrible that she'd made him wait all night and half the next day for food, and that her sole priority had been getting drunk.

And getting drunk hadn't even helped. Not only had the alcohol not dulled her agony, it had made her maudlin. If she'd actually known Sam and Catrina's phone numbers, she might have called them from that contraption in the hallway and said something absurd like, "If you two want to be together, I understand. I just don't want to lose your friendship."

Ugh! Thank GOD she'd thrown out her phone. That had been the right move after all.

"I drank one of the bottles of wine," she told Millie sheepishly. "I hope that's okay."

"Oh sure," Millie chirped. "That's what I left them out for. Got a small winery here in town." She grinned a little. "Downed the whole bottle, did ya? Not that I'm judging. I've downed a bottle or two on my own in my time."

"It's just… I had a really rough day." Then, because she hadn't told anyone and she *needed* to tell someone, she told. "I found my fiancé and best friend together. In bed. That's why I'm here by myself. They were supposed to be with me."

"Oh, my dear," Millie gasped, one hand over her mouth. "What pieces of hogshit."

Syra burst out with slightly shocked laughter. She hadn't expected that language from the woman across from her, who was dressed primly in a loose, mid-length rust-toned skirt and a billowy-sleeved white blouse. Though Millie didn't wear a head covering and had been driving an SUV, so Syra assumed she wasn't Amish.

"Yeah, so," Syra continued, sipping her iced tea. "That's why the first thing I did was get drunk."

"Makes sense." Millie had large, round eyes of a grayish-blue color, and they widened in commiseration, then narrowed in outrage. "I would have been hard-pressed not to take a shovel to both their heads."

"I didn't have a shovel, but I almost used a lamp," Syra admitted. "I was in so much shock I couldn't do anything and left. Then, for some reason I still can't fathom, I dumped my phone in the garbage and made my way here."

Millie made little *erm-erm* grunts of disapproval, shaking her head. "You let me know if you need anything," she said.

"What I really need is a phone. And a car." Syra paused, feeling guilty about burdening her host, who only wanted to rent out her sweet little cottage and not be dragged into a domestic saga. "I could manage for the next couple of days, but..."

Suddenly, she felt pathetic. But she wasn't pathetic. She was the type of person who took care of things. Never missed a deadline. Paid off her credit card in full every month. Didn't leave her friends in the lurch. Was chronically early for appointments. And last night was the drunkest she'd been since her first year of college.

But the woman sitting across from her was only seeing this other person, this newly-hatched Syra—one who'd made a series of rash, impractical decisions.

"I can't go back." The declaration was out of her mouth before she'd even consciously decided to say it.

"Not now. I don't know what might happen if I go back. I might do something to them. Or to me."

She stared into Millie's large egg-shaped eyes, wanting to see if the woman caught her drift.

"I understand," Millie said, softly.

"Is—is there any way… I could stay here longer? A couple of weeks? I'd pay you. I have my credit card with me."

Millie leaned in, her gaze overflowing with empathy. But Syra could already tell the woman was about to turn her down.

"I'm sorry. It's high season. The cottage is all booked up. Second you leave, I got the cleaning lady coming, and another group right after. On like that til November."

"Oh. Of course."

Syra was back to feeling like an utter idiot for throwing out her phone. If she had a phone, she could look around for another place to stay. She could email her boss, make up a reason why she couldn't come in on Tuesday. Or Wednesday. Or the whole week. Or ever again.

"I'd have you at my place, but…" Millie began.

"No, no. I completely understand. Listen, I'm sorry to—"

"It's that I'm allergic to dogs." She glanced under the table at Buster's snoring little body. "Can handle 'em for short periods, but after a day or two, my eyes would be swollen shut and I'd be sneezing up a storm." She rubbed one eye, which was turning pinkish in the corner.

"I get it. It's fine." Syra's chest sank despondently with the idea of having to return to Brooklyn and have her life completely change.

Millie took her glass to the sink and began washing. "There's cab companies in the drawer by the phone. You want me to show you how to use it?"

"I think I got it," Syra said, hoisting one finger into the air. "Stick your finger in the hole, like so."

Chapter Six

*T*hat night, harassed by dreams of Sam and Catrina, reliving their betrayal over and over, seeing them on that bed over and over, the *arf arf arf* of Buster's rough little barking pierced her torturous dreamscape and mercifully yanked her out of it.

She peeled her eyes open, for a long moment completely forgetting where she was and why a dog was barking.

One hand fumbled to the right side of the bed, where Sam always slept, and where she would reach for his warm, comforting body if she had nightmares. Feeling no warm Sam, the surrealness of her new reality crashed upon her. She was in a rented cottage in Lancaster County. She'd stolen a dog. Her heart was shattered and she no longer had a best friend or fiancé.

"Buster," she groaned. "Quiet."

She groggily sat up to look for him. Moonlight reached into the low-ceilinged room. Following the sounds of Buster's barks, she saw him on top of a chair across the room, his paws tapping at the windowsill. The window was open partway and she worried his nails would slip down to the screen and tear it open.

"Buster!" she shouted, then felt bad for raising her voice at him. Poor dog had no idea where he was or why he wasn't home. "Come on," she groaned, making her way over to him. She followed his sightline into the dark mass of woods behind the house.

"Let's go, Bus," she said, picking up his stocky, wrinkled body. As she turned, a sound wafted up through the window. That same odd, high-pitched *lalalala lalala laaaaa* she'd heard before. She remembered the moment when the face of what appeared to be a young girl had stared at her between a gap in the trees.

Putting Buster down on the floor, Syra backtracked and stared hard out the window into the dark night, but could see nothing despite a nearby streetlamp casting a hazy glow in the direction of the yard. "Weird," she whispered.

Could the girl really be out there in the middle of the night? In the woods? And why was she always singing? The hairs on the back of her neck were prickling on the edge of fear but she didn't know why. A little girl singing in the woods was bizarre but not threatening.

But it *was* strange she would be out so late, wasn't it? At least Syra assumed it was late. With no phone, she'd been using the clocks around the house to keep track of time, but there wasn't one in the bedroom. She'd gone to bed around 11 p.m. and it felt like she'd been asleep for a while.

Buster stopped barking so she picked him up, plopping his rotund body on the bed. Crawling back under the sheet, Buster rested against her leg. It took her a long while to drift off, as thoughts of the little girl were replaced with visions of her betrayal playing in a continual and tormenting loop in her mind.

Chapter Seven

*E*arly Sunday evening, Syra sat ruminating on her trip back to the city tomorrow. Much as she hated the idea, she had to go back. She hadn't prepared for any kind of lengthy time away. She'd return Buster first and to hell with Catrina if she was angry about the dognapping. Then she'd head to her apartment. Inform Sam they were finished, in case he somehow hadn't figured that out.

She had no idea what to do about the apartment; she and Sam had renewed their lease only two months ago. She couldn't afford it on her own and doubted he could either.

Thank god they'd only begun planning a small wedding. Beyond booking The River Café under the Brooklyn Bridge for both ceremony and reception (they'd probably lose their deposit), there had been no other expenses laid out.

She'd been dress shopping a couple of times but had held out hope she'd find something reasonably priced in a consignment shop or on eBay. She hadn't yet sent out invites, though she'd told several friends of their engagement and, naturally, had announced it on social media. Now she'd have to publicly *un*announce it. Anticipating that humiliation made her stomach harden into a ball of nerves.

Maybe—maybe she should quit her job, pack up, and go live with her parents in their retirement community in Phoenix. Start all over. But she hated the idea of running to her parents, giving up her job and city-living dreams because of Sam and Catrina. Why should *Syra* flee? Why didn't *they* flee?

She dreaded whatever drama was about to unfold. Sam would use his preternatural persuasiveness to blame everything on her. After all, they'd been having more irritants and disagreements since he'd been laid off. She felt he wasn't pulling his weight; he felt she wasn't being understanding. The typical stuff. Or he'd try to convince her that she hadn't seen what she'd seen. She could hear whatever ridiculously lame excuse he'd try on her.

It was so hot, and we were so tired from working, we took off our clothes and decided to take a nap. Jeez, Syra, what are you accusing me of?

Then there was an annoying drumbeat in the back of her brain. One nattering at her that infidelity was common and surmountable. That Americans took infidelity too seriously. That she should be more cosmopolitan, more European. That if Sam wasn't in love with Catrina, if he still wanted to be together, Syra should allow him this one transgression. Nobody's perfect!

But she knew this small but persistent current pushing in the opposite direction of her indignation was simply because she wanted to avoid the upheaval, expense, and trauma that was on its way. She only wanted everything to disappear, to reverse itself. The fastest, easiest way of doing that was if she forgave what had happened.

There was a knock at the door. Buster scrambled up from the floor and began his sharp, insistent barking. For such a small dog he could really project. Syra debated not answering the door. As a city gal, a door knock was generally cause for suspicion. But she was in a quiet, safe, rural area. A knock likely heralded a neighbor bearing a pie or something.

Millie stood at the door. And, indeed, she was carrying a pie.

"Am I disturbing you?" she asked.

"No, not at all. Was about to call a taxi and reserve a pickup for tomorrow. Maybe you can supervise my rotary phone usage."

They shared a small laugh. Syra was impressed that she still was capable of cracking a joke. Though, on some level, supervision wasn't a bad idea.

"I brought some shoo-fly pie," Millie said, elevating the plate. "Pennsylvania Dutch specialty."

"Sounds great. Afraid I finished off that tea you made or I'd offer some."

"No worries about that."

Millie placed the tinfoil pie dish on the kitchen counter and retrieved plates and utensils, relaying them to the wood-slatted table. The white plates were ringed with tiny blue flowers. Buster sat eagerly eyeing Millie as she sliced up the pie. At the first gooey bite, Syra groaned with pleasure as the sweet taste engorged her mouth.

"Delicious. What's it made of?"

"Molasses, mostly."

"Wow. I wouldn't say that's something I would ordinarily like, but this is amazing."

Buster whined. Syra ignored him, reluctant to give him a taste of something so heavily sugar-laden. She didn't need another thousand-dollar vet bill.

"I came over for another reason," Millie said, dabbing her lips with one of the cloth napkins folded on the table. "I was thinking about what you said, about wanting to stay longer."

Syra was silent, holding her breath. She didn't dare to hope that the guests who were to replace her tomorrow had cancelled. Another couple of weeks in this sweet cottage was exactly what her soul needed. Though she'd have to contact her editor and let her know she couldn't come in this week. What excuse could she give?

"I have another property," Millie continued. "I didn't mention it before because it's a bit unusual."

"Oh," Syra said, her tone hanging between hopeful and disappointed. How unusual was she talking?

"It's an old Amish farmette. There's no electricity, wifi, air conditioning, or television."

Syra was uncertain if this sounded delightful or hellish. "Is there a toilet?" she asked.

"Oh, my, yes," Millie said, chuckling. "Only the

most conservative of the Old Order Amish insist on outhouses anymore."

"Well, that could be fun." *Fun* wasn't the word Syra wanted, but in truth, anything sounded more fun than returning to her cretin of a fiancé and duplicitous (former) best friend. "How much is it?"

"I wouldn't charge you. Not for a week or two. Want to help you out. And as you'll be my first guest, you'd be helping *me* out. Letting me know what you like and what could use improvement."

Now the house sounded even better. Syra was worried about the added expenses of a new apartment —between a real estate agent fee and moving costs, it would easily rise into the thousands. That was New York for you. Anything that would save her money would be an excellent thing.

"The plan is to update," Millie said. "Bought the home at auction when the family moved to another settlement. But a part of me wonders if I should keep it the way it is. Tourists are big on the Amish. They might pay as much to stay in a house without electricity as one with it. This would certainly give them a real taste of Amish life."

Syra started to like the idea even more. For one, she was a real estate writer, a broad beat that veered all over the place: second homes, where to live, where not to live, where to vacation. She could write about her stay. Her editor might love the idea and chronicling her experience would give her an excuse to stay here longer.

For two, being "off the grid" appealed to her. No

electricity meant no computer, no phone, no chance to mess up by initiating contact with Sam and Catrina.

"There's plenty of board games and a few books, but that's it for entertainment," Millie warned. "So, I wasn't sure if this was something… well, something an English person could handle."

"English person?"

"Sorry. That means non-Amish."

Syra bristled a little. This "English person" was raised in New York City. If she could handle it there, she could, to paraphrase Frank Sinatra, handle it anywhere.

"One other thing," Millie added. "The property isn't exactly empty."

"Not empty?" Syra echoed. Was Millie about to tell her it was haunted? Or perhaps was overrun with mice?

"You see, there's a little daudy house—what you'd call a guest house—out back and, ah…" Millie started to seem uncomfortable, fidgeting and fumbling over her words. "There's a caretaker there."

She scraped her empty plate, clearly a nervous tic, and stared down at the table. When she looked up, her expression was almost apologetic.

"These days, he can be a bit… what my grandmother would have called *cantankerous*. With that and the house needing work and not having modern conveniences, I haven't had anyone stay there yet. But I kept thinking about what you said…"

"Is the man Amish?"

"I suppose you could say I took pity on him. In return, he does odd jobs and, hopefully, this year, we'll start fixing up the main house."

Syra realized that Millie's response had circumnavigated answering her question.

"Is he Amish?" she tried again.

Millie got up and took both their plates to the sink, then came back and wrapped the top of the pie with cling wrap. Buster, realizing he wasn't going to get a slice, whined several times, then wandered out of the kitchen.

"Yes and no," Millie finally said, seeming reluctant to share. "To be honest, he's… well… he's being… what the Amish call *shunned*."

For a moment, Syra thought Millie had said the man was being "sunned." She had no clue what that meant. He was busy getting a tan? Then her brain caught up with the word.

"Shunned? What is that?" Though she had a vague idea. The man was exiled in some fashion.

Millie waved a little. "He was excommunicated from the Anabaptist church. He's in a ban. That means—officially, at least—no one in the community is supposed to acknowledge him."

Syra had a vision of a *cantankerous* old man, hunched over, thumbs hooked in his suspenders, so disagreeable that even his own insular community wanted nothing to do with him.

Would she really want to live next to someone like that? Even for only a couple of weeks? But this was her chance to observe a real Amish person in the wild. A shunned one, no less. Could be good grist for an article.

She'd long held a curiosity about the Amish. Possibly because she was a native Lancasterian in a way. She'd been born in Lancaster County. Her parents had been taking advantage of her father needing to deliver a large order of timber to the area. They'd decided to enjoy a weekend at a local bed-and-breakfast, figuring it would be their last chance to travel before their first child arrived.

Infant Syra had other plans. Perhaps it was her curiosity about the Amish that had made her squirm out of her mother's womb a month early to take a look around.

Thus, it was on her birth certificate: Lancaster County General Hospital. Her mom had had a baby name picked out, but the new parents spontaneously named their newborn girl Sarah Jane, after the Mennonite woman who owned the bed-and-breakfast.

The woman had been so helpful when Mom unexpectedly went into labor, even calling her own obstetrician, insisting he get to the hospital to deliver her bed-and-breakfast guest's child. A few days after Sarah Jane's birth, infant and parents returned to Queens. None of them had been to Lancaster since. Until now.

"If he doesn't bother me, I won't bother him," Syra said about the caretaker. "Buster's okay to stay there?"

"Oh, sure. I won't come around much. I warn you there isn't a lot around there. Farmland far as the eye can see. You might get bored."

Far from boring, it sounded like exactly what she craved. A place as removed from the city as she could imagine.

"It sounds perfect but I should probably rent a car. I could get a taxi to the nearest rental."

"I can drive you over to a place near the Amtrak station, if you like," Millie said.

"I'd really appreciate that. I'll have to get in touch with my editor, too. Is there a library around here with computers?"

Millie grinned. "I've got wifi at my place. Happy to let you use mine."

"And you told this—this man I'd be coming?" She didn't want to surprise a moody old Amish dude who might jab a pitchfork at her.

"I knocked but he was probably out. Or he didn't feel like talking. He's a good sort, but had a rough time of it in life. I'll leave him a message later."

Syra nodded, suddenly feeling a kinship with the man. She empathized with someone who'd had a rough time of it and wanted nothing to do with people. Exactly how she herself felt these days.

She wondered what the old man had done to get flung out of his community. She almost asked Millie what his transgression had been, but supposed it was none of her business or Millie would have volunteered the information.

Chapter Eight

*T*he Amish farmette was white and surrounded by cornfields. The front door opened into a sitting area with large windows sprawling along the walls. The plentiful windows appeared designed to let in as much light as possible, which made sense for a house without electricity. A spacious kitchen brightened with another long row of windows stepped down into a mud room the size of Syra's city living room.

"Wow, it's bigger than I thought it would be," she said.

"Amish homes have to be," Millie replied. "This would have been rather small for the Yoders, who had six boys and six girls."

If Syra had been taking a drink at that moment, she would have spewed liquid straight across the room. "I take it birth control isn't a thing with the Amish," she said, laughing edgily.

"Some of the women secretly get an IUD," Millie

sniffed, smoothing back straggles from her braid. "But I don't think this was something Leah Yoder did."

"If she did, she should get a refund," Syra quipped.

It had taken about fifteen minutes to drive to the house from The Hansel and Gretel House, Syra following Millie's boxy SUV in her newly-rented Kia.

The gorgeousness of the passing scenery was so entrancing that Syra kept catching herself drifting over the center line of the narrow two-lane road. Her windows looked onto acres of glittery-golden wheat; butterscotch bales of hay piled at least fifty feet high; meticulous white farm houses; and horses, cows, and goats grazing in pastures smooth and green as jade.

As she sped deeper into Amish country, more horses and buggies shared the road with her. The buggies were black on the bottom with square gray tops, and the horses were dark and sleek with long, flowing manes. The animals had a no-nonsense, high-stepping canter, almost keeping pace with her car. If these horses were vehicles, they'd be Ferraris.

Passing the buggies, Syra gripped her steering wheel, preparing to veer if a horse darted in front of the car. Only after she'd passed several without incident did she begin to relax. Millie had told her that the buggies, while charming-looking, were quite dangerous and that accidents—some fatal for both human and animal—were common.

Millie explained that about five years ago, the community had capitulated to township pressure and installed LED lights and large reflective orange triangles on the buggies. But it would never be ideal to have horses trotting the same streets as cars.

There was no denying her gut was churning with nervous anticipation about living in an Amish house. Would she find herself in the pitch-dark with a nonworking toilet? Would it be too hot with no air conditioning? Too inconvenient without a microwave? Would she get so bored without television and computer that she'd go mad? What if there was an emergency?

She'd forced herself to focus on the marvelous colors and symmetry of the passing landscape. Many around here lived without electricity. They all must eat, bathe, and go to the bathroom.

As she and Millie had wended up a long, paved driveway, Syra noticed a black Ford Ranger parked off to the side. Must belong to the caretaker. Apparently, he'd left the Amish ways behind, or at least the horse and buggy.

She also noticed a smaller white house, a mini of the larger, positioned at the edge of the property, right along one of the cornfields. She assumed this is where the *cantankerous* shunned Amish man lived. It was pretty far from the main house, so she wondered if she'd even cross paths with him.

Buster pulled on his leash, excited for the considerable plot of dewy green grass to explore. She was tempted to let him off so he could run around, but didn't dare. A white ranch fence surrounded the property, but the dog could slip right through the rails. She'd already stolen him, she didn't need to lose him, too.

Before driving to the farmette, Millie brought Syra

to her own house and allowed her to use a computer in a cluttered office. Syra logged into her email account and determinedly avoided looking directly at several new messages.

Creating a new email to Catrina, she wrote, without addressing her at all: "Buster is fine. I don't know why I took him. I was not in my right head at the time. I need to stay away from the two of you for a little while. But I'll be back soon and so will Buster. We'll deal with all this then. Please know he is absolutely fine and is being well cared for."

That was as polite and calm as she could bring herself to be. Then she did the same for Sam.

"I'll be back in a couple of weeks and we can deal with the apartment and telling everyone the wedding is off. Please don't post anything online. I know you don't care about my feelings, but if you can do one thing for me, let it be this."

And to her editor:

"Hi, Liz. I'm going to be straight with you. I've had a life-altering event happen to me. I'm fine physically but emotionally I'm a wreck. I'd like to take my vacation and personal time for the next couple of weeks. I'm sorry for the short notice but I didn't expect this to happen. Additionally, I left the city and am staying in an Amish house. I could write about the area and the house when I'm back. I think it could be a popular story; we haven't done anything like this. Because there's no electricity or wifi I'm unreachable until I get a new phone (long story). Thank you, Liz. I'll make it up to you."

Liz was a decent person. She and Syra occasionally

had lunch together, though taking lunches was a luxury more than a daily occurrence. Both normally ate at their desks. And last year, Liz had lost her grandmother, whom she was extremely close to, and she'd taken a week off work. Syra also remembered her editor spontaneously taking off a day or two when her cat died. While no one in Syra's life had died, her future had, so she hoped that Liz would cut her some slack.

Then she sent an email to her mother, explaining that she was doing research for a story and wouldn't be reachable for a couple of weeks as she'd lost her phone. That should hold her mother, given that they only spoke once a week or so. Her father, even less. As for any city friends who tried to get in touch, most of them were so busy that if she didn't return a few calls or emails no one would report her missing. A benefit of city living, she supposed. One could disappear relatively easily.

The back of her neck prickled with the idea that Sam could be home trying to break into her laptop. If he figured out her passcode—which wasn't that difficult to figure out, it was their late cat's name, Puck, combined with the four digits of her birth year—then he might be able to get into her homestay profile and see where she was.

Would he come after her? How much could he want to be with her if he was sleeping with Catrina? Had he and Catrina really drunkenly tumbled into bed that one afternoon or had they been carrying on for weeks, or even months?

Inside the Amish house, Millie led her upstairs, where there were three bedrooms. Each had decent proportions for one or two people, but considering twelve children used to live here, Syra had no idea how they'd managed it.

"This one is fine," she said, choosing the bedroom that overlooked the red horse barn and a long cornfield that stretched into the solid blue sky.

The room's twin sleigh bed was draped with a white, diamond-patterned quilt. The walls were wood-paneled and two large windows were hung with green pulldown shades. Against the wall was a cedar cabinet and dresser. Crocheted placemats sat underneath two battery-powered lamps that looked like the kind of small lanterns you'd take camping in the woods.

Placed strategically around the house—on the bottoms and tops of staircases, on side tables, dangling from hooks in the ceilings—were varying-sized lamps and black and yellow DeWalt flashlights with lithium-ion rechargeable battery packs.

Millie showed her a charging station in the mud room. Syra only barely registered the instructions. The washing machine, powered by air compressor, had a wringer on its top that also baffled her.

"If you can't figure something out, go out back, and knock on Jonas' door," Millie chirped, noting Syra's intimidated expression. "He'll help you out."

This idea didn't appeal to her, but she figured she'd wash what few clothes she had in the sink and dry them outside.

The pair then walked down the long driveway to the empty stretch of two-lane road. Across the street was a small red shed. Inside, on a desk, was a button-dial landline with enormous numbers, as if the people who used it were elderly.

"It's a shared phone with a few Amish neighbors," Millie said. "And the one electrical outlet. I left my number right there." She pointed to where her name and number were taped to the desk.

"If I wanted to make a long-distance call?" Syra asked, staring at the big buttoned artifact as if it was a stone tablet etched with ancient and unintelligible writing. "Do I, ah, call collect?"

Millie smiled broadly, as if amused by the question. "No, go ahead and dial. We have an unlimited plan."

"Oh. Okay." Syra was relieved. Though she knew about "call collect" from older movies, she had no idea how to actually do it. Something about calling an operator. She'd never called an operator.

As Millie drove back down the long street and turned out of view, Syra shuddered. The heatwave of the past few days had dissipated. It was much cooler out and, other than her leggings, she had no warmer clothing. She'd have to find a store and buy a few things, using the local map Millie had left.

The broad sky had turned dazzling. The underbelly of the clouds was lit with breathtaking hues of pink and cherry red, rays slanting down like thick fingers, the horizon aglow and aflame, as if it was on fire.

There were no sounds except a wall of crickets loudly buzzing, and somewhere in the distance, a high-pitched ringing she assumed emanated from farm machinery, the sound traveling through a landscape devoid of tall buildings.

It hit her how far removed the farmette was. There weren't houses across the street or next door—only seemingly endless stretches of cornstalks, and behind them, jungle-like masses of plants and trees.

A feeling of desolation settled uneasily on her. She'd ever been this alone before. Even when she *was* alone, given that she lived in a bustling city, she was never *really* alone. City sounds constantly bombarded her—ambulances wailing, planes droning, neighbors vacuuming or banging for mysterious reasons.

Now she was *alone* alone. It made her feel out of sorts, hollow, and a bit crushed, as if the world had moved on without her.

Alright, she wasn't *completely* alone. There was someone else on the property. A cantankerous old shunned Amish man. But he didn't sound like the type to mosey over and start pleasant conversation.

Chapter Nine

rf... arf... ARF!

Syra groaned and rolled over. For several moments, she again had the disorienting sensation of not knowing where she was, of having the urge to drape her hand on Sam's warm, familiar body. But, this time, the disorientation quickly fled and she gained mastery of her surroundings. She was in Lancaster County. In Millie's Amish farmette. In an upstairs bedroom, furnished plain and simple as could be.

And Buster was barking. Buster, whom she'd stolen from Catrina. That bitch.

She peeled open her eyes and stared at the clock's intricate, gold-plated hands. It had been so long since she'd read a hand-clock that she scarcely knew what time it was indicating. After a few blinks, it crystallized: six-fifteen a.m.

"Buster, shut it," she moaned. But Buster wasn't listening. His sausage-like body was up on the room's only chair, which looked like it had been carved out of one large block of wood, its back slightly curved. His paws scraped along the window pane.

Irritated, Syra rolled out of the bed, which had a hard mattress that left her with a dull ache between her shoulder blades. Buster glanced at her. Feeling he had backup, he stopped *arfing*.

Syra squinted into the pale, gem-laced morning light, down to the long, viridian side yard. There, she saw a man. Shockwaves sent adrenaline streaming into her limbs as she realized the man—large and strolling with an assured, determined gait—was carrying an axe.

An axe!

And he was headed for the house.

She hurried down the creaky stairs of the narrow hallway, bare feet stomping on the wood boards, breathing in loud gusts. She was completely trapped— no phone, no one around to hear her scream. Buster's nails clanked on the stairs behind her, but he was hardly a guard dog and wouldn't do her much good.

She rushed into the kitchen in time to see the man's backside through the glass panes on the kitchen door. He was retreating down the long yard, away from the house. Then she remembered the old man who lived in the "daudy" house. It looked like the axe-man was headed in that direction.

She went to the counter, where several large knives gleamed in a magnet holder on the fiberglass back-splash. Removing the biggest one, she gripped it tight in her fist, and headed to the door.

"Back, Buster," she commanded, then padded bare-foot onto the house-wide porch. She was no match for a big guy with an axe, but was recklessly acting on instinct and adrenaline. With no phone, she could think of nothing to do but confront the man and ask what he wanted.

Her bare feet sank into the cold, dewy grass. She moved stealthily around the side of the house. When she saw the back of the man, taking in that he was wearing denim bib overalls and a white t-shirt, she called out, "Who are you?" Pushing through her constricted throat, the words came out a barely-audible, strangled whisper.

The man stalked to an area littered with tree trunks underneath a corrugated tin roof, threw the axe up high over his head, and brought it down with a *blonk* onto an upright block of wood.

Syra stood with the knife gripped tightly at her side. She became keenly aware of her attire—beige camisole and gray linen shorts, both of which she'd bought yesterday for sleepwear. She was even more aware that she wasn't wearing a bra. She was practically naked in front of this man chopping wood.

He had dark, thick hair with full bangs, a moustache, and a short beard. With denim overalls tucked into battered leather boots, he looked like he'd emerged out of a mobile home squatting on the edge of a swamp. He was also wearing clear safety goggles and bright yellow work gloves.

He had the axe over his head when he sensed her presence and looked at her. Returning the axe to his side, the man's gaze roamed downward until it got to the knife in her hand. He stared for a moment, then shoved the safety goggles up into his thick, floppy bangs.

"I knocked but you didn't answer," he said. "I need to start early before it gets too hot."

Syra could say nothing for a long moment, then managed, "I'm sorry, *who* are you?"

"Millie didn't tell you about me?"

Oh my God. The light dawned.

This man was the caretaker. Not an *old man* as she'd got it into her head he was. How exactly had she come to that conclusion? She couldn't remember. The man with the axe didn't look much older than she was. Maybe, if he scraped off all the facial hair, she'd see he was even younger.

More aware than ever of her clothing, or lack thereof, she pinned her arms over her chest, knife pointed towards the dank ground.

"Is that for me?" he asked, eyeing the knife. Now she heard the same sing-songy twang she'd noticed in Millie's accent, with a hard, rolling R. *Forrrr* me? Similar to a hint of Scottish brogue.

"Well, I saw you in the yard with an axe and I thought the man who lived out back was much older."

"Technically, it's a maul," he said, glancing at the axe—or whatever it was called—at his side. "I'm Jonas Martin. I live out there." He pointed a yellow glove towards the white shack at the edge of the property. "I won't bother you but you'll hear me doing chores around. And I start early."

"Okay. No problem. I'm Syra. Sorry about the knife. I wouldn't have really—" She gave a forced laugh, hoping he'd join in, but he only flipped his safety goggles back down, then attacked the block of wood. *Blonk.*

Well, bye then, she thought.

Retreating to the house, Syra couldn't help but focus on how high up her shorts were riding on her ass, and what this must look like from the man's perspective. If he was even watching, and she wasn't convinced he was.

* * *

SYRA SUCCEEDED in lighting the stove's pilot light without anything exploding in her face. Making scrambled eggs and toast, she lay the freshly baked bread on the large cast-iron pan as there was no toaster, then spread it with gooseberry jam, a local specialty.

But the coffee was a disaster. There was no regular coffee maker, only a press. She somehow ended up with a watery ground-filled slop. After feeding Buster, she sat at the kitchen table with her breakfast, taking in her surroundings.

The airy kitchen looked decorated by a great-great-grandmother. The prevailing theme was defiantly old-fashioned—white Formica counters and dark wood-paneled walls; linoleum floors with a bumpy, granite-like design; ruffled yellow curtain borders framing the sink windows; and above the kitchen table, a grandfather-style clock ticking loudly in the silence. (The clock would later give her a mild scare as it erupted with music on the hour, rotating wholesome melodies like *Amazing Grace* and *America, the Beautiful.)*

It truly felt like she'd stepped back into another time. The simplicity of the decor comforted and soothed her.

The "plain" aura of the family who'd lived here, all fourteen of them, fascinated her.

What must it be like to have so many siblings? To have to share the too-few bedrooms and the one (one!) bathroom? As a single child who'd always longed for a sister or two, a part of her thought it would be glorious to have that much family, but another part of her shuddered at the idea. So little privacy. So many personalities clashing and clanging.

She'd been raised in the Rockaways, in the borough of Queens, in an upper middle-class enclave that lined the beach. The neighborhood, Neponsit, was as close to a suburb as a city could get, with large homes—mansions, really—of various architectural styles: Victorian, Colonial, neo-Classical, Tudor. All had small but tidy front yards, often flying an American flag. Children played on the side streets until late at night, dunking hoops and kicking balls into soccer nets.

The area was ethnically diverse and filled with doctors, lawyers, CEOs, and local politicians. Her father owned a company that supplied timber to builders all over the east coast.

But Neponsit leaned up against the grittier aspects of the city. Thirty blocks south on the boardwalk was a homeless shelter. Men who hadn't showered in days or weeks would find their way into her neighborhood and sit drinking on the edge of someone's lawn, or pass out on the sidewalk. A fifteen-minute bus ride brought you to the center of Rockaway Boulevard with its graffiti muraled walls, dingy bars, and surf shops.

She loved growing up so close to the ocean. Perhaps

the milieu wasn't the clear waters of Miami, the vast sloping dunes of Cape Cod, or the dramatic coastline of Orange County, but it never occurred to her that there were better beaches elsewhere.

Yet, a few years after her high school graduation, that very beach would destroy their house. It happened during a hurricane. The only hurricane Syra could remember that raged so far up the east coast. Her parents had taken a settlement from the city, which was buying up destroyed properties, then moved to Phoenix, Arizona.

Perhaps the idea of being nowhere near the ocean appealed to them. But they only pointed to the state's no tax on social security benefits, lower cost of living, dry clime, and many golf courses. Her parents didn't play golf but claimed they wanted to learn.

Syra had one more year of college, so there was no way she would accompany them. Plus, she had no desire to live in a desert. At the time, she was attending New York University and living on campus. For senior year, she moved to Brooklyn with her college boyfriend. After they broke up, she met Sam. New York relationships, if they were to move forward into living together, tended to do so quickly. Living separately was too expensive to drag heels about it.

The city held many benefits that she loved (public transportation, a jaw-dropping array of ethnic foods, all the culture you could ever dream of), but she was also weary with its many difficulties (noise, litter, a populace that wasn't always nice—in fact, rarely was).

All of the downsides of city life were somehow exacerbated by the betrayal of Sam and Catrina. What they'd done seemed like the sordid business that happened in cities—a consequence of too much convenience, too much choice. Not the kind of thing that went on out here in Amish country.

After all, how easy could it be to cheat when you had a horse and buggy for transport, no phone, no computer? When everyone in the community knew everyone? When families all lived together on the same plot of land, or at least not very far away from each other? Did the kind of heart-wrenching betrayal that Syra interrupted happen in this time warp, this throwback to a simpler era? She couldn't believe it did.

In the "real" world, people were replaceable, disposable, interchangeable. Convenient to break up, convenient to leave. Even her parents had packed up and abandoned their community at the first sign of trouble, and left their only daughter at the first sign of a tax break.

Millie had said the family who'd lived here, the Yoders, had moved to help establish another settlement and left much of their furniture. A furnished house would bring them more money at auction.

And the community they were joining would be happy to provide them with furnishings, either used or handcrafted. Imagine that! A community waiting with open arms. Open arms willing to carve you a chair. Compare that to when Syra moved to Brooklyn. Not only had none of her friends offered to help her move, but the movers she'd hired had stolen two of her boxes.

The Amish community stuck together, helping,

supporting each other. But… how did that explain the axe-wielder out back? Jonas. She couldn't remember his last name. Miller? March?

According to Millie, he was being *shunned*. His people had stopped acknowledging him. Did this mean *everyone*? Even his family? She couldn't fathom it. Syra and her friends might go months forgetting to speak to each other, but they'd never make it an official *thing*. And while she'd didn't feel particularly close to her parents, she knew they would never stop speaking to her. No matter *what* she did.

Had Jonas committed an egregious sin to get shunned? Or had it been something absurdly trivial like wearing zippers or getting caught sneaking a beer? Now that she knew the man out back wasn't the stooped, cranky-but-harmless elderly gentleman of her imagination, but was about her age, the situation had a more unsettling feel to it. The man she'd seen—at least six-feet tall, broad-chested with bulging arms, and who could swing an axe, or whatever it was called, like a toothpick —didn't look harmless.

Perhaps she should abort this mission. Drive to the train station and flee back to Brooklyn. She'd have to return soon anyway, why not get it over with?

But her vague apprehension about this axe-carrying Jonas person wasn't nearly strong enough to override the dread of the real mess waiting for her at home. Besides, her curiosity about the man out back was piqued. He looked competent enough, why didn't he move on? Find another place to live, one that was his? What was keeping him here in a community that didn't want him?

And... what transgression did he commit that earned him a life in exile?

* * *

SHE WALKED BUSTER UP A LONG, winding hill overlooking miles of vibrant pastures dotted with red barns and ochre haystacks, all fringed with hazy, blue-gray mountains. The powder-blue sky, embroidered with the fluffiest of white clouds, seemed so much broader and lower than in the city.

She didn't pass one lawn that wasn't flawless. No rusty vehicles with cement block wheels, no discarded refrigerators with the doors pried off. It was a mystery where the residents even put their trash—which couldn't be an insignificant amount given the number of people, animals, and machinery on the farms. Say what you will about the Amish persistence in clinging to a way of life that no longer existed, but they took pride in their land. *Cleanliness is next to Godliness* is a proverb they lived by.

On the way back, she realized that she hadn't kept track of her route. As the sun lowered in the sky, dusk threatened, and hunger panged her stomach, she started to get nervous she'd soon be lost in complete dark.

Finally, she happened upon a street name she dimly recognized, which meandered to a horse farm she definitely remembered, and then to the white farmette on Turtle Way.

She wasn't cut out for life with no phone. What 28-year-old person was? But this was what convinced her she needed to try to exist without one. Having gone without a phone for a week, she was starting to believe she'd been addicted to hers. She didn't dare attempt to calculate how much she was inside of her phone in any given 24-hour period, but it was probably most of those 24 hours.

She also knew once she had a phone in her palm, she'd be checking her emails to see what bullshit Sam and Catrina had sent her, writing back impulsive screeds she'd regret, stalking the pair on social media, and forensically examining their digital histories for signs of how long they'd been sleeping together. As if that mattered!

The whole point of her time away was to be *away*. She'd have to be more careful about keeping track of her movements. Bring a pen and pad and write down her route if she had to. Or train her brain to do something it had never done—keep track of where she was.

She fed Buster, then made a meal of the odd assortment of traditional foods she'd acquired in Thelma's, the Pennsylvania Dutch specialty shop about fifteen minutes away. Blueberry, dill, and jalapeno-infused hard-boiled eggs, pepper cabbage, chow-chow, and triple-cheese macaroni.

The triple-cheese macaroni sat in the oven for an hour, so she ate the rest of the foods while waiting. The unusually-flavored eggs were rubbery. The chow-chow had a sharp vinegary smell but a rather sweet taste thanks to the sugar. (She hadn't been able to resist buying something with the quirky name of "chow-chow.")

After the distraction of cooking and eating, loneliness settled in—a cruel and almost debilitating loneliness. Modern conveniences jam-packed your life. Television, music, digital books, social media, internet rabbit holes, texting. Without any of it, she felt a cold void.

She couldn't remember a time when it wasn't available to her to share every thought with hundreds of people. Now every thought had to stay locked in her head.

She opened the bottle of wine she'd made sure to buy and sat on the porch. Buster perched on the other side of the screen door, whimpering at her. But until she found a way to securely tie his leash to something, she couldn't risk him darting off into the great, dark, Amish unknown.

She was on her second glass of wine and listening to loud crickets and what sounded like loons—a melancholy *woo-woo-woo* bird call that she couldn't identify. One of the thrills of being in the country was all the new sounds. Within this cornucopia of nature, she started to identify another sound…

The *lalala laala lalaaaa* singing of a little girl.

She placed her glass on a table made of a reclaimed barrel, and slowly stood, willing her ear canals to expand so she could home in on the sound. When the sound stopped, she had the peculiar sensation that she'd imagined it. That her city-fed ears, accustomed to the racket of traffic, sirens, and the wall-penetrating sneezes of her neighbor, had invented the *lalalalala* of a child, the same sing-song she'd heard days ago.

But as she had that thought, a little girl approached the driveway from the side of the house. She was wearing a plain dress that hung to her knees, and had long hair that was crimped as if it had been earlier tied in braids. She was walking towards the street under the lackluster glow of the lantern that Syra had balanced on the porch's railing.

"Hey!" Syra spontaneously called.

The little girl stopped and turned. They stood staring at each other, shocked into stillness. About fifty feet from her, the girl appeared to be nine or ten, with defined cheekbones despite her young age, and pale, luminescent skin. Syra thought the girl's shapeless dress might be sky blue, but couldn't be positive in the dark.

"Hi!" Syra called when she regained composure. "Do you live around—"

The girl turned and ran. It happened so fast that her light dress submerged in the impenetrable darkness before Syra could finish the question.

Must be a little Amish girl, Syra thought. *She's scared to death of me.*

The nearest farm, at least that she'd seen on today's walk, was a good ten minutes away. It was odd that an Amish family, children-oriented as they were, would allow a girl so young to wander around in the night, even if this was a safe, rural area. Could she be sneaking out? And why was she always singing that trippy little *lalalalaala lalalalala*?

Chapter Ten

The next morning, Syra was rudely awakened from a fitful sleep by the loud and grating sound of an engine. It had been a long time since she'd heard a lawnmower, but she recognized the guttural grinding of it.

It must be the caretaker. Jonas. He'd said he started work early, but she had no idea he'd meant working *loudly* early. Clasping one hand on her wine-throbbing forehead, she squinted at the hand-clock—6:15 a.m.

Unbelievable.

If this is what it was going to be every morning with this guy, Brooklyn might be preferable after all. Could she get him to hold off longer on the noisy tasks?

Shuffling groggily to the open window, she pressed her face an inch from the screen. He was riding a large, bright red lawnmower that looked more like a golf cart. He wasn't close to the house, but the traveling noise was grating and unbearable. Which he must know, as he was wearing bulky black earmuffs.

"Rmmdammit," she mumbled.

She shut the window, hoping that would muffle the noise enough to return to sleeping, but the sound stabbed right through the thin pane of glass. Downstairs, she fed Buster and tried to figure out the coffee press, this time managing to produce something resembling coffee. Then she went outside and sat on one of the porch's Adirondack chairs.

She could still hear the growling of the lawnmower somewhere out of sight, but the pristine morning air elevated her mood. Through the lawnmower's grumble, there was an abundance of birds making a variety of calls, trills, and warbles. The scene was so enjoyable that the lawnmower almost didn't annoy her.

She finished her cup of coffee and was about to return inside when Jonas lumbered around the side of the house. He stood in front of the porch, looking up at her.

He had thick, slightly wavy hair past his ears, with shaggy bangs reminiscent of a seventies hippy, and was encased in the same denim overalls, this time over a black t-shirt. And he wore that same stalwart, slightly grim expression.

It was the identical expression she'd noticed on the Amish people in passing buggies. As if life was a difficult undertaking, which she supposed it was without cars or electricity.

"Did I wake you with the mower?" he asked.

What a dumb question. If he was worried about waking her, why hadn't he waited a few hours?

"Yes, but not a big deal."

Ugh, why was she lying? Now was her chance to request that he delay noisier chores. But there was something intimidating about him, and instinct told her to get on his good side. Asking him to keep quiet in the mornings probably wouldn't do that.

"You'll see me under there today," he said, pointing to the area in front of the porch. "Wanted to warn you."

"Oh, um, under there?" She half-stood, trying to see where he was pointing. It was *underneath* the porch.

"Gotta set traps for the groundhogs," he said.

Yesterday afternoon, Syra had spent about twenty minutes taking much delight in watching two adorable, roly-poly little groundhogs wrestling and tumbling over each other. Their antics had happened right where Jonas was pointing.

"Traps?"

"Yawp. They're eating into the foundation. They gotta go."

"Oh," she said, stomach sinking uneasily. Then, with much naive hope, "You're bringing them somewhere else?"

He stared at her for a moment, something like contempt washing over his grim features. "So they can become someone else's problem?" he asked. Even with the sing-song accent, the disdainful tone was unmistakable. Inherent in the question was the addendum, *Like you English person would do?*

"You mean you're going to *kill* them?" Her voice was shrill with horror.

"Well, I'm not going to take them on a date."

Before she knew what she was doing, she was down

the three steps to the lawn and standing only a couple of feet from him. This close, she got the full brunt of how tall and broad he was.

"Please," she said, clasping her hands in a begging gesture. "Don't kill them. Not while I'm here. Please."

"Miss," he said after a moment of staring at her like she was an alien. "They're eating through the foundation."

"I know, but… please. Not while I'm here."

"When do you leave?"

"A couple of weeks?"

He kept staring at her with an unreadable, stoic expression. Damn, these Amish types were unemotional. In the rapidly brightening morning, she noticed his eyes were a muted, grayish-green color, like an olive.

"What's the difference if I do it now or when you're gone?"

It was a sensible enough question, but she resented its sensibility. She realized that the country, the true rural country, not the pretend-country that was her childhood neighborhood, was ruthless. Sure, the city was ruthless, too. But with *humans*. How many times had she blithely passed people on the street who looked almost dead, and didn't bother to ask them if they were alive?

"Because I won't be here, that's the difference," she said.

As he stared down at her, she thought his look was softening, though she could be mistaken. Then he announced, "They're on borrowed time," and headed with long strides back in the direction he came from.

Chapter Eleven

*A*round ten a.m., she managed to go back to sleep for another hour, the yard blissfully quiet except for the soothing caroling of birds hidden in the tree branches outside the window and the intermittent snuffles from Buster, who napped on an oval braided rug.

When she awoke, she headed to the phone shed and dialed the only number she knew by heart—her mother's. She hadn't planned on calling her mother until she was back in Brooklyn, but the lack of things to occupy her time in Amish country changed her mind. Her loneliness persisted. And the thought of Jonas murdering the roly-poly groundhogs made her even more depressed.

"Oh!" her mom said after Syra identified herself. "I almost didn't answer as I didn't recognize the number. Are you done with your article?"

"No, I'm still here," she said, wondering how much to tell her mother. Something about staring down a street didn't make you want to get into long, detailed discussions. The Amish must know this, thus their insistence on phones being outside of the house. Chatting on the phone was time taken away from more important tasks, like reading the Bible, tilling cornfields, or milking cows.

"Are you somewhere exciting?" her mother asked.

"Sort of." She paused. "I'm in Amish country. Lancaster. Where I was born."

"You don't say! What made you go there?"

"I guess I've always been curious and thought it would make a good article. I wouldn't mind checking out the b-n-b where you went into labor. Do you remember what it was called?"

"I'm afraid I don't, honey."

"Well, where was it?"

"In Lancaster somewhere. One of those small towns. Baby, this was almost 30 years ago."

"Do you remember the woman's name? Sarah Jane's last name?"

A long pause. Syra imagined her mother's incredulous face.

"Sarah Jane," her mother said (she switched between Sarah Jane and Syra—usually Sarah Jane when she was annoyed), "we were there less than a day when I went into labor. I hardly recall a thing. Now don't ask me what color the wallpaper in the room was, or how many horses in the front yard. I had bigger things on my mind, like pushing you out of my uterus."

"There were horses in the front yard?"

"I think so. But don't quote me on that."

"Won't help me much, anyway. There are horses in pretty much every yard here."

"If anything comes to me, I can certainly let you know. How can I reach you? Are you getting another phone?"

Syra debated telling her mother the real reason she didn't have a phone—the entire debacle. She'd have to tell her soon before her mom did something foolish like buy an expensive wedding gift.

Spotting a truck hauling enormous logs barreling in her direction, she figured it was not a good time to get into an emotional discussion.

"No, I'm trying to live without phone or electricity for a bit. I'm actually calling you from an Amish phone shed."

"A what?"

"Phone shed. Amish don't have phones in their houses."

"That's wild. How long will you be there?"

"Couple of weeks at most. Well, I thought I'd see if you remembered the b-n-b or the woman."

"You're the reporter, sweetie," her mother said. "If you find the lady, let her know that Devon and Marcus Fragos say hello. Though I'd be surprised if she remembers us."

"She wouldn't remember a woman who named her baby after her?"

"I'm not sure she knows that. I might have mentioned it when we went to pick up our things. But it's all a blur. Back then, they didn't skimp on the pain meds. Once the doctor determined you were fine, we only wanted to get home. Did you get a chance to look at those photos I sent you? Of the gowns? The one with the lace overlay and V-neckline is gorgeous and would really suit—"

"Listen, Mom, I'm on the street and there's a truck coming. Let me call you back later."

"But did you receive the—"

"I'll call later, I promise. Bye, Mom!"

Syra hung up as the truck hurtled by her, its large stacks of thick logs jiggling dangerously. She took refuge behind the shed until the truck turned a corner, hoping the small structure would protect her if the logs slid off the flatbed and rolled towards her like an avalanche.

Coming up the long drive, she saw Jonas. He stood under an enormous bushy tree, and was repeatedly bending, picking things off the ground, and plunking whatever they were into a plastic bucket. Although she had the ominous sensation it wouldn't go well, she decided to initiate conversation.

"What are you—" Her ankle buckled sharply to the side. "Ah!"

She'd stepped on something round, hard, and rather large.

"That," he said, pointing at the ground near her feet. Scattered all around were what looked like light-green tennis balls. "Walnuts. Gotta pick them up or you could break an ankle."

"Oh."

"And the groundhogs," he continued. "Gotta get rid of them too. They dig holes in the ground and a deer could break a leg. You ever see a deer with a broken leg? Nothing you can do about it. Not a thing. That's the end of the deer. You think groundhogs are cuter than deer?"

He stood almost glaring at her. Millie had been right that he was *cantankerous*. Syra couldn't think of a better word.

"No, but isn't there some alternative to killing them? What if they're humanely trapped and driven away?"

"*Humanely trapped*," he grumbled, as if that was the most ludicrous combination of words he'd ever heard. "You'd have to drive them five hundred miles away or they'd only find their way back."

"Can you do that?"

"No." He picked up a walnut and chucked it far off into the nearby cornfield.

"I'd pay for the gas and your time," she persisted.

After chucking another walnut, he glared at her again. "You're from the city, right?"

"Right."

"How many rats have you relocated?"

"But these aren't rats! They're cute little groundhogs."

He smirked—at least she thought it was a smirk, it wasn't easy to tell with his beard, which wasn't the typical long, scraggly Amish beard with no mustache, but wasn't particularly well-trimmed either. Despite how rude he was being, she was determined not to let him see how much his rudeness was affecting her.

In fact, she was determined to win him over. Sam

was always telling her, *Syra, life is so much easier when people like you. If you could keep some of your opinions to yourself, you'd have an easier time of it.* Getting on Jonas' good side might be the only way to save the pudgy groundhogs. But she had no idea if he had a good side to get on.

"Well, I'll leave you alone, but I have a question," she continued.

He stared at her, obviously preferring that she would just leave him alone.

"Last night, I saw a little girl in the yard. I'm pretty sure I've seen her a couple of other times, too. She seems kind of young to be running around late at night. Any idea who she might be?"

"All the Amish do is breed," he said, derisively. "Could be anyone."

"But she was right there." Syra pointed at the driveway.

"Probably cutting through the yard on her way home."

"Yeah, I guess so. It's weird though. She's always singing." Syra came close to imitating the girl's childish trill but the man didn't seem the type who would find this charming.

He waved his arm off into the cornfield. "There are farms all around here. Every single one of them has ten, twelve, fifteen kids living on them. If you've only seen one, count yourself fortunate."

"Ha." She thought he was joking, but the stern expression on his face made her doubt herself, so the laugh came out more like a spurt of ill-defined sound.

"I was born here," she said, hoping this information might soften his attitude towards her.

"Yeah?" he asked dubiously, examining her from head to toe. It wasn't a lustful look by any means—more as if he couldn't believe that anyone who looked like her could be a native. "Never seen you before."

"I wasn't raised here, just born. It was a fluke. My parents came down for a weekend and my mom went into labor. So, they rushed to the hospital." As he continued to squint doubtfully at her tale, she added, "Now you have to be nice to me."

It was a risk, saying something like that. Something that was a tad flirtatious, a tad pitiful, a tad bossy. It could backfire—make him see her as weak, as someone eager to have his approval. But this time, his beard-coated smirk was more like a half-smile.

"I'll try," he said before slinging another walnut into the cornfield.

Chapter Twelve

*I*t was around eight p.m. when Millie drove up the long drive in her boxy SUV. Syra was sitting on the porch reading one of the few books she'd found in the shelves in the sitting room. It was called *Shunned*. (There were also piles of a newspaper called *Die Botschat, A Weekly Newspaper Serving Old Order Amish Communities Everywhere*, and a thick advertisement circular called *The Busy Beaver*. And several Bibles.)

The book appeared to be an Amish romance, with a pretty woman in her twenties on the cover, her auburn hair, topped by an organdy *Kapp*, parted straight down the middle, and her gaze modestly turned downward.

Given the title, Syra hoped the book would give her insight into the harsh practice of shunning and what was happening to Jonas. But the writing was stilted and the plot hadn't gotten to the shunned part yet.

She smiled as Millie approached with a pie in hand. "Shoo-fly?" Syra asked, hopefully.

"Peach."

Syra pulled a mock sad face. "Kidding. I'll take the peach."

* * *

INSIDE THE KITCHEN, Millie sliced up the pie while Buster sat at her heels, watching her every movement expectantly.

"My husband used to love my cooking," Millie said, stepping around Buster and bringing two plates to the table.

"Can't cook to save my life," Syra laughed.

"I imagine in the city you don't need to do much of that."

"Nope. Got delivery for everything."

Millie looked pensive, as if she was struggling to decide something. Then she said, "I used to be Amish. We girls are all taught to cook, sew, clean, from a very young age. Then there's embroidering, crocheting, quilting, braiding and weaving rugs."

Her mouth drooped wearily, as if reciting all the work she'd once had to do was enough to tire her out. Syra thought about her own childhood—one essentially of leisure, with enough time to get herself into various typical teenage troubles. If it hadn't been for bucketloads of homework and various extracurricular activities, probably far more trouble than she'd managed to get in.

In a way, she admired how the Amish put their kids to work. She was tired of reading about mothers who turned to alcohol because they were so exhausted and frustrated, but were also unwilling to tell their kids to make their own meals or get out the vacuum.

"Why did you leave?" she blurted. "I mean you don't have to say if you don't…"

Millie sighed, forked some peach pie into her mouth. "I'm not ashamed of it. I worked in my family's quilt shop. A local English couple came in all of the time. Then the wife got sick, and the husband continued coming in to get her patterns and fabric. Over the years, our little chats grew to longer chats." She stiffened her back, staring daringly. "After his wife died, there was a lot of sneaking around, leaving hidden notes for each other, things like that. We had to make a decision, and so I made it. I was 23, he was 50."

She pushed some pie crust pieces around with her fork, still looking a bit rebellious. It was clear she'd suffered her fair share of criticism about this choice she'd made.

"We were married thirty years, no children," she said. "Michael died a few years ago, leaving me a decent chunk of change. I began buying properties to rent. This is my second."

"How do you know Jonas?"

"I know the Martins because I opened my own quilt shop, and they came in a lot from the time Jonas was a baby."

Syra wondered how it was that Millie had left the community but members apparently had no issues spending money in her store. There seemed to be inconsistency in the rules. Not only why Millie could essentially remain part of the community while Jonas was banished from it, but why battery powered lights were fine while electric ones weren't. What was the difference other than the battery powered ones gave off a fluorescent glare that probably ruined your eyes?

"The two of you met by now I presume?" Millie asked, sounding a little worried for the answer.

"Yes. And you're right, he's definitely cantankerous."

They shared a chummy but slightly forced laugh, allies in putting up with moody men. Buster had installed himself at Syra's side, a pleading look in his googly brown eyes. Against her better judgement, she sliced off a very thin piece of pie and placed the plate on the floor. Within a second, the slice was gone, as if the dog had simply inhaled it.

"Speaking of Jonas," Syra began, uncertain how her question would be received. "I was wondering if you could tell me why he's shunned. I understand if you can't. But I'd really like to know, if possible."

Millie grimaced and hunched over, as if the explanation was weighty enough to affect her physically. "I suppose with you two being on the same property, you have a right to know. So you know he's not dangerous."

She sighed, wiped her mouth. She was makeup free. Syra could tell that, as a youth, Millie—with her large, grayish-blue eyes, long, oval face, and nose that was a bit crooked but perfectly suited her—must have been extremely striking in an atypical way.

Syra could picture the older man—Millie's eventual husband, Michael—setting his sights on young Millie in the quilt shop despite the company of his wife; how Millie must have appeared in her long, formless solid-colored dresses and sheer heart-shaped *Kapp*s, demurely showing the "English" couple pattern books while the husband furtively eyed her up.

"You won't repeat this," Millie said.

"Of course not."

Syra's neck prickled, an excitement jittering in her gut. It wasn't often she got to hear such juicy personal drama as the reason for a shunning.

"Jonas did the worst thing a man in Amish culture can do—besides kill someone," Millie said, lowly.

Syra made a concentrated effort not to hang her mouth open in anticipation of whatever spicy gossip she was about to become privy to. It didn't sound like Jonas had worn zippers or sneaked a beer.

"Mind you, this is all second-hand," Millie clarified. "Officially, I've been out of the community for a long time. But my sisters still write me and sneak visits. They tell me everything that goes on." She nodded knowingly. "This is how I heard it. He and Lydia Chupp were sweethearts. Lydia, I saw her all the time. The most beautiful girl. Like a little doll. Pale-blonde hair, eyes the color of the sky in summer evening, kind of a deep violet. You'll have to trust me on that one, as the Amish don't believe in photos."

"You should have seen Jonas back then," Millie continued. "The most handsome boy. A sweet person-ality too, never gave anyone any trouble. Hardworking, athletic, church-oriented. All the girls were mad for him, but he only had eyes for Lydia."

Syra had a hard time picturing the groundhog-hunting axe-man as "sweet," but it didn't surprise her to hear he'd been so handsome. He still was and would be even more so if he shaved, cut his hair, and wore something besides shapeless denim overalls.

Millie went on, "They began officially courting. But because of her young age—as I recall, she was 17 and he was 22—the families decided that the pair should wait a year before marrying." She cleared her throat, starting to look more uncomfortable. "But one evening, it was early summer I believe, the two of them disappeared."

"Disappeared?" Syra echoed.

"Yes, vanished. Everyone thought perhaps they'd left the Amish. This happens. If the young folk want to leave, they usually do it in the dead of the night. But it was a shock, considering how happy they'd seemed, how well they fit in. Jonas wasn't a fence-crowder. He seemed content working on his family's dairy farm, going to church, dating Lydia. His father had bought him the fastest horse at mud sale, one with a perfect white diamond on its head, and had the best buggy made for him. Search parties were sent out, but to no avail."

"No one called the police?"

"Oh, nooo," Millie drawled, slowly shaking her head. "Amish believe in handling their own, though I heard there was some discussion about it, especially when money that Jonas had saved was found sitting in a drawer. But about a week later, they reappeared as suddenly as they'd left."

"Where—where were they?"

"They refused to say." Millie clucked and smoothed

back her hair again, appearing to get some enjoyment out of relaying the dramatic tale.

"That's what got him shunned?"

"No one was happy about that, but no, that isn't what got him shunned." Millie took their plates to the sink, turned, and folded her arms, resting against the white Formica counter. "Soon it became obvious that Lydia was pregnant."

Syra's jaw dropped a little but she said nothing. She assumed that, in the Amish world, premarital sex was verboten. But she also knew that two ragingly hormonal young people who'd run off together were fairly likely to have had it. It sounded as if being told to wait a year before they could consummate their passion had proven too difficult for the couple.

Millie continued, "In the church, when this happens —which it does once and a while—the pair get married as soon as possible. There's no debate about it. And now we get to what got him banned." Millie raised a brow, having an unerring sense when to drop her pauses for maximum dramatic tension. "He refused."

"Refused?"

"Yes, refused to marry her."

Syra took in this news. While it was the kind of thing that went on in the "real" world all of the time, in the Amish community, this infraction was taken much more seriously.

"Did he say why he wouldn't marry her?"

"Not so far as I know."

"Forgive me for speculating," Syra said. "You know

this world and I don't. Is it possible he had reason to believe the baby wasn't his?"

Millie heaved a sigh. "Anything is possible but it's unlikely. Young Amish girls are kept on a very short leash, and Lydia's parents were even stricter than most. If she wasn't at home with her family, she was at school, church, or working on the farm. Jonas was the only boy she'd been allowed to go on dates with, and he would have only brought her to sing-alongs, then straight home. It's not… not like…"

"The English," Syra finished.

Millie grinned in acknowledgement. "Even me, bad girl that I was, only managed secret notes and a couple of stolen kisses with Michael before I left the church. This district never practiced that horrible 'bed courtship' that some of them do."

"Bed courtship?"

"Yes, on a first date, couples get into the girl's bed. They're supposed to kiss and fondle, but sex isn't allowed. You can only imagine how that was for the girls. Many of them came out of it pregnant. I'm sure a lot of it wasn't consensual. Not that girls are even taught what consent *is*."

Syra's mouth slowly dropped open again. "That's awful."

"Our district never did that, thank Jesus."

"The marriages aren't arranged, are they?"

"Oh, no. But it's the men who take the lead on everything. They ask the girls out, and the girls really have no choice but to give them a few dates. Refusing causes all kinds of gossip."

"So you think the baby was definitely his."

"He never denied he was responsible. If he had, that would have been taken into consideration. From what I heard he wouldn't say anything at all. Neither would she. So, that was the punishment that came down from the bishop. He was excommunicated. He left shortly afterwards."

"Do you think he came back here to... make things right somehow? Did Lydia ever marry anyone else?"

Millie returned to the table, sat, and drew a deep breath. "No, she didn't. But there won't be any making it right, I'm afraid. A few months ago, something terrible happened."

Syra leaned forward. Hard to believe there was more coming.

"Lydia, bless her," —Millie placed her hand over her heart— "was killed in a buggy accident."

Millie went on to say that the young woman's horse had bolted for some reason, perhaps upon hearing a loud noise, and the buggy flipped over with Lydia and her young daughter, Beulah, inside.

It was an open buggy, the most dangerous type to be in. The road wasn't well traveled, and it took a while for anyone to come upon the mother and daughter, and even longer for help to be summoned as the Amish neighbor who'd found them didn't have a cell phone. Beulah, who is nine, had her leg trapped under the buggy and couldn't run to find help.

Lydia had an internal injury and died before the ambulance arrived. She was only 27 years old.

"Imagine being a child stuck inside the buggy while

the life drains out of your mother," Millie sighed. "From what I hear, the poor girl hasn't been right since."

Syra realized she had her hand pressed over her mouth. She lowered it and tried to look composed.

"It was shortly after Lydia died that Jonas appeared here on the doorstep." Millie pointed to the windowed door where Syra had first seen him retreating with an axe in hand. "He said he was having a difficult time finding employment. He assumed the Yoders still lived here—I suspect one or two of the boys had kept in touch with him—and hoped they could suggest some work."

Millie's mouth turned down and her gaze roved to the small grandfather clock above the table.

"I offered him the job of caretaker and the daudy house. Given how poorly he treated Lydia, perhaps I shouldn't have. But being an outcast myself, I suppose I have a sympathy."

Syra leaned back and expelled a puff of air. She must have been holding her breath for the last part of the story. Now she began to suspect that the little girl she'd seen in Millie's driveway—the girl always singing —was none other than Jonas' daughter. Beulah.

Intuition told her to keep the sighting from Millie. If the little girl and Jonas had been together, he seemed to prefer no one know about it.

Millie rubbed the corners of her eyes, a consequence of Buster's presence, and within ten minutes had excused herself for the evening.

In the long seating area off the kitchen, Syra lay on the one couch, trying to read the *Shunned* book. But between the small print and the inadequate light from the battery lamp, her eyes were failing her. At least she had the answer to the question that had been plaguing her—what Jonas had done to get thrown out of his world.

He must have known refusing to marry Lydia would guarantee being banished, depriving him not only of his family and community, but his daughter. And Lydia's life would never be the same. Millie said the teen's pregnancy had ruined her chances of finding a husband, as was expected of Amish girls. Lydia had lived at her parents' farm with her daughter until her life was tragically cut short by the buggy accident.

At least, Syra thought, Lydia's pregnancy hadn't resulted in the community ostracizing her, as many other communities would have done. It had punished the proper person.

Jonas Martin.

But why would he refuse to marry her? According to Millie, he'd been deeply in love with Lydia. And they'd been planning to get married anyway—the pregnancy would have given him the opportunity to do it sooner.

Perhaps Jonas hadn't loved her, after all. Syra thought of Sam. He'd been the one to pursue her, hurry along their relationship, suggest they move in together, *and* propose marriage. And look what he'd done. Who can tell what goes on in men's hearts?

Before she'd met Sam, dating had seemed like nothing but a long series of men who courted her—sometimes aggressively—only to lose interest once she returned it. It always made her feel like an idiot.

Laying the book on her chest, she drifted into sleep. Mercifully, she didn't slip into a dream of Sam and Catrina. Instead, it was Jonas' face before her. His sad, muted green eyes, the grim expression that would sometimes lighten with a reluctant half-smile. And then the odd, singing little girl. Her prim, solid-toned dress and casually flowing hair, and otherworldly face.

Chapter Thirteen

*L*ife without electricity resulted in Syra going to bed much earlier than she did in the city. The battery-powered lamps were meant to be used outside and not for long periods of reading, her only real way of passing the time after dark. (There wasn't even a radio around, as Millie had told her music wasn't allowed in the community either—except sing-alongs which were mostly done in German.) Anticipating nightfall became part of Syra's routine.

She hadn't realized how much light constantly bombarded her in the city—even down to her bedroom at night, with the winking lights of her wifi modem casting the room in an eerie blue tint. So, within a week of arriving, she was an early bird, retiring around 9:30 p.m. and rising with the first blush of dawn.

This morning, she sat enjoying coffee on the porch, listening to the piercing warbles of the birds and the unbroken wall of buzzing crickets and cicadas. She'd tied Buster's leash to the bottom of the steps' railing, so he could sit outside with her, something he appeared to relish, pointing his snout straight up, sniffing at the fresh country air.

These past days—only a week of them—felt like a month or longer. Time slowed and stretched without the distractions of modern life.

Speaking of distractions, Jonas appeared from around the side of the house. The sight of him made her insides clench with agitation, even more than usual. Given her awareness of what he'd done to Lydia, and how his daughter had grown up without a father in a community where family was such a high priority, Syra saw him in a new light, and it wasn't a good light.

Gone were the bib overalls. He was wearing jeans and a long-sleeved, nondescript white shirt, so he looked less like a lumberjack. Remembering how Millie had said that the Amish girls had been "mad" for him, Syra reluctantly admitted to herself that she could see it.

With his boyishly handsome face, olive-green eyes, and tall build, he would have been an attraction anywhere, let alone in the provincial community. But he also would have had that laughable bowl cut the Amish men wore—his full, wavy hair would have been perfect for it. Not to mention the suspenders and barn door pants ensemble. But perhaps he'd managed to pull it all off. If anyone could, it was probably him.

"Alright, I'll do it," he said, without preamble.

"Do what?" Syra asked, straining to sound polite.

"The groundhogs. I've been thinking about it. There's a big, overgrown field by a goat farm, about twenty miles away. I can release them there. They might find their way back, but… I'll deal with that then."

"Well," Syra said, hiding her expression behind her coffee mug. "Thanks."

He paused for a long moment, bent to pet Buster, then straightened back up.

"You don't sound very grateful about it."

This galled her. Why on earth did she need to sound *grateful* for him doing something humane?

"Oh, sorry, I didn't realize that was a prerequisite. *Thank you so much*."

She didn't want him to change his mind and kill the rascals, but she couldn't curb the sarcasm lacing her tone.

He stood blinking blankly at her, then walked silently away. About halfway to the red horse barn, he called, "You're a strange one, you know?" without turning around.

At least I didn't ruin anyone's life, she mentally retorted.

"Jerk," she muttered underneath her breath, then brought Buster back inside to make breakfast.

IN THE EARLY AFTERNOON, she set Buster in the Kia and drove all over Prairie, hoping she wouldn't get lost as she was using the paper map that Millie had left for her. Much more difficult than the navigation app she was accustomed to. The map forced her to pull over occasionally to figure out directions. How the hell did people used to rely solely on paper maps?

On a main road was a series of antique outlets and flea markets. She spent a few hours exploring. Inside a large warehouse, vendors sold ingenious upcycled items: lamps made out of old clocks, clocks made out of old car parts. There were quilt and repurposed furniture merchants and all manner of collectibles, crafts, and vintage pieces.

Not wanting to carry anything heavy back to the city, especially as she anticipated having to move, Syra kept her purchases to food. Organic tomatoes and corn, homemade bread, Pennsylvania Dutch specialties like pickled asparagus and F.R.O.G. (fig, raspberry, orange, ginger) jam. (She said a big, silent *No, thank you* to the bacon jam.)

Back at the farmette, she took a shower. As she came downstairs, curls wet on her back, she was startled to see a man sticking his face almost flush against the glass pane of the kitchen door. It took her a frightening moment to process that the bearded face was Jonas. She pressed her palm to her heart to slow its spasming, then glared at Buster, who was sprawled right by the door but hadn't made a sound at Jonas' arrival.

"What good are you?" she asked the dog.

Opening the door, she automatically smiled, though she couldn't get the things Millie had revealed about Jonas out of her mind and preferred to avoid him.

"You coming with us?" he asked, thrusting one thumb over his shoulder. "This was your idea."

"With us?" she asked, confounded by the suggestion that she was supposed to go anywhere with him and someone else.

"To the field out by the goat farm. Let loose Jack and Jill. I could use some help."

She stared past him and noted that the flatbed of his truck had the gate flipped down.

"You trapped them?" She didn't bother to ask about the names.

"Would I be standing here otherwise?"

She could think of no excuse to turn down his invite (more like an order), so she said, "Let me refill Buster's water bowl and I'll meet you outside."

After he retreated down the porch steps, Syra did what she really wanted to do—pried a small knife off the magnetic holder on the kitchen counter and stashed it in the outer pocket of her tote bag.

* * *

JONAS BARRELED down the twisty side roads at a high rate of speed. The groundhogs in the flatbed must be wondering what the hell was happening. Her tote was clutched on her lap, her hand draped over the pocket containing the knife. Why had she felt compelled to bring a weapon? She really couldn't explain it. But he was so tall, broad, and muscular. So grim and bordering on nasty with her.

And the only thing she *really* knew about him was that he'd once knocked up his teenaged girlfriend, then refused to marry her, guaranteeing her a cloistered life with her parents, probably clucked at disdainfully by everyone she knew. And his daughter had grown up without a father in a conservative community where that must have been a huge deal.

Syra's train of judgment went even further—straight down to Lydia's buggy accident. That would never have happened if Jonas had been around to drive his family places, like he should have been.

She wasn't ordinarily a judgmental person—except when it came to expecting her fiancé to be faithful to her —but the way Jonas had handled things really rankled her. She had little doubt that he'd been the one to entice Lydia into having sex. After all, he'd been older than she was.

And look at him. He was physically imposing, even intimidating. Millie had described Lydia as being like "a doll." The naive girl could have felt she had to go along with his desires even if he hadn't explicitly threatened her.

Syra thought of times in high school and college when she'd been impaired due to alcohol consumption and how more than once she'd found herself in frightening scenarios with young men who became sexually aggressive with her. Fortunately, she'd always managed to extract herself, usually by the skin of her teeth. She had friends who weren't as fortunate.

"Thanks for doing this," she said, her tone flat.

He didn't respond but in her peripheral vision, she saw him shrug. They kept quiet for the short ride past endless rows of corn, past a wire-encircled field of goats, then to a vibrantly green meadow of overgrown weeds.

They pulled to the side of the stretch of empty road, and Jonas flipped open the flatbed. Wearing a thick black glove, he slipped one trap out by its handle. The befuddled animal inside banged against the steel sides, looking for an escape.

"Want me to take the other one?" she asked, hoping he'd say no.

"Nah, they're pretty heavy. We'll come back for Jill. Or maybe that's Jack."

They traipsed out to the middle of the meadow and Jonas set the trap down. "Now," he said, "I'm going to open the door and when I do, I need you to give a quick, sharp kick to the back. Otherwise, he'll stay in there all day."

Syra looked at the creature. He had his little paws up on the sides of the trap, studiously sizing up his situation. To her, it seemed as if the animal would instantly find the exit, but Jonas must know what he's talking about.

"Hopefully, he'll go out straight ahead," he continued. "But if he comes at you, you need to run. How fast can you run?"

"He might come *at* me?"

Squinting, Jonas examined her with a solemn expression. "Sure. Why do you think I brought you here? You're my decoy."

"Your *what*?"

"Decoy. You don't think I want them coming for *me*, do you?" He pointed to the woods at the edge of the field. "Hightail in there. Can you climb a tree?"

"*What*?!"

"How high can you climb? Because they can shimmy right up a tree."

"Oh my God," she sputtered. "Forget this. I'm not—"

He began laughing. The first time she'd seen him do so. She realized he had a faint gap in his front teeth, which made him even more boyish looking.

"I'm kidding," he said. "You'll be fine. They're more scared of you than you are of them."

"Very funny," she said, shaking her head disapprovingly but unable to stifle a small smile. She'd had no idea he had a sense of humor, though it was a twisted one.

"When I slide up the door, give the back a quick kick. Ready?"

She nodded, though after his perverse teasing, she was anything but ready. He moved to the side of the trap, bent, and unlatched the door.

"Kick!"

She thrust at the end of the trap with the sole of her sandal. The roly-poly groundhog sped out faster than she'd thought he could move. With a lumbering but effective gallop, it disappeared into the thick weeds. Then she and Jonas went back to the truck and repeated the procedure with the second groundhog.

"Bye, bye, sucker!" he called at the animal's retreating posterior. "And don't come back!"

INSIDE THE TRUCK, Syra didn't plan to strike up conversation, but silence was an unnatural state for her, so she asked, somewhat slyly, "Didn't that feel better than killing them?"

"They'll probably be back in a week or so. Then I'll have to do it all over again." He glanced sidelong at her. "But yeah, it did feel better than killing them."

She felt ridiculously paranoid that she'd hid a knife in her tote bag. The man had spared two groundhogs who were well-fed with devouring Millie's house. Why on earth did she think he might want to harm her? Sure, he hadn't treated his young girlfriend right, but that didn't make him a predator.

In the confines of the front seat, she could smell him. A heady masculine brew: Rugged earth, snipped grass, sawdust, plain soap.

No cologne. Not that she'd expected any.

She glanced at his arm on the wheel, trying not to be obvious about it, and noted the fine dusting of hair a few shades lighter than the hair on his head, glistening with the sun's rays pouring through the window. Noted his bulky knuckles, the tanned skin stretched taut over them, and the silver watch with a thick black leather band that, if she leaned and sniffed a little to the left, seemed to have been cleaned with linseed oil.

Realizing she was too intensely examining his arm and sniffing at him, she turned to watch the gorgeously green farmland, her emotions in a knot. He was so dynamically masculine in a way she wasn't accustomed to—it unmoored her a bit, but she couldn't deny that she was attracted to him as well. Biology was a bitch.

"What brings you way out here?" he asked, surprising her with what sounded like a conversation starter.

"A break from the city," she said, knowing this sounded coyly vague.

He went silent. Syra's attention once more turned to the outdoors. Passing a horse farm with a plump baby pony frolicking next to its mother, she wished she had a phone so she could take photos.

"I suppose Millie told you all about me," he continued.

She was struck mute, not knowing how much, if anything, she should admit to knowing about him. The last thing she needed was to make her host feel that she'd betrayed her confidence.

"Oh, she only said... that you grew up Amish, like she did."

He cast a doubtful glance her way. "She didn't tell you about me getting the boot?"

"She might have, um... she didn't say much," she finished, unconvincingly. But as he'd been the one to bring it up, perhaps it was a prime opportunity to pry a little, see what he'd reveal and whether his account matched that of Millie's.

"What makes a person get shunned?"

"By 'person,' I assume you mean the one driving." He made a *humph* noise, but as if he were more amused than outraged. "So, she did tell you."

"A little," Syra admitted.

"I figured she would. I've never known Millie to resist a juicy bit of gossip. It's in the Amish blood, since we can't text or email. Well, I can. *Now.* To answer your question, I was nearly engaged to a young Amish lady, and it didn't work out. That's not well received around here."

"Is that it?"

"That's most of it."

Syra watched the passing greenery for a long moment, then said, blithely, "That's kind of coincidental. Because my engagement didn't work out either." With this common ground, she theorized he might reveal more of his own story.

"Yeah?"

"Yeah. That's why I'm here. I discovered him cheating on me. With my best friend. Sounds kind of cliché now that I say it out loud."

They said nothing more until they approached a stop sign on the empty road. Then he said, in a somber tone, more thoughtful than she'd heard out of him yet, "That must have been rough."

"It was and is." She sighed, squirming uncomfortably. "Especially the way I discovered it. Up close and personal. I wish I could empty the vision out of my head like you empty out a piggy bank."

At the stop, a buggy from a crossroad drew out quickly in front of them. The driver was a bearded man in the typical uniform of straw hat, white shirt, and dark suspenders. Sitting next to him was a boy of about seven, gripping the front of the buggy. The horse had emerged from the side road so swiftly that Syra had the impression the cantering animal hadn't been drawn to a complete stop.

"Those things aren't safe," Jonas muttered. "No seatbelts, no nothing."

Knowing that he was probably thinking of Lydia's buggy accident, Syra didn't respond. They rolled through the sign and she tensed as they caught up with the buggy, the horse's clomping growing louder on her side of the vehicle. The sound faded as they picked up speed and left the buggy behind.

Since she'd revealed so much about her broken engagement, Syra decided she was entitled to press him a little more. "Why did you decide not to get married? I mean, you don't have to tell me if you don't…"

He didn't answer for long enough that she began to regret the question. But then he said, "I guess she and I weren't meant to be."

It didn't come out with any particular emotion, just a stated fact. He wasn't about to confess the cause of his banishment. Why Syra had imagined that he would was beyond her.

Having witnessed Jonas take the trouble to respect her wishes by relocating two troublesome but cute groundhogs, and sensing him grow so somber when the buggy pulled in front of them, her view of him began to soften.

Could he *really* be the type who would get a young girl pregnant then abandon her? And not have anything to do with his child all these years? And if he *had* done those things, what could be the reason?

At the farmette, he unloaded the empty traps and slammed the flatbed gate shut. He stared down at her and she again noted the pretty olive tint of his eyes.

"I hope they stay gone," he said. "If they come back,

Millie will want me to take care of them the permanent way. And I'll be obliged to do it. I'm on her dime."

"I understand. Thanks for giving them a chance."

He nodded at her, then ambled towards the large barn area, traps swaying creakily in his hands. It occurred to her that he hadn't really needed her help. He could have walked behind the traps and given them a kick by himself.

Chapter Fourteen

*T*his time, when she saw the little girl wandering down the driveway, Syra made a spontaneous decision to follow her. Wanting to enjoy the beauty of the starry periwinkle sky and the bright, swollen moon, she'd been sitting in the dark without a lantern.

About ten minutes after she sat, the girl's softly-pitched *lalalalaala lalalalala* rang out eerily from the dark-ened yard.

Syra's pulse picked up and she rose stealthily from her chair, trying to keep it from creaking, and peered over the porch railing. The girl was wearing the same long dress of a pale color—either light blue or green—with slightly puffy medium-length sleeves. There was an efficient and graceful fluidity to her movements.

Syra had no time to ponder her next move or she would lose the girl, so she hurried down the porch's few steps and sneaked up behind the broad walnut tree. She was wearing her favorite flipflops, the only shoes she had with her, but they were quiet and had solid, dependable soles.

The girl continued nimbly down the drive. Syra hastened from tree to tree with jaw clenched and elbows askew, hoping she wouldn't twist her ankle on a hard walnut or stumble into a groundhog hole. Country lawns were a minefield of various dangers—or at least this one was.

The girl was plainly visible as the voluptuous moon shimmered down its bright silver light. Her long hair was in two braids and Syra could even see that she was barefoot.

At the bottom of the drive, the girl crossed the empty two-lane road. Syra had no more trees to hide behind, so she stood watching, wondering if she should continue following. But she figured if the girl turned and saw her, she'd wave and walk away. After all, she wasn't doing anything wrong.

But the girl didn't turn. At the opposite side of the road, Syra suddenly lost track of her. She realized the girl must have gone directly into the giant stalks of corn. Syra kept on the road parallel to the field, trying to look like she was out for a casual stroll in case the girl reappeared in front of her.

The tiny *lalalalala* had disappeared as well. Syra's heart was thumping. It was scary being out in this dark, empty country, and right next to a cornfield, where anything—animal or human—could lunge out from its towering, concealing stalks.

About five minutes later, the rows of corn came to an end. Syra caught a glimpse of the girl as she walked with that hurried but balletic gait down a long, sloping lawn. At the end of the lawn was a rambling white farmhouse. Syra hadn't seen it before, as every time she'd left Millie's, she'd taken the main road, not this smaller side road.

Now she saw how close the young girl lived to the farmette. And the girl was obviously familiar enough with the territory to cut through a cornfield, plunging straight into the tall, closely-knitted stalks with no concern she might get lost in them. Syra watched until she could no longer see the girl and assumed she'd headed into the white farmhouse, which was completely dark.

Did the girl's family know she was sneaking out at night? Or was she leaving with permission? Perhaps Amish girls were free to roam as they pleased as this was a rural area presumably without the myriad menaces of a larger town or city. But hadn't Millie said that Amish girls were kept on short leashes?

A chilly wind accosted her. Syra clutched her arms around her goose-fleshed arms, hurrying back across the empty main road. She took note of a lone light glowing in the window of Jonas' little house.

* * *

THE NEXT MORNING, she sat on the porch drinking coffee. She had a week or so left here, she figured. Then she would have to get back to reality, a reality so ghastly that when she thought hard about it, her heart raced.

But she couldn't lose her job. Staff writing positions, especially ones that still came with perks like occasional travel, weren't easy to come by. Liz was going to run out of patience soon. But Syra had zero desire to leave. Not only because it was so relaxing and beautiful in Amish country, but she'd rapidly become accustomed to being unplugged from the world.

It had rather slowly become clear to her that being plugged in, and online especially, left her feeling low-grade empty, anxious, and angry all of the time. Being perpetually accosted with the world's ills and human beings' predilection for careless and aggressive behavior didn't do much for one's mental state. Her job required her to regularly post her articles and no matter how benign her content, someone, somewhere, wanted to be mean to her about it.

She still shuddered remembering the piece she'd written that advised against buying a home in certain areas of the west coast because of frequent wildfires. The backlash was noxious and far beyond what was warranted. She'd even received a few death threats.

And though she tried to keep up with what terms and ideas were currently considered offensive, it was a relentlessly morphing and unforgiving landscape. One wrong move, no matter how well-intentioned, and you were flung to metaphorical Siberia.

But these weren't the only reasons she was loathe to leave her unplugged cocoon. She was more intrigued than ever about the little girl. And Jonas. She was curious to stick around for whatever might happen between the two because she was almost certain they were meeting up in secret.

Why Jonas had refused to marry Beulah's mother so long ago, Syra didn't know. The important thing was that he'd returned. Better late than never. Knowing that the girl had lost one parent, he must have decided it was time to step up. But being excommunicated, he couldn't simply knock on the girl's house and introduce himself. He needed to ease back into her life, and do it clandestinely. How the two had found each other, she had no idea.

At the bottom of the porch steps, Buster emitted a series of yelps, the type he made when he was excited about something. Jonas had come around the side of the house and was crouched down petting the dog.

"He likes you," she called.

He looked up at her and smiled. His hair was shorter and trimmed back farther from his eyes, the mustache and beard neatly tamed. With the faint gap between his two front teeth, he was very boyish looking, even with the facial hair.

When he stood, Syra saw he wasn't wearing the gauche bib overalls but a nice pair of dark jeans with a tucked-in blue-and-black flannel shirt. A gleaming silver buckle drew her attention to his waist and flat stomach.

She was definitely attracted to him in a kind of animal way, one that made it tempting to walk down the steps, grab him around the belt, and yank him to her. She half-wondered if he had decided to clean up for her benefit, but pushed the thought out of her head.

"How long have you had him?" he asked.

"He's actually my friend's dog. Ex-friend. The ex-friend I caught with my ex-fiancé."

"Don't tell me you stole him."

When Syra pointedly didn't answer, he looked a little shocked, then turned up his palm in a *don't tell me more* gesture.

"She'll get him back soon enough. She took something of mine, so I guess I felt I had the right to take something of hers. It was childish."

"He seems like he likes it here."

Jonas planted his hands on his hips, and glanced all around the yard, giving off the impression that he was about to say something, but not doing it. Then he cleared his throat, kicked his black-booted feet into the grass, said *Ahhh* a few times, then finally looked at her.

"I'm going to get out the mower and wanted to… okay, no…"

He shuffled and looked around again.

"Ahhh, need to fix the… that fence out by the road —" He pointed away from the road.

"Are you okay?"

"Course, I just… I haven't done this kind of thing in a while, so… oh, heck, I wanted to know if you'd join me in the daudy tonight. That came out wrong. For dinner. Nothing special. But since we're both here, I don't know…" He trailed off into mumbling, massaging the sides of his mouth, and seeming as if he was about to wander away.

"Yeah, sure. That would be great."

He stared at her, blinking steadily, as if he hadn't expected this answer.

"Well, alright. How's, uh, well, do you want... how about six?"

"Can we make it seven?"

"Sure." Still looking dazed, he ambled off without saying goodbye.

Syra smiled to herself.

AT SEVEN O'CLOCK EXACTLY (SHE was allergic to being late), Syra knocked on the door to Jonas' daudy house. She carried a bottle of white wine, though she didn't know if he drank. If not, she'd look like a lush drinking without him, but whatever. Her belly was fluttering. She wanted one drink to soothe her nervous edges.

He answered and had somehow grown even more handsome. How had she not noticed before how good-looking he was? And that his facial hair suited him perfectly, and even his dark, shaggy mane had a great deal of charm to it?

She had on a cute sundress she'd unearthed in a nearby vintage store—knee-high with a flower pattern. Her legs were long and slightly muscular from summers paddling around in the rough Atlantic, so she liked to show them off when possible.

But Jonas hadn't changed clothes. He was wearing the same flannel and denim he'd been wearing in the morning, even though he must have been working all day.

She realized, with acute embarrassment, that she'd probably misinterpreted his invite. In her new dress, with her unruly curls subdued in a ponytail, wearing shimmery pink lipstick and black mascara, and carrying wine, it became crushingly obvious that she'd come prepared for a date. But he'd merely tossed off the invite in order to have a little company.

"Hey!" she said, almost belligerently. "Brought some wine! Not sure if you drink!"

She couldn't stop herself from practically yelling in his face.

"Yeah, I drink," he said, waving her inside. "And if you think the Amish don't drink, you'd be wrong about that. Course, like everything, they do it on the sly."

Syra laughed too airily, taking in the small house. She immediately noticed the lighting—it was the kind of warm but radiant light she was accustomed to. "You have electricity?"

"Yawp. First thing I did was wire the daudy. That and get wifi. They kicked me out, so I'm sure not living by their rules anymore."

He took the bottle from her, and walked to the small, open kitchen. She hadn't told him she didn't eat meat and wondered how to handle it if he was preparing a roast or something. She'd noticed the local cuisine was meat heavy, another thing that kept her cooking at the farmette.

"Making pasta," he said, indicating a large stainless-steel pot on the stove. "Figured it was something everyone liked, and I'm not much of a cook. And salad, with everything from the garden. You good with that?"

"Perfect," Syra said, taking the glass of wine he proffered and relieved she wouldn't have to have the no-meat conversation. He walked her in a small circle around the house, which was only two rooms, though the second room, presumably his bedroom, had the door shut.

"What does 'daudy' mean anyway?" she asked.

"That's Pennsylvania Dutch for grandfather. When people get older and need more care, they move to smaller houses on the kids' land. No one goes into a nursing home. Even if it gets really rough, and it does."

"That's admirable."

They sat on a small couch, Syra thankful that the wine was already doing its job of smoothing out her nerves.

"When do you go back to the city?"

He'd already asked this question a few times, and it gave her the odd sensation that he was eager for her to leave. But she dismissed the feeling. If that were true, he likely wouldn't have invited her over for dinner.

"Probably next week. Though to be honest, I'm conflicted. I love being cut off from everything. And everyone. I wasn't sure I could handle it at first, but now I really enjoy it. Plus, it's so beautiful here. I really feel at home."

Taking another sip of wine, she realized she was outpacing his own drinking, and decided to slow down.

"But I need to return Buster," she continued. "And get back to my job. I rushed out an email to my editor from Millie's computer but I don't even know if she's answered me. I've got nothing right now. No phone." At his slightly bewildered expression, she said, "Long story."

"You're welcome to use my computer, if you like." He waved at a small dark wood desk in the corner, on top of which was a silver laptop.

"Oh, thanks. If you don't mind, I'll come back tomorrow and check emails. It's tricky because I'm also trying to avoid whatever ones my exes sent."

Soon, they moved to the kitchen, only about thirty feet from the sitting area. A small house, yes, but no smaller than many city apartments. Jonas served the pasta, mixed with olive oil, cherry tomatoes, and shredded aged parmesan. In the middle of the table was a big wooden bowl of leafy salad.

"This looks great," she said. "Thanks for inviting me."

She'd noticed that the tips of his hair were wet, indicating he'd showered at least, so she felt less awkward about going to more trouble than he had in terms of appearance.

"Thanks for joining," he said, looking bumbling. He seemed uncomfortable with anything that hinted at intimacy, so Syra instinctually slipped into a persona that was slightly louder and more animated—one more aggressively platonic.

"Tell me about growing up Amish," she said, forking lettuce into her mouth. She wasn't sure it was a topic he was keen on, but she was intensely curious.

"It's what it appears on the surface. A real strange

way to grow up. Though not so strange if you're in it. For years, I thought people like *you* were the strange ones." He grinned. "But I've been out for a decade."

Earlier, Syra had noted a Bible on his small desk. The red fringed bookmark in the center indicated he might be reading it. "But you're still religious? I see the Bible over there."

"Old habits die hard, let's say." He looked embarrassed. "When you grow up being told that everything you do, everything you say, every part about the way you live should be about getting closer to Jesus, you don't shake that very easily. But I'm coming to understandings about God in my own way. Not throwing the baby out with the bathwater, I guess."

Syra didn't know what to say to that. She hadn't been brought up religious other than going to church for Easter or Christmas Eve, and even that was more about tradition than religion.

"How many siblings do you have?" she asked, recalling the populous Yoder clan.

"There's my twin sister, Hannah. And four older sisters, and two older brothers. My oldest siblings, Phineas and Ezra, I hardly know them. They'd already moved out and had their own families by the time I was born. Then I had a younger brother named Elam, but he died in his sleep when he was eight. Heart condition no one knew about."

"I'm very sorry."

He nodded somberly, then said, "You should know I have different views than what I grew up with. I happen to think birth control is a wonderful invention."

She laughed.

"And flossing. My parents were against it. Too worldly. My teeth have been paying for that ever since. Flossing, can't keep me away from it. Second you leave, out comes the floss."

She laughed again.

"And I'm definitely not on board with only giving an eighth-grade education."

"Eighth… grade?" Syra repeated, a little dumbfounded.

"That's how long Amish go to school for. I was 14 when my schooling ended." He sighed, dolefully. "When I left the church, or rather was ordered to leave, I had to get help with everything. Driver's license, social security number, bank account, health insurance, high school diploma, you name it."

"You didn't already have a driver's license for those buggies?"

"Nawp. Don't need them. Did I tell you Amish get away with a lot? Amish bring in so much tourism, own so many businesses. Add in religious protections and no one is inclined to mess with them. No matter *what* they do. Luckily, I found a group of ex-Amish willing to help. Without them, I don't know where I'd be."

He put his head down, and they both lapsed into silence while eating. Syra's naive and romanticized view of Amish life was taking a serious hit. And who takes a stance against flossing of all things?

"Sorry if I made you uncomfortable," she said. "It's very different from anything I know, that's all."

"I get that. I've been out of it for so long that it's all very different from what I know in some ways, too."

"So… why return?'"

She hoped she wasn't being too intrusive in her questions, though she probably was. He sighed, his lips moving slightly, but no words forming, as if he was practicing for what he was going to say.

"Because my sister told me my mom is sick. She refuses to see a doctor. Kind of an Amish thing. In case it's really bad, I want to be here. Maybe she'll change her mind and see me."

He looked so defeated that Syra's heart went out to him. What a difficult thing to be exiled from your family, your community, everything you'd ever known. Whatever had happened between him and Lydia, they'd both been so young. It seemed as if he'd been punished enough.

"Can't say I've ever read the Bible, but doesn't it say to forgive?" she asked.

"Don't get me started on the Amish incongruities," he drawled, rolling his eyes. "Cars are the devil's work but being *driven* by a car is fine. Kick bicycles are okay but no pedals! You can take a train, but not a plane. Battery powered lights are no problem but electric ones the road to hell."

"I wondered about that!"

"You want to hear the best one?" He grinned but the expression wasn't lighthearted. "When I was a teenager, bunch of men went to the bishop and said, 'God makes the sun, so why can't we have solar panels?' The bishop thought about this for a while, then agreed.

So, my father installed solar panels on our roof and told me why it was allowed. I said, 'But Da, God makes lightning, and that's electricity. So why can't we have electricity, too?' Don't ask me how I knew that. We're not taught science in school. Maybe it was a good guess."

"What did he say?" Syra asked, already knowing the answer wouldn't be good.

"He made me sleep with the cows for talking back. Ever sleep with a bunch of cows? You don't get the stink off you for a month."

Syra had walked by many dairy farms in the area and indeed the stench was thick and unbearable. She pictured teen Jonas trying to sleep in the mud, next to the moaning cows, the reek of cow dung in his nostrils, simply because he'd asked a logical question.

"Not to mention, erm, solar panels create electricity," she said quietly.

"Yeah, that too." He laughed, sharply. She began to get the feeling that being evicted from the Amish wasn't something entirely negative for him. Seemed as if he had too much of an inquisitive mind for them.

"Is it the bishop that makes all the rules?" she asked.

"Pretty much. He's supposed to uphold the *Ordnung* —the district rules. But he has a lot of power and can add or take away from them. Classic example, allowing solar panels."

After dinner, exhaustion crept up on her. She'd only had two glasses of wine, but was accustomed to going to bed early. She was also torn about what, if anything, to do with the chemistry between her and Jonas. She couldn't tell what it consisted of. Was it attraction? Was it merely the stark differences between them creating a sort of friction that she was mistaking for attraction?

If she stayed later, would it turn sexual? Should she nudge it into sexual territory? Was she thinking too much like an "English" person, who had to make everything sexual? Though she hated Sam right now, he was the only man she'd been intimate with for the past five years. She wasn't quite ready to move on in that regard.

Nor did she know what Jonas wanted. He wasn't exactly giving off flirtation vibes, but they weren't strictly platonic ones either. She'd been decrypting male vibes since she was a young teen, and her skills at knowing if a man wanted her sexually or not were fairly sharp, but she found herself at a loss with Jonas.

She decided to allow her very real desire to take Buster out for his bathroom break make her decision for her. "I guess I should walk the dog before he uses the mud room," she said.

In her dating life before Sam, if she'd told a man she wanted to leave his place and he didn't want her to, he'd start a little song and dance of persuasiveness. It was a good way of gauging how much he wanted her. But Jonas only said, "Probably right," and walked her the short distance to the door.

She looked up at him. She'd always been attracted to men with dark eyes, like Sam had. Perhaps because her own eyes were hazel, and she'd spent her entire life staring at them in the mirror, she preferred eyes that were different from her own, the darker the better. But she couldn't deny that the shade of Jonas' eyes was very alluring, drawing her to him in some indefinable way.

Suddenly, she was seized with the powerful desire to reach up and brush the hair out of his eyes so she could better see their pretty olive color.

Before she knew what was happening, she'd actually done it.

"Thanks," he said. "I need a haircut."

Oh my god, Syra thought. *What the hell did you just do?*

"Nooo," she stammered. "Your hair looks perfect. I don't—ugh, I've had too much to drink." Realizing she'd only had two glasses, she added, "I'm a lightweight."

He grinned. She was hugely relieved that he didn't appear insulted by her inappropriately intimate gesture.

"I can't believe I did that," she stammered more. "I'll get out of your hair. Ha! No pun intended."

She tried to open the door but couldn't manage it for some reason. He leaned in and pushed the lever. "It sticks. We don't bother to lock around here."

As he pulled the door open, Syra's gaze traveled to the linoleum floor. Right next to the doormat was a pair of shoes—black plastic clogs with airholes. Small.

A child's size.

She heard herself yammering, but what she said was a blur of indistinct words. Probably thanking him for dinner again. Then she was blessedly out the door, hiking up the long, dark lawn towards the main house, her thoughts a wild jumble.

The last time Syra had seen the little girl, she'd been barefoot. The clogs at Jonas' door indicated not only that the little girl in the pale dress was Beulah, but that she was definitely visiting him. Did the adults caring for the girl know about this?

Just then, she stepped on something hard and round. Her ankle snapped to the side, and she nearly stumbled to the ground. Damn walnut.

* * *

AFTER WALKING Buster to the opposite side of the street so he wouldn't do his business on Millie's property, Syra was heading up the drive when she spied a silhouette sitting on the porch.

Her heart began to thump even though she knew the filled-in shadow must be Jonas. She not only recognized his large body shape but who else would it be? Her brain was still attuned to city threats. Though to be honest, she felt safer in the city, with its constant lights and streams of people, than she did out in this dark nothingness, with dogs and what sounded like coyotes howling off in the distance.

As they approached, Buster began straining on the leash, wriggling towards the figure. Jonas crouched, rubbing Buster's head as the dog planted his paws on Jonas' knees.

"Hey, there," Syra said.

She didn't know why he was sitting on the porch when they'd said goodbye to each other not half an hour ago, but she liked that he was. Maybe he missed her company. He stopped petting Buster and straightened. It was too dark to see whatever expression he had on his face.

"The Amish are told not to lie," he said. "But like most people, we lie all the time. I told you a lie at dinner and it's bothering me. So, here's the truth. It's not my mother who's sick. It's my daughter."

Syra went into mild shock that he admitted he had a daughter. So everything Millie had told her about him was true.

"Her name is Beulah," he continued, without any inflection in his voice other than his usual slight twang. "Her mother died recently in an accident."

"I'm sorry."

"She's staying with my sister, Hannah. And Hannah's husband, who's Beulah's biological uncle. It's a little incestuous around here."

"Ha!" Syra said, then chewed on her lower lip, as if this would take back the unsuitableness of her outburst.

"I stay here because it's close to Hannah's house. Anyway, Lala comes up and spends time with me. We play Checkers and other board games."

"Lala?"

"Beulah. Everyone calls her Lala."

"Oh."

"Here's the thing," he said, staring at his feet and kicking them a little. This appeared to be his go-to move when he was uncomfortable. "Ever since the accident, she doesn't speak. She only sings."

They were quiet for what seemed a long time as Syra adjusted to this new information. So... that's why the girl she'd seen around was always singing. And apparently singing her own name. Lala.

"I don't know if it's an emotional thing or a head injury or what," he continued. "They brought her to the hospital after the accident but the doctors couldn't find anything wrong. Amish don't have health insurance, so that was about as much as anyone wanted to spend. With me only selling firewood and taking care of Millie's properties, I don't have the money for a specialist either. Even if they'd allow me to bring her to one, which they wouldn't."

"Does she know who you are?"

"No. She comes up to play Checkers because Hannah told her I'm a friend of Millie's and a champion. In case she mentions me to anyone, this won't get my sister in trouble. Because we don't know if she'll suddenly start talking."

He squinted and squeezed his temples, as if the conversation was giving him a headache.

"But I'm trying to figure out what to do," he continued. "If I try to get custody, that means taking her away from the only life she's known. All her cousins, both sets of grandparents, her friends. She doesn't even *know* me. To do that after she's lost her mom doesn't seem right. The Amish life is a hard one for women. But, from what I've seen on the outside, it's hard there, too. Just in different ways." He jammed his hands in his front pockets and stared down at the ground. "I don't stand much of a chance of getting custody, either. I abandoned her."

Syra could sense shame radiating off him. Buster

stretched up his legs seeking more attention. Jonas rubbed the pooch's head again before saying, "Anyway, I thought I'd share that. Goodnight." He gave her a short wave and abruptly loped down the long yard.

"Night!" she called but wasn't sure if he'd heard her.

Chapter Fifteen

*T*he next morning, she walked with her mug of coffee to where Jonas was working at the edge of one of the huge cornfields. He was busily spiraling white plastic tape around the spindly trunk of a white cherry blossom tree.

She'd spent much of the night wishing she had internet access so she could do research on people who could no longer talk, only sing. She'd never heard of such a thing. Was it a neurological condition? Psychological? A combination of both?

Was it dangerous for the girl that the community was allowing her condition ago unchecked, or was it protecting her from an "English" medical industry that might want to poke, prod, and medicate her into an even worse condition, then charge a fortune for it?

"What's that for?" she asked him, indicating the tape.

"Deer. Males rub their antlers against trees to mark them, which destroys them. So on goes the repellant tape, and they can't do it anymore. That's the theory, anyway."

Syra had regularly seen a family of deer—two adults and three slender, speckled fawns, young enough that their stick-thin legs were still wobbly—picking across the perimeter of the grounds before bounding into the corn. It was one of her favorite things to see every morning.

"Huh. Where do you learn all this stuff?"

"Grew up with it, I guess."

He cut the tape and pressed it on the tree, the trunk of which resembled a tall, lithe mummy. He was back to wearing his denim overalls. Syra now thought they looked damn fine on him. As he moved on to a tree that was about ten feet away, she thoroughly checked out his backside.

"I'm sure you know all kinds of things I don't," he said, depriving Syra of her view by crouching and pressing more tape on the base of the trunk.

She tried to come up with any knowledge that was unique to the environment she'd grown up in. "Well, I can get on a subway car first, no matter how crowded it is," she said with pride. "I have a sixth sense about where it's going to stop on the platform."

"See? That's something I'd never be able to do."

He looked up at her and smiled before continuing his wrapping. The smile sent Syra's heartrate into a buoyant rhythm, causing her hands to jostle and almost slosh coffee on her chest.

It was a glorious day. At eight a.m., it wasn't yet hot. The broad sky was powder blue with only dangling ribbons of cloud, the surrounding countryside brilliantly green, the air luxuriously dewy. How many summers like this had she missed, cooped up in the claustrophobic city, squeezed between air-and-sun-blocking buildings?

Maybe she could talk to Liz about working remotely. But although she loved being in the country, she wasn't sure she could handle it permanently. She knew no one here except Jonas and Millie, and she hardly knew them. If the groundhog dilemma was any indication, she didn't have the heart to survive the country, with its inherent brutality. She would let those roly-poly groundhogs chomp through any foundation of hers.

"I wonder if I could take you up on the offer to use your computer," she said. "To email my editor."

"Sure," he responded, distracted with twining the tape. "It's on the only desk in the room. There's no password. Feel free."

INSIDE JONAS' small house, Syra walked to his desk. His laptop was open and she pressed the space bar. The fact that he was so nonchalant about sharing his computer with a near stranger was a notch in his favor. In her mind, this meant he didn't have a secret life stashed in his laptop (as she was sure Sam did). She was tempted to check his search history, but refrained from acting on the impulse.

Inside her email provider, she entered her address and password. This time, she couldn't help but see that the screen was riddled with new emails. She skimmed quickly but Sam and Catrina's names still leaped out at her. She was inexorably drawn to a subject line from Sam that read, in all caps, "PLEASE TALK TO ME."

She steered her gaze away from it, went to the search bar, and typed "Liz" to bring up her editor's reply to her last email.

"Hi Syra, I'm sorry to hear that. It should be a slow week but will start picking up soon. Can you give me an ETA?"

That was so short. Syra sensed Liz was annoyed. Which she supposed her editor had a right to be. In her reply email, she took her most obsequious tone, this time delineating the dirty details of finding Sam and Catrina in bed together. She thought this would sound gut-wrenching enough to excuse her sudden departure. Even so, she also found herself embellishing the narrative in an effort to garner more sympathy.

First, she said she'd "blacked out" from the shock of what she'd walked into—which was close to the truth of her "shellshock" but more dramatic. When she "awoke" from her "blackout," she was at Penn Station and spontaneously decided to take the trip she was scheduled to take with Sam and Catrina. Again, close to the truth but more desperate-sounding. She sprinkled in buzzy mental health terms like "holding space" "centering my pain" "grounding myself" and "practicing self-care."

These were all things she was really doing, so she didn't feel too bad about using whatever popular terminology would get her more time off. She wrapped up her email with a plea for one more week, and promised to produce a story on living without modern conveniences.

Logging out, Syra sat feeling discombobulated, uncertain if her email to Liz would save her job or guarantee her termination. Three weeks away from work was a lot of time for a personal relationship crisis—at least as far as the corporate world was concerned.

Seeing a spiral notepad with a blank page on top, she decided to jot "Thank you!" on it for use of Jonas' computer. Not seeing a pen anywhere, she slid open the center desk drawer, at first without any thought that this was a violation of Jonas' privacy.

As this thought *did* occur to her, it was too late, for her attention landed on a white business envelope perched on a dictionary. The writing on the outside of the envelope was distinctly feminine and addressed to Jonas Martin, Millsburg, Ohio.

Her gaze traveled to the return address.

Hannah Chupp.

Jonas' twin sister. The woman taking care of Beulah.

Syra eyed the door as she felt herself sliding the letter out of the envelope. She'd only take a fast glance. Her heart was pumping as she poured over the loopy but clear handwriting.

"Jonas,

Millie Otto bought the Yoder place at auction. I hear she's planning to gut it. This is where he put it. I know it. He was helping build their extension at the time it disappeared. It would be the perfect place to hide it. We can't have Millie or whoever she hires finding it!

What if you came back and stayed there? Offered to do work for Millie? She's always liked you. You'd have plenty of time to search. It could be in the walls, under the floors, inside the attic or basement.

Four boys aren't good enough for him, he's obsessed with having a girl. Now that Lydia's gone, he seems to think Lala belongs to him. If you stand any chance of getting her, you've got to find it. Jonas, it must be found!

If you come, I can let her up to see you. We'll have to sneak it, but when he's down for the night, the dead wouldn't wake him. Lala sleeps far away from the boys, and her room has its own door to the yard.

Be warned she hasn't been the same since the accident. She wanders miles from home sometimes, lost in her own little world. She's quite the restless explorer, like you! I also think it might be best if you're the one to ask her about—"

There was a strong thumping sound outside the door. Adrenaline shot into Syra's veins and her trembling hands made it difficult to fold the letter and stuff it back inside the envelope. Jonas was on the other side of the door, stomping his feet. She slid the drawer closed as he appeared in the open doorway.

"Get what you need?" he asked, slapping the inside of one boot.

"Yes, thanks."

It felt like all the blood had drained from behind her face and she was breathing too rapidly. She didn't have the constitution for sleuthing around.

Hiding things was an unnatural state for her—she generally liked to share, divulge, gurgle with honesty and confession. She'd never liked this trait of hers. People who could keep silent, who could curate their thoughts, revealing only the carefully vetted ones, glided through life with much more ease. Just as Sam had always chided her.

"By the way," Jonas said. "Wondering if you've ever seen a corn maze."

"A—what?"

"Corn maze. A maze cut into a cornfield. You try to find your way out. That's what we do for entertainment around here." He shrugged self-deprecatingly. "There'll be food and hay rides and things. If you're interested."

"Yeah, sure, sounds cool." Her voice was tuned too high. She stood up from his desk, barely feeling her legs.

"Great. How's this afternoon?"

"Absolutely!"

For a moment, he looked at her strangely. She knew he could tell that something was off—it was smeared all over her face, staring out guiltily from her eyes. It was embedded in her flighty, hallow falsetto.

"What time?" she asked.

"How about we meet at the truck at four."

"Sounds good!" Before she hurried past him and out the door, she caught sight of his expression, which seemed equal parts puzzled and amused. "See you then!" she called behind her.

As she hiked back up the sloping lawn to the main house, she could feel his eyes burning into her back. Or was she imagining it? She didn't dare turn around to confirm one way or the other.

The letter's contents wormed their way into her mind.

Something was hidden in Millie's house. Something

Jonas and his sister desperately wanted. And whatever this thing was could determine if he got custody of Beulah. Her previous sense that Jonas was eager for her to leave the farmette had been correct.

Her arrival had interrupted his search.

Chapter Sixteen

*O*n the ride to the corn maze, Jonas acted perfectly normal. So normal, Syra accepted that her reaction hadn't given away the dastardly thing she'd done. She promised herself that would be the last time she'd cross that kind of boundary. He'd kindly allowed her to use his computer, trusted her to be alone inside of his house, and look how she'd repaid him. He wasn't Sam, and she had no right to start prying around in his business.

They drove about half an hour to a town called Blue Ball. Syra had giggled at the name, thinking Jonas (uncharacteristically) was making some sort of sexually crass joke. But then he went on to name other nearby towns with bizarrely suggestive names, including Intercourse, Fertility, Peach Bottom, Rough and Ready, Lickin Valley, Honey Hole, and Virginville. Syra had nearly doubled over with laughter as he reeled them off.

At the corn maze entrance, Jonas paid their entrance

fees and collected a printout with hints to help them navigate the maze.

Its theme was "Famous Lovers." They stood at the first numbered sign posted inside the field. The corresponding number on the printout read, "Scarlett O'Hara" with four choices of her "famous lovers" for answers. Their answer would determine which way they should turn.

"Oh, that's easy," Syra said. "Rhett Butler."

"I'll take your word on that. So, we go right."

They turned and walked in circles through the maze, the green corn towering over them on all sides, stalks rattling in the light wind, the dirt below their feet stamped with the footprints of the many who'd come before them. There were other people in the maze— Syra could hear them chattering through walls of stalks —but it felt as if they were alone.

Soon, they came to another numbered post and the corresponding name on their paper said, "John Book."

"Who?" Syra asked.

"I know this one. The movie *Witness*. With Harrison Ford."

"Oh, right." With her curiosity about the Amish, she'd watched the romantic thriller set in Amish country many years ago, but didn't recall much about it.

"The girl's name was… ah… Rachel! They filmed right around here at the Krantz place." He pointed them to the right. "Never thought that movie made much sense," he continued. "An Amish widow that age would have had five kids, not one. And she wouldn't have flashed her boobs at a big city cop."

"In her defense, he *was* Harrison Ford."

They chuckled and she had the urge to loop her arm through his, but resisted. After about ten minutes, they were hopelessly lost, as the numbered posts only appeared once in a while. The rest of the time, they had to guess which way to turn. After many turns that only led them back to where they'd started, he said, "No fear, I have my secret weapon."

"Google maps?"

"Even better."

He took a small compass out of his pocket. Between that and the picture he'd taken of the maze map posted at the entrance area, he soon began leading them confidently towards the exit.

Syra enjoyed being with a man who did a manly thing like whip out a compass and free them from a byzantine cornfield. But she also couldn't help wishing he hadn't led them out so fast.

The pair signed up for a hayride. The stacks of hay were set along the perimeter of a large flatbed tractor trailer. Syra squished in next to Jonas, the earthy smell of hay strong in her nostrils. The trailer took off, winding all around the multiacre farm. As it bumped over a hill, Syra was thrown sideways. A small wave of pleasure sparkled through her as she pressed into the muscles of Jonas' shoulder and thigh. He put his arm around her for a few moments before she righted herself.

After the hayride, they roasted marshmallows on long metal rods over a fire pit, chatting without any pauses. It surprised her how easily they chatted, given their dissimilar backgrounds, and how reticent he'd been when they'd first met.

He opened up more about leaving the Amish, and how hard the lessons on living in the "real" world had been on him. Like the time he'd naively left his wallet on the dashboard of his unlocked truck. The wallet contained not only all the money he had, but his brand-new social security card. It was swiftly pilfered.

"I had no idea people stole things," he said, laughing. "In the bubble I'd been brought up in, something was yours or it wasn't."

"That's a nice way to grow up," she said thinking of the myriad things she'd had stolen in her lifetime. "Until you move out of it."

"You got that right."

She was fully entranced by the radiance of his grayish-green eyes in the late afternoon light. There was no point in struggling to arrange her expression into something more aloof. She wouldn't be able to do it, and she didn't want to do it. If he could deduce by the dreamy glow on her face that she was attracted to him, then fine.

On the drive back, the sky was streaked with a spectacular display of cherry red, cotton candy pink, and apricot hues. A few times, they pulled to the side of the road, where they could better admire the sky between gaps in the trees or from a high hilltop.

"Do you ever get tired of looking at this sunset?" she asked.

"How could I get tired of looking at something so beautiful?"

He was staring at the horizon, not at her. But Syra's

insides flushed pleasurably, because his declaration had an unmistakable double meaning to it. So she imagined, anyway.

As they approached the farmette, the deepening evening sky had turned a luscious scarlet, reminding Syra of Millie's description of the color of Lydia's eyes.

She tried to imagine what Lydia had looked like. Extremely young, fawn-like, with a perfect little upturned nose, limpid eyes, and thick lashes. Syra was only guessing based off Millie's rudimentary description. But her imagination had turned Lydia into a kind of Amish Barbie doll.

But she'd never know for certain. It's not as if Lydia had any social media presence she could examine. As the Amish didn't believe in photos, Beulah would have none of her mother. Would she eventually forget what her own mother looked like? Would that matter?

The "English" were obsessed with images, to the point where images seemed to run their lives. And yet, how much in a photo told the truth about anything? She and Sam had plenty of photos of themselves appearing deliriously happy together. And had they been? No. Ditto photos of her and Catrina. Had they truly been loyal best friends? Apparently not.

If only there was some way that Syra could help Jonas find the thing that could be hidden in Millie's house. She couldn't suggest joining his hunt as that would mean admitting she'd read the letter from his sister. Nor could she conduct her own search, as she didn't have a clue what to look for.

"That was fun," she said, hopping down from the

truck. She didn't add that it was fun mostly because he'd been there.

"Just how us hicks get our thrills."

Syra was surprised but pleased that Jonas was keeping pace with her as she walked toward the main house, not veering off to his side of the yard. Was he going to suggest accompanying her inside? If so, what should she say?

Hearing them approach, Buster started barking. He probably needed to pee, and she felt a little bad leaving him alone for four hours. She turned to face Jonas. It was on the tip of her tongue to invite him in. He could at least come with her to walk Buster. But they'd just spent a large chunk of time together. If he wanted more time, she felt he should voice that. He may have left Amish life a decade ago, but she was willing to bet he was still hardwired to take the lead on courtship. If that's even what was happening.

"Guess I better walk him," she said.

"Guess so."

They stood awkwardly. He didn't appear to want to suggest coming inside with her, but nor did he appear to want to leave.

"Thanks again," she said. Then, without thinking, she hugged him.

He was so wide, she could barely get her arms around him. Then the hug ended as quickly as it began. It occurred to her this might have been a breach of Amish etiquette on her part. He may not belong to the life anymore, but Syra knew that deeply-ingrained customs could keep a tight hold. Proven by his still reading the Bible.

She was in the process of turning when he suddenly leaned over and kissed her on the cheek. She was so taken aback by the gesture that she laughed out loud.

"Sorry," he mumbled. "If that…"

"No, no," she stammered, devolving into her nervous habit of giggling when hit with intense emotions. "It's fine. Haha. Okay, see you tomorrow."

She practically sprinted up the porch steps, regretting that she hadn't taken that small window of opportunity to turn her mouth into his.

Hopefully, if her inane laughter hadn't turned him off forever, she'd have another chance.

Chapter Seventeen

*T*he next morning, she failed to see Jonas working on the grounds as usual. She walked around inside the house, staring out the windows one by one, scanning the sprawling property. Then she sat on the porch sipping her coffee, hoping to see him.

But she didn't. He was probably inside the barn, which contained a large tool area. She didn't want to track him down and give off the impression she was stalking him.

Besides, what if he was avoiding her? After his cheek kiss, innocent as the gesture was in the "real" world, the dynamic between them had definitely shifted. Perhaps he was regretting what he'd done.

Or given that she'd laughed in his face when he'd done it, he was humiliated. How could she explain that she often laughed at inopportune times, that it was a nervous tic? She'd even laughed in the middle of sex before. Well, she wouldn't tell him *that*.

Should she go find him? Apologize for laughing,

clarify that she'd only done it because she'd been surprised and pleased? Should she confess she'd been reluctant to wash her face last night because she didn't want to wash away the feeling of his lips on her skin? Should she mention that she'd thought about him all night long?

God, no. She couldn't tell him any of that. She had to get ahold of herself before she saw him lest she blurt out one of these imbecilic mental ramblings. Browse the vintage stores, go buy some of those wacky Pennsylvania Dutch specialties. Splurge on a moon pie.

Buster sat at the bottom of the steps, occasionally whining, as if he too was anticipating Jonas' arrival, and was disappointed that it hadn't happened yet. His whines increased and rose to a few short, rough *arf arf*s.

When the pup's barks didn't herald Jonas' arrival, Syra leaned over the porch railing, wondering what was agitating him. That's when she spotted the gray-brown hindquarters of a creature scurrying to the underside of the porch steps.

"Oh, shit," she breathed. She'd only caught a glimpse of the retreating backside of the critter, but it appeared to be a groundhog. Either a new one, or perhaps Jack or Jill—or both—had found their way back to the house, as Jonas had predicted.

She went down the steps to where the creature had vanished. She crouched, keeping a safe distance from the area, but hoping to confirm what she'd seen. Perhaps it hadn't been a groundhog but a large rabbit or even a stray cat.

Underneath the porch was a dirt floor that disappeared into darkness. Maybe there was a way to scare whatever it was out of there. If she threw a rock in its direction, it might run off and not come back.

Untying Buster, who kept wrinkling his snout and sniffing towards where the animal had scampered, she walked the dog inside. Grabbing one of the claw-like lithium battery flashlights, she walked back outside, keeping an eye out for Jonas. She'd gone from hoping she would see him to hoping she wouldn't. Then she returned to the bottom of the porch and crouched down below the steps, shining her flashlight under them.

She made ridiculous sucking noises with her lips, as if this might call out the animal, as one would call a cat. Finding an apple-sized rock half-submerged in the dirt, she dug it up, thinking she could toss the rock near the critter. Hopefully, it would run off. Better that than Jonas catching sight of it and plotting to kill it.

"Come out here, dammit," she said lowly, crab-walking closer to the porch's underbelly. Shining the flashlight around, this time its beam landed on a hole in the dirt, one about a foot across and several inches deep. Getting on her knees, Syra crawled closer and lifted the flashlight higher, until its light slanted directly into the hole.

There was something solid and angular poking out from the dirt. Whatever the thing was appeared to have been dug up by the groundhog. She was about to flick off the flashlight and backtrack when a part of Hannah's letter to Jonas came to mind.

It could be in the walls, under the floors, inside the attic or basement.

With her heart pounding, she took a final visual sweep around the yard, intensely paranoid that Jonas would suddenly appear. Then she sank to her knees, crawled completely under the steps, and dug the thing out with her bare hands.

* * *

IT WAS A BOX.

A plain wood box, soft brown in color, with the rings of the tree it was carved out of clearly visible. About a foot long and five inches deep.

There was a small, dirt-encrusted clasp holding the box shut. On its bottom left side was an etching. She sat on the toilet seat upstairs and carefully wiped the dirt around the etching with a wet washcloth. Within several seconds, she could see that the etching spelled out, in simple font, J. MARTIN.

Oh my God, she thought. *This is it. The thing hidden in the house that Jonas and Hannah want back.*

She spent several minutes wiping the clasp, getting it as dirt-free as she could. When it was good and clear, she placed the box on the floor, and thoroughly scrubbed her hands, trying to dig all the dirt out from underneath her fingernails. She sat down on the toilet seat again, staring at the box.

How could she tell Jonas she had it? What could explain her crawling underneath the porch? No one randomly crawls under a porch. She'd have to tell him she'd seen a groundhog. That would spell its doom. She wasn't at all confident she'd twice be able to talk him out of killing it.

She cleaned the sink with soap, then found paper towels and a spray bottle of disinfectant in the sink cabinet and wiped the dirt off the linoleum floor. Now she knew why ugly linoleum was in every room—the dirt easily lifted away.

Then she took the small garbage bin where she'd deposited chunks of dirt caked to the box, spied out several windows to make sure she didn't see Jonas, and hurried out with the bin, dumping clumps of dirt underneath the porch steps.

Chapter Eighteen

The box was under her bed.

She couldn't think of anywhere else to hide it in case Jonas entered the house while she was out. But... he wouldn't come in, would he? Unless he'd been coming in every time she was away. Millie hadn't given Syra keys, so she'd only been locking the doors from the inside.

She paced the bedroom, staring out the room's windows, keeping her eyes peeled for Jonas. Buster lay on the braided rug, curiously tilting his head at her.

If you stand any chance of getting her, you've got to find it.

If only she could think of some other way to tell him how she'd found it. He would see it was muddied with dirt. She couldn't say she'd creeped under the porch, exactly where the groundhogs had been, *apropos* of nothing.

Even if she lied—told him she *thought* she saw a groundhog, but did not—or that she saw something *else*, he'd still investigate. He'd see the new hole. He'd see more foundation destruction. He'd know the groundhog —or more than one—was there and he'd set a new trap. This time, it would be a killer trap.

Could she get the box clean enough to claim she'd found it inside of a closet? That wouldn't work either. No matter where she might say she'd found it within the house, it could be a location he'd already checked. He'd know she was lying.

Sitting on the bed, keenly aware of the wooden box beneath her, a sore ache spread within her gut. There was a war going on within herself—the desire to hand Jonas the box, walk away, and come what may for the groundhog.

And the desire not to do that.

The desire to do something else. Something she shouldn't do.

"I can't open it," she said aloud. Spending so much time alone was making her slightly unhinged. Human beings need someone to bounce things off of and she had no one.

In the past, she would have gone to Catrina for advice. She was the one friend who would understand Syra's desire to open the box. Catrina loved drama and secrets. She too would want to know what was inside.

I could just flip it open, Syra thought. *Flip it open quickly, and see what's inside.*

Just take a quick peek.

In the bedroom that overlooked the driveway, she saw that Jonas' truck was gone. He'd taken off to do some kind of errand. She stared at the empty spot where his Ranger was usually parked. Then she went to the other bedroom, reached under the bed, and slid out the box.

Chapter Nineteen

$\mathcal{T}$he smell of dust, the smell of age, the smell of history.

Inside was a stack of folded paper. The paper was thin, slightly-yellowed onion paper, the kind people use to mail abroad to save on postage. The individual papers were stacked, each folded multiple times into medium-sized squares, and tied with black string.

At first, she thought the knot might be too tight to open, and there was no way she could cut the string and then give the box and its contents to Jonas. But burrowing into the knot with her nails, she was able to fairly easily untie the string. She sat in the second bedroom's one chair, keeping her eyes and ears open for Jonas' return.

Her heart was pounding furiously, her hands shaking. Her body certainly knew what she was about to do was wrong. So why was she doing it?

Something about the urgency in Hannah's letter to Jonas.

If you stand any chance of getting her, you've got to find it. Jonas, it must be found!

What if whatever was in this box *shouldn't* be found?

Much as Syra was starting to like Jonas—his sparing the groundhogs, his cooking her dinner, the cute gap in his teeth, his olive-green eyes, and his gentlemanly kiss on the cheek—the reality was she didn't know him at all.

Sure, they'd exchanged stories at the corn maze. But she was jaded enough to know that men could and did pretend to be one thing when they were actually another. Look at Sam.

It was quite possible that Jonas had turned on a charm offensive in a calculated attempt to control her. For one, if she stumbled upon the thing he needed—which she *had* stumbled upon—then she'd be more likely to simply return it. After all, the box had his name on it. It had to be his.

Syra couldn't and shouldn't dismiss the things that she knew about him.

At 22 years old, Jonas had disappeared for a week with his 17-year-old Amish girlfriend, Lydia. Lydia had come back from the excursion pregnant. Jonas admitted the resulting child was his.

Lydia may have been over the age of consent, but she'd still been awfully young, and Jonas had been five years older. Syra had mostly tamped down her unease with the age difference, given that Amish customs were different, the women were expected to marry and begin having children earlier than in the "real" world, and the pool of available co-procreators would be much smaller.

But Syra's disapproval with his refusal to marry

Lydia and raise his daughter jabbed her despite her increasingly strong attraction to him.

These letters could contain the reasons why he'd made such an irresponsible decision. They could contain the answer as to whether or not he should get custody of a vulnerable young girl. A girl who'd already suffered so much trauma that she'd stopped speaking.

And, deep down, Syra knew there was another compelling reason for her to read these letters.

She could feel the beginning of her falling for Jonas Martin. The kind of falling that wasn't based in anything except a visceral *feeling*, a tugging, magnetic sensation. Nothing practical, nothing rational.

She needed to know if she should allow herself to continue to fall.

Chapter Twenty

She unfolded the first letter on top of the batch, not knowing if they were in any kind of order. The letter was only one page. The handwriting was in neat, plain shorthand with flourishes that looked young and feminine. The ink was black and slightly thick. There was no date.

The first line of the letter deepened Syra's queasiness, for it began with, "Jonas." She glanced out of the window, double checking that his truck was still gone. She was about to plunge into his past and was grappling mightily with whether she should.

She would read this one letter. Only one. Then she'd retie everything and invent some way she could have found the box.

Jonas,
It was so nice to see you at church

yesterday after your illness. I hope you're feeling better? You looked quite well. You always look wonderful to me. Mem says you can continue tutoring me even though I'm done with school. She thinks it's good to keep my math and reading up for work in the store.

I wish I could see you before next Sunday. I hope you'll be at the Borntrager's for the volleyball game. I always love to watch you hit that ball! I'll put my heart out there and admit when I go so many days without seeing you, I get very sad. But chances are you won't get this letter until after church when I can sneak handing it to you. I hope you have one for me.

Lydia

Syra leaned back into her chair, brimming with emotion. The letter was so lovely. So innocent. Lydia seemed so in love with Jonas. Ugh, the whole thing was tragic!

Eyeing the empty driveway, she glanced at the hand-clock over the bed. A little past noon. She'd read one more. She refolded the first letter, placed it to the side in the box, and unfolded the second.

Jonas,

You looked fetching today at church. Fetching! I saw that in a book. Thank you sooooooo much for your letter. I read it over and over and over. I wish it was a bit longer. Can you write on the back too so it's longer next time? Maybe I'm being too demanding. I'm supposed to be sweet at all times. But I admit sometimes I feel greedy when it comes to you. I want more than a handshake. I want more than you secretly putting your hand on mine when no one is looking. I want more, more, more.

I know you'll be at Esther Miller's wedding so I won't despair too much that I won't see you until next Sunday. I'll give you this letter then and hope you have one for me. I thought for a moment that Harley Yoder saw me slip the last one into your hand. He is always staring at me! I know as soon as I turn 17, he's going to ask me on a date. I'm going to say NO. At least when I turn 17, I can go to the youth group and stop being watched so much.

I should have been allowed last year!

It's not fair! All my sisters were allowed at 16 but after what happened with Sadie getting engaged so quickly to Menno Miller, my parents want to hold onto me longer. I think it's to keep me doing chores and cleaning houses!

Can't wait to see you. That sounds forward but I don't care. Righteous lips are the delight of Kings, he who speaks the truth is loved!

Lydia

SYRA SMILED TO HERSELF, folded up the second letter, and placed it back on the pile. She sighed. What a precious little courtship. Absolutely nothing at all like hers had been with Sam. She and Sam had only gone on two dates before they'd had sex, and their emails had been sexually charged before they'd met in person. Looking back, she wondered if she'd even *known* him before she'd committed herself.

How wonderful it must be to get to know someone slowly through letters and community get-togethers. She was thoroughly disabused of her idea that the Amish life was an ideal one, but perhaps the community had the right idea about courtship—at least this kind, not that bizarre "bed courtship" Millie had mentioned.

And she was impressed with Lydia's courage and spunkiness. She remembered Millie saying that Amish girls didn't have much agency when it came to dating, and yet Lydia was intent on turning down Harley Yoder because it was Jonas she wanted.

Yet… something between them had gone wrong, torn the young lovers apart. Something that was cause for Jonas and his sister to desperately want these letters back.

Also, there was another party involved—a nameless "him" who'd been the one to bury the box when he was helping to build this house's extension. Who was he? And why would he bury the box?

So far, the missives were so precious and delightful that Syra was crawling with shame that she was reading them. The impulse to shut the box and return it to Jonas was strong. The only thing stopping her was the inability to come up with a convincing story to explain how she'd found it.

Chapter Twenty-One

*I*n the afternoon, she took Buster for a long walk around the neighborhood, stopping to allow him to sniff and bark at various farm animals: horses, goats, chickens, cows, black bulls.

At a goat farm, a heavily pregnant goat waddled right up to the wire fence, her belly jiggling from side to side. Syra tied Buster to a nearby rail and spent time rubbing the friendly goat's head. After about an hour, she walked back towards the house, still admiring the views on all sides, while thinking about Lydia's letters to Jonas.

Her vague plan was to spend her remaining time getting to know Jonas better. Perhaps launching her own charm offensive. Then, the day before she left, she'd casually tell him she'd seen a groundhog scurry under the porch. When she'd inspected beneath the stairs, she'd spotted the hole and the half-buried box.

Hopefully, by then, he would be fond enough of her to agree not to kill the critter (or critters), but to relocate it again. But the reality was, there wasn't much Syra could do to control the situation. If the little beast kept returning, it was dooming itself. At least Syra would be back in the city and not have to watch it happen.

Approaching the farmette, she saw Millie's boxy maroon SUV parked in the driveway next to Jonas' black truck. Her heart sped up in an excited rhythm to see that Jonas had returned from wherever he'd been. And it would be nice to talk to Millie, who probably came to—

Syra jolted to a sudden stop, eyes adjusting to the figure who exited the passenger side of Millie's car. Millie came around to the road side, and stood alongside the figure. At first, Syra couldn't move. In the time it had taken her brain to identify the figure, her body already knew.

Sam.

She couldn't imagine how it was that Sam was with Millie. Her immediate irrational urge was to turn and run away. Millie was smiling, but appeared a bit uncertain. Sam had an unreadable expression. Syra decided she couldn't flee, she needed to confront the situation.

"Your friend said it was an emergency—" Millie started, but her smile deteriorated as she absorbed the look on Syra's face, which couldn't have been pleased. "I agreed to drive him here, but, um…" Millie trailed off. Syra got the distinct impression that the woman realized she'd made a mistake.

"He's not my friend. This is my *ex*-fiancé, Sam." She stressed the *ex*, in case Sam was wondering.

"Ohhh," Millie breathed, her expression sagging. Then she glared at Sam but refrained from speaking.

"I'm sorry," Sam said. "But I really needed to see her." He had that deferential look on his face, the one that usually won people over.

"Well, I don't…" Millie said, flustered, then trailed off again.

"It's fine, Millie," Syra said. "I'll handle it."

"I only want to talk," Sam said. "Then I'll leave. They got ride shares out here?"

"Of course," Millie snapped, huffily. She was still half-glaring at him, as if she didn't know if she should berate him or not.

"Let me put Buster in the house and we can talk," Syra said.

* * *

ABOUT FIVE MINUTES LATER, she sat with Sam on the porch. Millie had reluctantly left, appearing as if she didn't know if she should try to corral Sam back into the car. She'd thrown a few more poisonous glances at him for good measure before driving away.

Syra was gratified to see that Sam looked terrible. Puffy bags formed under his eyes if he wasn't getting enough sleep, and in the bright sunshine, they were plainly visible. As were gray strands of hair threaded around his temples that she'd never noticed before, possibly because their Brooklyn apartment had little natural light. She hoped the baggy eyes meant a guilty conscience was robbing him of sleep.

But he was dressed sharply in bright white chino shorts and a button-down shirt overlaid with an intricate diamond pattern. He ordered most of his clothes from expensive catalogs and tended to spend Sunday mornings poring over them. He currently looked as if he was on his way to a summer cocktail party in the Hamptons.

"How did you find me?" Syra asked, sipping her glass of water. She hadn't offered him one.

"I spoke to your mom."

Unbelievable. Her mother, the traitor. But she knew Sam could charm the birds out of the trees when he wanted to.

"What lie did you tell her?"

"No lie. I told her we'd been in an argument and I wanted to find you. She told me you were in Lancaster somewhere and she actually seemed eager for me to come get you. Only you hadn't told her exactly where you were. Then I found a notebook on your desk with a bunch of scribbles. One said 'Hansel and Gretel.' Google did the rest."

Damn, she vaguely remembered jotting down the name of the cottage in a notebook when she was looking for places to stay. Of course, she hadn't thought to cover all her tracks when she'd fled from the apartment.

"Then you lied to Millie," she said.

"She wasn't there, a family was, but they called her when I explained the situation."

"You mean when you lied to them, too."

"What did you want me to do? Tell a bunch of strangers our personal business?"

She said nothing, taking another sip of water, her solar plexus clenched with nerves. Despite her animosity towards him, his voice was so familiar to her that it began stroking her senses in some revoltingly strange way. As if it wasn't Sam visiting her, but Brooklyn itself.

"Nice area," he said. "This was where you'd planned for the trip?"

"I don't want to talk about that. Why did you come? In case there's any confusion, we're broken up. The wedding is off. I was planning to return next week, and we can sort everything out then."

"Syra, I—"

"I don't want to hear it!" She tried to lower her voice, not wanting to alert Jonas to what was happening, as he must be around somewhere. "What you did is unconscionable," she hissed. "With Catrina of all people."

"Listen, I can sit here and apologize, and I'm going to. I apologize a million times over. But I thought you'd want to hear what happened."

"You had sex with my best friend. In *my* bed. What kind of piece of trash are you? Actually, you're an insult to trash."

She was starting to tremble, and couldn't stop her voice from climbing, becoming strident. She only wanted him to leave. There was nothing, absolutely nothing, he could say that would blunt the outrage of the situation.

"Syra…" he sighed, spreading out his hands in a

gesture of defeat. "I'm not here to excuse anything. We both feel terrible."

"Oh, please!" she scoffed. She knew that Catrina probably didn't feel terrible. Deep down, her ex-friend was probably impressed with herself.

"I can't even tell you how it happened," he continued. "One minute, she was crying because James pulled some shady shit on her, and the next, we were naked. It doesn't help that we began drinking." He pulled a funnel of air through his nose, and blinked several times. "It was inexcusable. I'm not expecting you to forgive me. But it's not like we were having an affair. I thought you should know it was a one-time thing. It just *happened*, and…"

"That makes it worse, Sam," she spat. "I could understand if you fell in love with her because you two had been working together. But you were *suddenly* naked? What's to stop you from becoming *suddenly* naked with anyone else? If you'd *suddenly* become naked with my best friend, then *anyone* is up for grabs."

"As I've told you a million times, I don't even *like* Catrina."

"Oh my God!" she cried, throwing up her hands histrionically. "So you ruined our relationship for a woman you don't even like. I'm supposed to feel better?" She stood and pointed towards the road. "Would you please leave?"

He sat for several moments, then reluctantly stood, brushing his bright white chinos with his hand before staring at her.

"Catrina wants her dog."

"Oh, does she!" Syra yelled. "She's calling the shots now, is she?"

"It's her pet. She's been pretty patient, not calling the cops."

"Go!" Syra hollered, pointing to the road again. "See if you can get NYPD to come to Lancaster for a dog!"

"Be reasonable. Why do you need Buster? He doesn't have anything to do with this."

"She owes me a grand for his vet bill!"

Syra was full-on yelling now, her voice resonating with a faint echo as it propelled through the countryside.

"Fine. I'll give you the money."

"*You'll* give me the money? For a woman you supposedly don't even *like*?" Syra knew him. He was pretty cheap. There was no way he'd be willing to pay off a thousand-dollar vet bill unless he was still sleeping with the dog's owner.

"I'm sure she'll pay me back soon as she can. If I cash app you right now, will you give him to me?"

"No! But you can pay my half of the River Café deposit!"

He swiftly closed the space between them and abruptly was right up in her face. "Listen, it's not your dog."

"Oh my God," she breathed, studying the ferocity in his eyes. "You didn't come to apologize or explain. You came to get Buster. You're here doing her bidding. You must still be fucking her. There's no doubt about it."

"What does it matter? We're not together, right?"

"Leave!" she demanded.

"You need anything, Syra?" came a deep, twangy voice from the bottom of the porch.

She turned to see Jonas. He stood holding his axe, one big hand on the handle, the other tucked under its blade. His stance communicated he was prepared to use it if need be.

Sam retreated a few feet and stared at Jonas, his mouth open in a little "o." Syra felt a deep satisfaction at his astounded reaction to Jonas' presence.

"I'm—I'm okay. Thanks," Syra said.

"You sure?" Jonas flexed his wide shoulders, jutting out the axe.

"I don't want any trouble, man," Sam murmured.

"Then you should listen to the lady and leave."

"I just came to collect the dog. It—it isn't hers."

"It's hers for now."

Syra relished watching Sam be out-alpha'd by Jonas. But she didn't want their confrontation to escalate, so she put her hand up at Jonas in an *I got this* gesture.

"Sam, I'll be back next week," she said, switching to a placating tone. "Buster will come with me. What's the big deal? You and Catrina have each other, can't I have him for a little while?"

Sam hesitated, appearing to assess the risk of pressing the issue when a burly guy armed with an axe stood between him and the road. "I don't see why it's so important, but fine, I'll tell her."

Jonas pointed down the driveway with his free hand. "There's the exit," he said, his delivery as if he was genuinely helping out a neighbor. "Take a right at the road and you won't get lost."

Chapter Twenty-Two

"Y ou probably already put two and two together, but that was my ex," Syra said.

"Yeah, I kind of figured that." Jonas waved for her to enter his daudy house.

It was early evening, the sky had deepened to its usual deliciously rich lavender, and she had brought Buster on his post-dinner walk. Then she spontaneously continued to Jonas' little house, wanting to thank him.

After Sam had agreed to leave, Jonas had ambled away, saying, "I'll be splitting heads—I mean *logs*—right over here if you need me," and giving one last mildly-threatening thrust of the axe. Then Syra had stood on the porch watching until a car pulled up and drove away with Sam inside of it.

"Want a drink?" Jonas asked.

"Sure. Can I let him off the leash?" she asked, indicating Buster.

"No problem."

Glasses of white wine in hand, they sat on the small couch in the sitting area while Buster sniffed around.

"I'm really sorry you had to see that," she said. "He tracked me down, then lied to Millie about who he was. He only came to get Buster. He wasn't here to get me back, that's for sure."

Ever since Sam had left, Syra wanted to let Jonas know that her ex's arrival hadn't changed her mind about him. If anything, it had hardened her even more against him.

"I admit I loved the look on his face when you showed up brandishing an axe," she added, smiling.

"I grew up Amish and that means non-violent. But I'm not against a little show for the English. Especially when they're assholes."

They laughed. She called Buster over as he was attempting to stuff his head inside one of Jonas' rain boots standing by the door. She also noted that the child-sized plastic clogs were still there. Apparently, Beulah hadn't been over for a few days.

Clearing his throat, he said, "Syra, you're probably wondering why… why I haven't…"

She waited, but felt she knew what he was going to say.

"Why I haven't tried to…" he continued, and she didn't think he was ever going to get the words out, so she jumped in.

"Why you haven't made a move on me?"

"Something like that." He grinned a little, seeming grateful that she'd been the one to voice it.

"You kissed me on the cheek," she said, hoping her

own smile negated her burst of laughter when he'd done it.

He looked embarrassed. "See, it's that…" He cleared his throat, took a quick sip of wine, and began the eye contact avoidance he did when he was uncomfortable. "I didn't grow up with any kind of dating life. Lydia and I had only begun courting and we'd only had a few kisses before…"

He lapsed into silence, then gathered himself.

"Amish aren't brought up with physical affection. We don't talk about things, important things. I had one serious girlfriend after I left. It didn't work out, probably because I don't know how to be in a relationship." He finally shifted his focus back to her. "I want you to know I think you're interesting. And smart. And… I guess it goes without saying that you're very attractive. I'd like to know you better. But I still don't know what I'm doing. I don't want to mess up another one."

She'd heard variants of this speech from men before. It was a version of *It's not you, it's me.* But with Jonas, she knew it was genuine. He wasn't handing her excuses rather than admitting he wasn't interested. He was grappling with his unique upbringing, one that had left him singularly unprepared to navigate the outside world, both in practical and emotional terms. He was also dealing with the situation involving Beulah.

And the box. He needed to get the letters back for whatever reason. To do that, he needed Syra to leave the farmette so he could continue searching for it. Becoming involved with the home's guest wasn't exactly a way of encouraging her to leave.

"I think you're all that, too," she said. "Including being very attractive." The smile that spread across his face at the compliment almost made her lean in to kiss him but she stopped herself. "You have a lot on your mind with Beulah. It's right to prioritize that."

"So maybe... I was hoping we could be..."

"Friends?"

"Yeah, friends... *first.*"

One side of her mouth curled up contentedly. He wasn't shutting her down for good. He was doing what she couldn't ever remember another man doing—wanting to get to know her as a human being before a sexual being.

"I'd really like that. I leave next week, but you have email right? And a phone?"

"Damn right I do."

She watched him carefully for signs of enthusiasm at her announcing her departure, but saw none.

"Can I ask you a question?" Her mild alcohol buzz was fortifying her determination to try to get clarity on the point most bothering her. "You mentioned you and Lydia only had a few kisses. But Beulah is yours? You don't get a baby from kissing."

He seemed to slip into a trance, to the point where his wine glass, which he had balanced on his thigh, listed to the side. She eyed it, wondering if he was about to have a lap full of wine. But he took a breath, righted the glass, and sat up a little straighter.

"Yes, she's mine."

He continued to gloomily avoid eye contact, and she

refrained from asking him the obvious question—why he didn't marry Lydia.

"I'd rather not talk about it," he said in the abrupt tone she hadn't heard from him in a while. Considering it came directly on the heels of what she'd felt was a tender moment between them, it caught her off-guard.

"Of—of course," she stammered. "It's none of my business."

His mood downshifted so severely that she settled her wine on the nearest surface without finishing it, then chirped, as if she couldn't tell how the room's atmosphere had dulled, "I'm going to head back. Getting past my bedtime!"

He walked her to the door, and as he was opening it, he said, "I'm sorry, Syra. That was rude."

"No, you have every right—"

"That kind of thing destroyed my last…" He sighed, his look soft and apologetic. "It's hard for me to talk about some things. Things are complex. Lydia and I…" He trailed off, then said, "We did have a child together. That's definite."

And that, clearly, was all he was going to tell her.

She put her hand on his arm, a gesture of empathy. As she was about to leave, he leaned down and pressed his mouth on hers. But only for a moment.

"Goodnight, Syra."

THAT NIGHT, she came out of a dream of trying to turn on a light, but no matter how many times she flipped the switch up, the room remained blind dark. When she awoke, her heart was pressing against her ribcage with frustration.

She heard Buster whining, and squinted her eyes open to see him on top of the chair in the corner, his paws on the windowsill. As she groggily shuffled to the window, she already had a feeling what she would see, based on Buster's body language.

The little girl was retreating down the driveway, in a pale dress, her hair long and loose.

Chapter Twenty-Three

Jonas,

I don't understand why you ignored me at the Yoders today. Is it because Harley Yoder thinks I belong to him? That he looks at us suspiciously? He's an oaf. He would never understand our connection, never.

I can't tell you how much it stabbed me to the core when I greeted you. You were so quick about it, then wandered off into the backyard with your friends. You didn't even touch my hand or look me deep in the eyes as you normally do.

Has something happened? Did someone say something to you? Everyone is too caught in their own worlds to think anything of us. Besides we have been friends forever.

Am I being too demanding? Did you not mean anything and I'm feeling rejected for no reason? You send my emotions into a tizzy (as Mem would say) with the slightest word or look.

Can we meet at the gazebo on the river and you can tell me what's wrong? I don't know what to think. I cried a lot yesterday.

Lydia

Syra folded the letter and stared out the bedroom window onto the green meadow and the cornfield beyond. She preferred to read in this room as it gave her a clear view of the driveway, where she'd see Jonas if he came to the front door.

She hadn't meant to read another letter, but the way Jonas had deflected her question about Beulah's conception had sparked the irrepressible urge to delve into his past again. So had when he'd kissed her. It had been so fast she hadn't even known what was happening until it was over, but she couldn't get it out of her mind. As if she'd never been kissed before.

What had Lydia once written? *I want more, more, more.*

Syra touched her lips and murmured, "I hear you, Lydia." Funny how the letters seemed to perfectly reflect what she herself was feeling about Jonas—a whole bundle of lust tied up with an uneasy, distrustful feeling.

This letter was the first one to have a darker tone to it. Syra knew what it was to think a boy liked you, then have him turn cold when his friends were around. She couldn't imagine trying to decode male behavior in such a cloistered religious clan, where the girls weren't even supposed to have lustful feelings. Where the girls weren't allowed to be forthright and demand answers. Where they were supposed to be "sweet" all the time.

Lydia was also very young—16 when she was writing these notes. Jonas would have been 21 or 22. Worlds apart at that age.

Glancing out the window again, she watched Jonas stride to his truck, open the gate, and begin shoving cords of wood onto the flatbed from a little wagon. Even though she had all the downstairs doors locked to prevent any surprise visits, she stiffened when she saw him, her pulse coursing with guilt.

After spending about ten minutes loading, he climbed into the truck, peeled down the drive, and took a right towards downtown.

She folded up the last note and set it on the small side pile she'd already read. She had every intention of shutting the lid and returning the keepsake box to its hiding spot under the bed.

But she needed to know what happened next, as if she was engrossed in a riveting bestseller. One more couldn't hurt.

Jonas,

Yes, I know the Yoders keep eyes on things and are the gossips of the world. Fine. I accept your apology. But you had never done that before, even at the Yoders. It made me feel so worthless and unwanted.

I'm not sure you completely accept or understand everything I'm feeling. I think of so many things that I know I'm not supposed to. I think of them all the time. If I'm sewing, I'm thinking of them. If I'm cleaning, I'm thinking of them. Milking cows, same thing. Always. I'm so glad I'm not in school anymore because I would not be able to think of the lessons in front of me.

My English friend (I won't say her name here) gets books from the thrift store and gives them to me when she's done with them. I hide them (I won't say where here!). I know a lot more than Mem thinks I know.

I suppose if Harley or Mem or Datt or any of my aunts or sisters or anyone else does ever grab a letter out of my hands they will be furious. But I don't care. Mem doesn't believe in hitting us girls but I suppose I'd be in for a beating if these were found. But I'll take the beating.

For without telling you how I feel, I'll wither up and die!

Lydia

Jonas!

I saw you looking at Katie Renno! I SAW you. You think you're being very sneaky but you're not. Yes, she is quite beautiful with her curly red hair. But she doesn't know you or care for you the way I do. Besides she has her eye on Simon Eicher, everyone knows this!! Except you, I guess!!

Jonas,

Sorry about that note. I admit I got jealous. It seemed like you were staring at her through the whole sing-along! If you say you weren't, then you weren't.

Mem had me and Gertie canning all day. Peaches, blueberries, and pickles. We also baked an elderberry pie, a peach pie, and three dozen buttermilk cookies. Of course, Gertie then went and darned all the boys' socks and sewed about a hundred dresses. That's the way she is, always making me look lazy! I'm so tired. I guess I'll go to bed and dream of you. I'll try to hand this to you at the doddies on Thursday.

I think we should be able to creep out at night and take a walk around! I don't think anyone will notice or care. Except maybe Harley Yoder! I expect he might follow us. He's downright awful.

Lydia

THESE LAST FEW notes had Syra feeling ill-at-ease with herself. Things were getting more personal between Jonas and Lydia, with the jealousies and squabbles typical of a young couple in love and insecure about it.

Syra was ashamed that she'd read three more letters when she'd planned to read only one. She excused it by telling herself the notes were so short, that three of them equaled one. Short as they were, like any good soap opera, they were filling her mind with questions.

Who was the red-haired Katie Renno? Did she have anything to do with why Jonas didn't marry Lydia? Who was this Harley Yoder character who kept cropping up, acting possessively towards Lydia? He was beginning to sound like the villain of the narrative.

Syra was developing an affection for Lydia. It couldn't have been easy growing up this way, expected to can, sew, clean, and work hard from a young age, and act as if the world hadn't changed at all in the past two hundred years.

And Lydia's personality was much feistier than Syra had expected from Millie's description of her. Lydia was so plucky, Syra kept forgetting the poor girl was no longer alive.

She studied the pile of letters. There weren't many left. She could tear through them before Jonas returned. Then she'd know the whole story, or at least enough of it. After all, she'd gone this far, why not go all the way?

Still, an internal war raged. What she'd read so far was all pretty innocent. There was a good chance that things were going to go downhill, and badly. Nothing else could explain why Jonas had refused to marry the mother of his child. What would Syra learn about him? Would it affect her opinion of him to the point where she wouldn't want to keep in touch?

This idea depressed her, for the coming months would offer her nothing positive—no spot of sunshine, only the stress of finding a new apartment, cancelling a wedding, and informing her parents and friends about the incident she'd rather not talk about.

Jonas gave her a sliver of hope that the near future could contain something to look forward to. She pictured making frequent visits to Prairie. Perhaps, once she got a new place, Jonas would come to Brooklyn. And, hopefully, things between him and Beulah would soon be settled, then Syra could get to know the girl, too. That part, especially, gave her a cheerful rush. The *three* of them together in some fashion.

She was so attached to this vision that she strongly considered returning the keepsake box to Jonas and allowing whatever had happened between him and Lydia to remain in the past. For her to remain ignorant of the details.

But she'd always wonder what had happened. And Jonas would never tell her.

Unable to make a decision one way or the other, she pushed the box back under the bed.

Chapter Twenty-Four

"Syra, honey, I had no idea——"

"Mom, if a man tells you he's arguing with his girlfriend, and you know that girlfriend is out of town, maybe that means the girlfriend doesn't want to talk to him!"

What she didn't add was that her mother, unlike normal a person, wouldn't know this because she'd never had a fight with her husband. At least that Syra had ever seen.

"I'm sorry," her mother said, sounding contrite. "You should have told me you weren't speaking to him."

Syra leaned out of the phone shed, keeping her eyes on the empty two-lane road, alert to any big trucks that might barrel around the corner.

"That would have meant telling you everything and I couldn't," she said, her throat constricting. She hadn't wanted to tell her mother about the breakup until she returned to Brooklyn but she'd have to. "Sam was cheating on me—with Catrina—so the wedding is off. Naturally."

She rapped it out, because if she didn't fling it out of her mouth, then she'd falter halfway through and never say it. Complete silence on her mother's end. Syra wondered if the call had dropped at the most inopportune time.

"Hello?"

"Yes, yes, I'm here," her mother said, faintly. "I'm so stunned. Sam and Catrina? Are you positive?"

"As positive as a person can be who walked in on them naked in bed."

Her bottom lip started to quiver from the memory of seeing them and the looks on their faces—shocked, and had there been a dollop of irritation at the interruption, too?

To hold back tears, she concentrated on a buggy that swerved around the bend in the road, the horse sleek and black. There were several people inside of it. It was Sunday, church day, and she was going to see a lot of them on the road. By now, she knew that the Amish didn't have typical churches, they held services in each other's homes, taking turns being hosts.

"Oh, Syra," her mother moaned. "That's horrible. I was so nice to him when he called. If only I'd known. I would have had a few things to say to him."

"Yes, he told me you were *eager* for him to come get me. I can't say I understand *that*."

"I only want you to be happy. You've always seemed happy with Sam."

Syra stared off down the road, mouth furrowed at

the corners. Had she been happy with Sam? Maybe. But no happier than she'd been without him. Her mother's words felt like more evidence that her mom was more interested in a married daughter than a single one.

The horse was practically on top of her now, so she shrank farther back into the shed. The large animal swiftly clomped by her, mane flying. The men in the buggy wore their church black felt hats rather than the usual straw hats. What had Jonas told her they called the hats? Telescope hats. He said he had no idea why they were called that.

"When are you going home?" her mother asked. "Should I stop looking at wedding gifts?"

Syra rolled her eyes. What a ridiculous question. "Unless you're buying them for someone else," she said.

"Have you two considered counseling? These things happen, you know. It doesn't mean you have to throw out the baby with the bathwater."

This was the exact same phrase Jonas had used about God. But this time the hokey idiom was like skin on a cheese grater. Sam wasn't God. He was barely a man.

"Oh my God, Mom! No. *And* he's not even sorry. *And* he's still with her."

Seeing another carriage whip around the bend, she decided to end the conversation. She was getting flamingly irritated with her mother. Who knew her mom had such outdated views on relationships. *These things happen?* Given how devoted her father was to her mother and vice versa, it had never happened with *them*, so why was her mother giving Sam this kind of leeway?

Since her parents lived in Arizona, they had only met Sam a handful of times over the years. He'd always gone out of his way to ooze charm around them. She supposed her mom couldn't conceive of the smooth charmer she knew as a duplicitous cheater.

"Sorry, I was only trying to help," her mother said. "Is there anything I can do? Why don't I come out to Brooklyn? Or you come here?"

"No. Not yet. Please cancel any gifts and don't bring up the wedding unless it's a practical thing you need to know about. I'll call River Café when I get back. Be glad I found this out before you two paid for anything major. Sorry I got you excited for half a second about something in my life."

"Sarah Jane, how can you say that? Of course I'm excited for your life. I just don't know much about it."

Because you live in freaking Phoenix, Syra wanted to point out, but didn't bother. The clomping of the second horse increased faster and faster until the carriage was almost upon her.

"Mom, tell me quick, do you remember anything else about the Mennonite woman I'm named after? Like her last name?"

"No, honey. I can't even remember what I had for lunch yesterday."

Her mother was only 63, but talking like she was ancient. The horse and buggy streaked by her, so fast she didn't get a good look at how many people were inside of it. The speed of some of the horses was truly impressive.

"I'm only saying, that's kind of a big thing," she kept on. "Naming me after someone?"

"Not really. I liked the name. As I told you, I was in pain, exhausted from a 12-hour labor, and loopy from pain medication. When you have a baby—*if* you do—you might have a better understanding of why I don't remember every detail of those few days."

"What were you going to originally name me? Before you switched it to Sarah Jane?"

"Oh, let's see. I think Josephine, after Jo March in *Little Women*. Wouldn't that have been fitting, since you turned out to be a writer."

"Well, that's nice…" Syra said lamely, silently grateful to the Mennonite woman who'd saved her from a name she liked even less than Sarah Jane.

Chapter Twenty-Five

Jonas,

My darling, I'm still smiling about Thursday. Gertie is constantly teasing me about how happy I look, thinking I've taken her advice to pray more. But Sadie is suspicious. She's the smart one. She keeps asking me 'Are you smiling because of Jonas?' Can you imagine?

I'll risk it all here by saying your kisses are divine. Imagine if anyone saw this, they'd accuse me of worshipping an idol. But isn't it wonderful we're allowed to go for walks alone? And when you can tutor me in the barn? We'll have an entire afternoon to ourselves. Or at least an hour before I need to milk cows!

I miss you already.
Lydia

$\mathcal{W}$ell, this was getting heated. The pair were managing to sneak off together and get physical. Given that Millie had said Amish girls were kept on short leashes—and that Lydia's parents were even stricter than most—Syra was impressed with the couple's craftiness. But perhaps Lydia and Jonas were expected to get engaged and her parents were being lenient.

Syra folded the last note, placed it on top of the read pile, and looked at the rest. One more couldn't hurt.

Jonas, Jonas!
There is no doubt about it, my darling,
my feelings are bursting out of my chest. I
keep replaying your kisses over and over in
my mind. It was sheer heaven getting you
alone in the barn for reading time. Of course,
we didn't get much reading done, did we???
I can concentrate on nothing else but you.
Mem has to ask me to do chores several
times before it finally sticks in my brain.

She even asked me if I was sick! My birthday is next week and then I'll have more time to myself and be watched less!!

The only bad thing is that I'm sure Harley Yoder will take this as his opportunity to ask me on a date. It's even more important that we stick to the plan.

See you on Sunday.

Lydia

SYRA PLACED the next letter into the read pile, then closed the box's lid. What was their "plan," she wondered. A part of her was jealous of the whole thing —the secrecy, the pining, the delayed gratification. It must have ratcheted up their ardor until it was ready to burst into white hot flame at the slightest touch.

Imagine what it must have been like to be almost 17, newly swollen with lust hormones, and meeting up with a young, swaggering Jonas Martin in a remote barn for an hour? Syra's body tingled hotly at the thought of it.

So unlike her own dating years. No mystery. No longing. No delayed gratification. Just herself and various boy-men blundering full-speed into each other, frantic to make a connection strong enough to convince them to leave behind the tiring and degrading dating scene. Look how *that* had worked out.

By now, Syra was fairly certain she was going to read through all the letters but couldn't manage to admit the bald truth to herself. As long as she kept pretending that she was spontaneously reading one and then one more, it was somehow less unethical.

It reminded her of a friend who'd buy "loosie" cigarettes from a man who sold them on a corner. When Syra asked why her friend would travel to the corner several times a day, paying a dollar for each cigarette, when she could simply buy a pack, her friend said that as long as she didn't commit to a pack, she didn't feel like a "real smoker." So long as she bought one at a time, she could convince herself she wasn't addicted, and could stop whenever she wanted.

Syra was using a similar mind trick. As long as she read one, two, or three letters at a time, and not the whole batch, then she wasn't *really* snooping into Jonas' most personal affairs.

She told herself she wasn't addicted, and could stop whenever she wanted.

In the early afternoon, Millie drove up the long driveway as Syra sat reading on the porch. As Millie approached, her look conveyed she didn't know how she'd be received, given that she'd delivered Sam to the door. Or even that he might still be here.

"Everything okay?" Millie asked, tentatively. She had a pie in her hands, so Syra knew the woman was really contrite. "Shoo-fly," she said, holding up the pie with a wavering grin.

The smile that erupted on Syra's face must have let Millie know all was forgiven.

With hot tea served, pie slices dispersed, and Buster sitting in his usual spot by the table, googly eyes begging, Millie and Syra sat across from each other at the kitchen table.

"He seemed so nice," Millie said, regretfully. "Said he was a friend of yours from the city and had to tell you something important. Never occurred to me it was... *him*."

"Don't blame yourself. He fools everyone. It's fine. We spoke and he left."

Millie breathed a sigh of relief. "Well, that's good. I've been feeling real guilty."

"Please don't. Millie, this pie is the best thing I've ever had. I've never seen it before or I'd eat nothing else. Did you make it?"

"Oh, no. Picked it up at Thelma's. Can't make a shoo-fly close to hers." Millie opened a big shoulder bag hanging on the back of her chair and dug out a small notebook and pen. "I hope you don't mind, but I'd like to ask some questions about the house."

"Of course."

"No electricity. How's that going?"

"Oddly, I'm pretty used to it now. The hardest thing is being without a microwave, but I've managed. And the battery powered lights kind of bother my eyes, so I don't read as much as I'd like."

"Are you cool enough with no air conditioning?"

"In the day, it's a bit warm, but it's been fine at night."

Millie nodded, jotting notes. "It would certainly save me a lot of money if people want to rent the house as it is. Have a real authentic Amish experience. Minus having to milk cows and pray."

Syra laughed. "I like it but not sure how it would be for a larger group. They'd probably at least want a bigger refrigerator. Oh, and the water is either freezing or hot. Seems to be no in-between."

"I'll have Jonas look into that," Millie said, continuing to jot notes.

Syra finished her thin slice of pie and decided to slice off another. What the hell. She'd been walking so much she'd burn it off. Buster whined and wiggled. She broke off a small piece from her slice and let him scarf it out of her palm, hoping he didn't immediately drop from a sugar overload.

"Millie, can I ask you a few things?" she said, hesitantly.

"Certainly."

Syra had gone over in her mind how to approach Millie about topics she'd learned from the letters, but the only way seemed to be to come straight out with them.

"Do you know a Harley Yoder?"

Millie looked surprised. "Yes, Harley was one of the Yoder boys who lived here before the family all moved to the Indiana settlement."

"Did he ever date Lydia?"

"Date Lydia?" Millie seemed perplexed. "Not that I'm aware of. Soon as she was old enough to date, she began going steady with Jonas. And that was it, so far as I know. The girls here don't date more than one boy at a time like English girls do."

Millie didn't say this judgmentally, but Syra felt a bit judged nonetheless.

"Jonas and Lydia, did you see them together much?"

She knew Millie must be baffled by the questions, but was unable to stop herself from digging further into the mystery of their relationship. Millie was the only link between the past and present. Besides Jonas. And she'd get nowhere with him.

"Not much, no. Saw them go by in his buggy a few times, that was it. I was excommunicated. But my sisters told me all about them. They tell me everything."

"They seemed happy?"

"So far as my sisters could tell." Millie finished her slice and peered closely at her. "Why so many questions about them?"

"I don't have much to entertain me here," Syra smoothly lied. "I can't really read because of the poor light. And there's no TV; I don't have a phone. So... guess I've started making up stories in my head."

"I see." Millie paused. Syra couldn't tell if she bought this admittedly weak explanation. "How do you know Harley?"

Syra shrugged. "Jonas and I get talking. He mentioned him a few times, that's all."

"You two getting along?" Millie asked, slate-blue eyes twinkling. The news that Syra and Jonas were spending time together appeared to override the mystery of why Jonas would talk about Harley Yoder to her.

"Sure, you know…" Syra said, vaguely.

As Millie stood and gathered their plates, Syra noticed a slight self-satisfied smile on Millie's face. She seemed pleased to have potentially played matchmaker.

Chapter Twenty-Six

Jonas,

Thank you so much for wishing me happy birthday, my darling. I know we're not supposed to care about those worldly things, but I do and you're the only one who said anything. I do so love that about you.

Now for some bad news. Harley Yoder did indeed ask me on a date and Mem is encouraging it. I told her I don't want to but I might be obliged to go on one. That is unless the plan starts. What shall it be?

Also, I can swear that Harley was staring at me when I handed you the last note so we must be much more careful. I feel we've gotten a bit careless.

. . .

Jonas, Jonas!

Very bad news! Gertie is so nosy and I have no privacy in this house! She dug into my dresser, below all my stockings, and found my pile of notes. I caught her as she was reading one of them! To get her to not say anything to Mem I've agreed to do all her outdoor chores for the next month!! With that and my own chores and cleaning English houses I will have hardly any time to see you.

It's too dangerous to have notes around so I've decided to burn them. Oh, my darling, burning your precious words is the worst punishment I can imagine!! I love to sneak one or two out to the barn and read them over and over and now I can't do that. I HATE living here and having no privacy and being treated like an infant!

You are older than I am and have no idea what I go through. You have some free-dom!! I'm sick of living here and tired of all my sisters and Mem and all my aunts *too! Everyone always watching me, watching, watching, watching!*

Jonas, would you ever think of going away?

I'm so sad I need to go out by the chicken pen and burn your wonderful letters. I hate my life!!

Lydia

*S*yra slipped the box back under the bed and decided to take Buster out. Dusk was deepening and it was her favorite time to walk, marveling at the spectacle of colors staining the sky. Across the street, she let Buster do his business and sniff around the edges of the cornfield on the remote side road that led to Beulah's farm.

Lydia's last letter was weighing heavily on her mind. The poor girl sounded so frantic, so miserable. Reading about her state of mind had triggered flashbacks to Syra's own rebellious and melodramatic teenage years. Desperate to gain autonomy. Desperate to have more freedom and be treated more like an adult.

There had been frequent arguments with her mother—how late she could stay out, what kinds of clothes she could wear, whether she could put on makeup, whether she could sleep over friends' homes, whether she could have mixed gender get-togethers. On and on it went. By the time Syra was Lydia's age, her mother had basically given up and Syra was essentially following her own rules while still living under her parents' roof.

Imagine being a 17-year-old Amish girl who couldn't even pass notes to her boyfriend without risk of a beating.

One line in the letter stood out above the rest: *Jonas, would you ever think about going away?*

This sure sounded like the seed being planted for when the pair disappeared. Syra imagined they'd tried to run away, to break loose of their restrictions. In the excitement, they'd quickly consummated their passion, only to realize they didn't have enough funds to get very far, and had returned home defeated. With Lydia pregnant.

Millie had mentioned that Jonas' drawer still contained money he'd saved up—one of the clues that had made the community doubt the couple had run away. Had he simply forgotten it? That seemed like a big thing to forget but it was possible.

And the prime question—what had happened either on their excursion or after they returned to break them apart? Not only break them apart but make Jonas refuse his responsibility, get him exiled, and send Lydia to a life of "spinsterhood"?

Buster, who was ahead of her on the leash, was staring back behind Syra. She'd been so consumed with her thoughts that she hadn't noticed the dog had stopped until she was almost on top of him.

Buster began barking as Syra's wrist was grabbed,

and everything was a blur of something bad ambushing her. Instinctively, she tightened her grip on the leash as what was happening took shape—Sam was trying to wrest Buster away. She was so shocked that she went catatonic and couldn't move except to refuse to give up her hold on the leash.

"Give me the fucking dog, Syra," Sam growled.

"No!"

Buster was hopping and barking. Sam let go of her wrist and grabbed the leash, trying to pry her fingers off of it. She had to make a split-second decision. She opened her hand wide and let the leash pull away from her.

"Run!" she yelled.

Buster took off like a shot, his leash dragging behind him. Sam gave chase. Syra watched, still dumbfounded at what had just happened. She had no idea if Buster would get lost. Something told her that the dog was better off tearing around Amish country than being with Sam.

She saw Buster rapidly outpace Sam, who stopped at the end of the cornfield, then turned and started back in her direction. Syra didn't know what to do. A small part of her brain was urging her to run away as well. But this was Sam. She'd lived with him for five years. Made love to him countless times. Consoled him through various crises, cared for him during various illnesses, including one hernia operation. Had more in-depth conversations with him than with anyone else in her life.

So, she couldn't have predicted that he'd walk up to

her and grab her wrist again, this time quite painfully, his face a mask of barely-contained fury.

"Why the hell did you do that?"

"Let go of me!" she cried, trying to wrench her wrist out of his pinching grasp.

To her utter amazement, he began dragging her towards the cornfield. It made no sense. Buster was gone and Sam should leave. Why was he pulling her? This wasn't Sam. This was a stranger who looked exactly like him.

"Stop!" she commanded. They were only a few feet from the tall, imposing rows of corn, looming over both of them. "Sam! Get off… *stop*!"

"You're such a little cunt, Syra. You think everything is about you. You'll tell everyone I'm the bad guy when the truth is you drove me away. Drove me to Catrina. *Drove* me to her!"

He yanked her a few rows in. The green stalks engulfed her. He thumped his palm on her chest and she fell backwards into the corn, broken stalks crackling loudly, crisscrossed on all sides of her.

The hard stalks were unexpectedly sharp and cut into her bare legs and arms. Now she fully realized she was in danger. In danger with Sam. This other Sam, an angry, physically violent Sam, one she'd never met until this moment.

Realizing she stood no chance of fighting him off, she put up one hand in a placating gesture. "Okay," she begged, sounding powerless and desperate. "I'll get him back. I'll call him."

"Too late," he practically spat.

He stood over her, one arm held back, as if he was going to strike her. He'd never hit her before, or even come close to it. This scenario was unfathomable. But it was real. Her brain went into hypersurvival mode, doing whatever it needed to do, saying whatever she needed to say, to come out of this cornfield alive.

"He'll come to me," she said, breathless. "I need to call him."

"Fuck you, bitch!" He came at her, and she knew that this was about to get very bad. Very, very bad. He was much stronger than she was. And she was sprawled on the ground, cornstalks slicing into her hands and legs, impeding her movements and vision.

How was this happening? Who was this Sam standing over her? Where had he come from? Had he always been like this?

She ripped out a scream that he quickly stifled by getting on top of her and pressing his hand on her mouth. She furiously wriggled underneath his heavy weight. Sam wasn't a big man and yet it was as if he'd gained masses of muscle and had the strength of ten men. She was not going to be able to save herself. The despair of this knowledge sent her soul into freefall. The very man she used to love, whom she planned to spend her life with, was going to do her terrible harm. He may even kill her.

"Get off her or I'll shoot your brains out."

The voice was like a screech. Thin, high. Female. Young.

"Get off her now, I mean it. I shoot straight. That big head of yours is right in my sights."

Sam did nothing for what seemed a long time, then slowly slid his hand from Syra's mouth but didn't move to get off her. All Syra heard was her own raspy breathing.

"You got three seconds, Mister," came the young female voice. "Then I shoot you right in the back of the head."

"Okay, okay," Sam said, his voice back to the man she knew. He began to stand, looking behind him. "I'm off."

Syra clutched her sore chest, where his weight had mercifully lifted. She coughed several times, then tried to sit up so she could see who was talking. How a young girl had such confident ferocity in her voice.

And was speaking like she had a gun.

Sam walked out of the cornstalks; his hands held up. Syra sat on the churned-up dirt, breathing heavily, trying to recover enough balance to get to her feet, but she had no strength to lift herself.

"You better start running, or I'll take your head off," the girl ordered. "I been shooting since I was a tot, lot smaller creatures than you. I seen what you be doing. No one will fault me for blasting your brains on the road."

Now Syra recognized the curly twang of the Amish. In the time since the attack had started, the sun had rapidly faded below the horizon, and it was mostly dark out. Through the stalks she could see that a little girl—about ten, hair in two braids, and in a formless, pale blue dress—was standing with a long rifle pointed at Sam.

"Alright, alright, I'm out," Sam said.

Syra could tell he was scared. She knew him well enough to know that. The only other time she'd heard that slight quake in his voice was the night before his hernia operation. How scared he'd been of the anesthesia.

"I'm going," he said.

"Run!" the girl ordered. "Run now or you'll never run again!"

Syra didn't see him start running but suddenly he was nowhere to be seen. The girl had turned, the rifle pointed down the road.

Then Syra realized something else—the girl was the little girl she'd seen on Millie's property. Jonas' daughter. Beulah.

"Oh my God," she groaned, her hands at her throat and chest as she tried to slow her panicked breathing. "I can't—can't believe—he did that—"

The girl rested the rifle at her side, and turned to stare at Syra. Syra crawled up on her knees, then managed to stand but felt as if her legs might buckle. So much adrenaline had flooded her veins that she was trembling as if it was the dead of winter.

"He's gone, Miss," the girl said.

"I can't—believe—*fuck*—piece of *shit*! Mother*fucker*!"

Syra couldn't stop spouting curses even though she dimly realized she shouldn't be doing so in front of the girl. But she'd lost control.

"You're living at Millie's right, Miss?" the girl asked.

Syra couldn't answer, then finally nodded jerkily.

"Come, I'll walk you in case he comes back."

* * *

As THEY HEADED up the road, Syra repeatedly called out for Buster. But her voice was cracked and weak, as if Sam had strangled her, which, so far as she could remember, he hadn't.

The entire incident was already muddling in her mind. Had he *really* pushed her into the cornfield? Had he really sat on her chest, smothered her mouth with his hand? Had his face contained that much fury, like he had another man entirely living inside of him? It seemed impossible. But, yes, he'd done it. All of it. Her ribcage ached from where he'd shoved her and sat on her.

"You're bleeding," the girl said, pointing at Syra's legs.

Syra glanced down and noted blood trickling along one leg, but felt nothing.

"You're Beulah, aren't you?" she asked, squeezing her arms.

"Lala. But let's keep this secret. You promise?"

"I—I was told you can't speak. Only sing."

She didn't have the capacity right then of determining whether saying this betrayed Jonas' confidence. They reached the main road and waited as a buggy clomped past.

"Yeah, they think that," Beulah said as they crossed the road. "Please don't tell them I can talk."

"I won't. I promise. But… can you tell me why?"

At the other side of the road, they stopped. Syra was struck by how long the rifle was in Beulah's small hand.

It touched the ground. The girl stared at Syra with big, luminous eyes. Syra couldn't determine their color, but they looked like what she imagined Lydia's eyes must have looked like. She was otherworldly looking altogether—pale, incandescent.

"Because," the girl said, "they keep asking me what my Mamma said before she went to heaven."

"Oh. Um. Who's they?"

The girl looked back in the direction of the farmette —towards where Jonas' daudy house was hidden in the shadows of the deepening night, with a single light glowing in the window.

"My *Aenti* Hannah. And Jonas." She turned to look back at Syra. "My father."

Syra took a deep breath. So Beulah hadn't been fooled by Jonas' and Hannah's "Checkers champion" story.

"How do you, ah, know he's your father?"

"I'm not stupid," the girl said, imperiously. "He looks exactly like *Aenti* Hannah. And people *always* say I look like *Aenti* Hannah."

"No, you're not stupid," Syra mumbled. She couldn't say the same for Jonas and Hannah. The "Checkers champion" story they'd concocted was, of course, inane given that the siblings had such a strong resemblance to each other.

"I was out to shoot rabbits, dusk is the best time to get them," the girl continued. "Then I heard you."

"Lala, if you don't mind my asking, where did you learn to speak like that? I thought Amish were non-violent."

"Sure, but we hunt." She looked at Syra as if this was patently obvious. "My *Onkle* Levi hides western books in the tool shed. Sometimes I read them."

Syra couldn't help but smile a little. Seemed as if the Amish hid a lot of things.

"Well, thank you." Syra wasn't sure if a handshake with an "English" person was acceptable in the Amish world so, still disoriented with shock, she saluted. The girl looked puzzled, then smiled. That's when Syra saw the girl had the same faint gap between her two front teeth that Jonas had.

He has to be her father, Syra thought. *That would be too coincidental otherwise.*

"I'm very sorry about your mother, Lala."

The girl said nothing, only looked down, her smooth, motionless face reflecting the brightening moonlight, making her look for a moment like an alabaster carving.

"And don't worry," Syra added. "Your secret is safe with me. I owe you one."

The girl glanced up and smiled mysteriously, then crossed back over the main road, an odd, ghostly specter in a pale dress, carrying a long rifle. Syra realized the girl was barefoot.

Unreal. A barefoot little Amish girl who wielded a gun like a pro and spat threats like a bounty hunter.

Syra was ashamed at how she'd crumpled in front of Sam. She'd been so taken off-guard by his attack that by the time she realized the danger she was in, she'd been on the ground, toppled over like the wooden block tower game where you take out one block at a time until the structure crashes down.

It reminded her of other times in her life when she'd been at the mercy of one man or another—either she'd had too much to drink, or she was wearing high heels, or she was alone and it was dark. All the times merely living her life had conspired to take away any chance she might have against a man's greater strength. How each time she'd had to pacify the man in some way, to rely on him feeling unthreatened enough to take mercy on her. How wretched it made her feel, this simple lack of physical strength.

Yet the girl hadn't crumpled. She hadn't pacified. She'd scared the shit out of Sam. How did this little girl have so much bravery? Sure, she had a rifle. That helped. But she also had to know how to hold it, how to keep her hands from trembling, and to have the exact words that would defuse a raging adult male.

Thank god the girl had been able to speak after all. Why would Jonas and Hannah be asking the girl about what Lydia had said before she died? Beulah had been trapped in the buggy as the life slipped from her mother. What a horrific thing for a child to endure. Why would two people—Jonas and Hannah—who cared for the girl's well-being interrogate her about something so traumatic?

Fearful that Sam was hiding in the shadows, she quickened her pace. She wanted to ask Jonas to drive her around the area to help her search for Buster. But she had no idea how she would explain her appearance —cuts all over, probably dirt and cornstalk remnants in her hair. Her skin didn't bounce back like it used to—any strong emotion entrenched in her epidermis, created wrinkles, folds, and swells that didn't fade for hours. Jonas would certainly see that something had just gone very wrong.

As she approached the house, she emitted a loud gasp. Buster was sitting at the bottom of the porch steps, where he normally sat when he was tied to the railing.

"Bus!" she cried, and the dog began wriggling his behind.

Chapter Twenty-Seven

*A*fter finding Epsom salts in a kitchen cabinet, she soaked in the tub, first running scalding hot water, then ice cold to balance that out, as she could never reach a medium temperature. Her palms and the back and sides of her legs were covered in tiny slits, like paper cuts.

She'd locked the doors and placed a lamp on the ledges of three downstairs windows, as three working lamps were all she could find. She also kept the largest knife in the magnet holder close to her at all times. She didn't feel safe anymore, not with Sam knowing where she was staying, though she had her doubts he would return. Between Jonas and his axe, and Beulah and her gun, he'd likely had enough of Amish country.

But how was she supposed to go back to the apartment and retrieve her belongings? She'd have to get a friend to agree to go with her, but who? She didn't want to put any of her friends in danger, as the only ones she could think of who would accompany her were women.

She sunk deeper into the tub, holding her throbbing head. She didn't normally experience headaches unless they were hangovers. This must be a consequence of so much adrenaline gushing through her veins.

After soaking for at least half an hour, her fingertips were pruned, so she drained the tub, then used the showerhead to wash her hair. With no dryer, she squeezed her curls tight with a towel, then pulled them back from her face with a scrunchie. Luckily, her face hadn't been cut in the stalks.

Downstairs, she made tea and sat at the kitchen table, still in disbelief at what had happened. How much more could Sam do to her? He'd destroyed their relationship, slept with her best friend, then assaulted her.

How could she have been so wrong about him for so long? If she'd been this wrong about Sam, who else was she wrong about? Catrina, yes, she knew that. Anyone else? Everyone? Was every single person she knew hiding a different, darker, more diabolical version of themselves?

And how was *she* any different, really? What would Jonas think if he knew she was furtively reading his most personal missives? Gobbling them down like candy? Using these intensely private moments of his life for her own enlightenment and, dare she admit it, entertainment?

A knock came at the kitchen door window and she let out a little scream, so startled that her whole body jumped on her chair. Buster scampered to the door but didn't bark.

"Sorry!" Jonas called through the window. "Did I scare you?"

Opening the door, Syra nudged Buster aside with her foot. She had her sleepwear linen shorts on and a sleeveless t-shirt with no bra. But she was in such emotional disarray that it didn't occur to her to be bashful and excuse herself to go cover up.

"Yeah, it—it's okay," she said, nervously laughing. She was relieved to see him. Nothing bad would happen to her so long as Jonas was here.

"I was headed to the country store. Thought I'd stop by and see if you needed anything." He entered the kitchen. "Locked the doors? There's nothing in here worth stealing, I assure you." His expression of mild amusement transformed quickly into concern. "Syra, what's wrong?"

She made her way back to the table and collapsed into her chair, folded like an accordion. "My ex, Sam, was still around. I ran into him. Um." She began twisting her lip, not sure how much to tell him. She definitely couldn't mention Beulah, but would something in her voice give that away?

Jonas came and stood over her. "What happened?" He plucked her arm up, examining her wrist, which she now realized sported a large red mark. "Did he do this?"

"He—he wanted Buster." She kept shaking her head, staring at the plain white wall hung only with the grandfather clock and a paper calendar whose date read November from the year before. "I can't believe how he was. It—it was like no Sam I've ever seen. I don't even think it was about Buster. His real concern is what I'll say to everyone about him."

She knew that Sam was excessively preoccupied with other people's opinions. It was why he dressed in clothes he couldn't afford. Why he got his hair cut at a trendy salon where it cost him three-hundred dollars rather than in a cheap barbershop, even though his hair would look the same. Why he'd spent months obsessing on whether his layoff from the investment firm would cost him future jobs. But it hadn't occurred to her that other people's opinions would be his primary concern about being caught in bed with Catrina.

Jonas sat down, and pulled the chair closer to her. "We should call the police."

"No, no. I stole a dog. He came to get Buster for the owner. And he'll say I tripped and fell."

"Tripped and fell?"

"Yeah, I—next thing I knew, I was on the ground in the cornfield." She pointed out the windows on the opposite wall, though she wasn't pointing to the correct cornfield. "I feel like he pushed me. But… maybe… I don't know. I'm sort of forgetting things."

The shock and adrenaline of the attack was eating away at her memory. Things came to her in flashes. It even seemed unlikely that Beulah could have shown up at the right moment and threatened Sam with a rifle. If only Syra could tell this part to Jonas—how proud he would be of his daughter. Wouldn't he?

"Listen, why don't I drive around and find him," Jonas said.

"I'm sure he's called a car and is gone." She smiled,

weakly. "And I don't want you getting in my mess. But thank you."

"I don't understand, Syra," he said in a low tone, staring at the red mark on her wrist. "He grabbed you, pushed you... then what happened?"

She pressed one thumb into her banging temples, as if confused. Worried the look on her face would give something away. "Then he... I yelled at him. And he left."

"Just left?"

She nodded. They sat silently for what seemed a long time. The throbbing in her temples subsided. Then he slowly reached over and took her hand in his—she couldn't tell whether this was to examine her wrist again. His skin was slightly rough but she liked that, it spoke of a man who did actual work rather than one who pretended to be working while sleeping with her best friend.

"I'll stay here tonight," he said.

The idea of him sleeping over pushed aside her shock and numbness, giving her a pleasantly euphoric sensation.

Then she remembered the keepsake box under her bed.

Had she even put it back under the bed? She *had* to have. She *always* did. But *had* she? Why was she not absolutely positive she'd returned it under the bed? Had she shoved it back far enough so that if he stood in the doorway, he wouldn't see it?

"N-nooo. It's okay, Jonas. I'm fine."

"Just for tonight," he said. "There are enough

bedrooms. You won't see me. I promise."

"Mmm, no. It's nothing. Now that I think about it, I'm pretty sure I tripped."

"Syra…" He spoke quietly, but sounded bewildered and a little hurt. "I'm not here to do anything but help. If he comes back, I won't hear anything way out in the daudy." He glanced at Buster, sprawled on the floor with his head on his paws. "And I don't think this one here is much protection."

Realizing she was gnawing on the inside bottom of her lip, she knew she must look too distressed for what a sleepover offer warranted. Especially as they'd already expressed their attraction to each other. But her fear that he would sniff out the wooden box was overpowering. Just the fact that he was in the same house with it made cool sweat erupt all over her body.

"Syra, I swear——" He patted her hand and stood. "I won't come anywhere near you. I can sleep down here."

She took a deep breath, let it out in a slow hiss. If he left briefly, this would give her a chance to make certain the box was definitely under the bed, and pushed far back enough that if he happened to stand in the doorway, he wouldn't catch sight of it.

All night, she'd have to play virginal maiden, keeping him out of the bedroom. She didn't even want him in the same room with the box, as if it would send out SOS signals.

"Alright," she said, defeated. "Just for the night."

"Let me grab my toothbrush and a couple of things. Oh, and floss." He grinned. "I'll be back in ten."

Chapter Twenty-Eight

Sam was standing over her. He'd gotten into the house. She tried to scream but nothing would come out of her throat. She tried to move but was paralyzed.

Sam came at her swiftly, his hand reaching for her in the dark. Her heart nearly burst out of her chest, and she thrashed, finally emitting a strangled sound of fear and rage.

"Syra," Sam said. "Syra!"

She kept trying to cry out and thrash him away from her, to scream for help, but her throat wouldn't work, and the frustration of her immobility sent tears streaming down her cheeks.

"Syra!"

Sam was sitting on her bed. Right next to her—but no. It wasn't Sam.

"It's okay. You're having a nightmare."

Jonas. It was Jonas.

She grasped his bare forearm, pulled him towards

her, and the next thing she knew, he was curled around her as she sucked in loud gasps of air, trying to slow her breathing.

What had she been dreaming? Sam. Sam pushing her hard, knocking her backwards into the cornstalks. How they'd snapped and bundled around her, restricting her movements, holding her down like straps as he came at her, ready to sit on her chest and press his hand over her mouth. How weak she became, raising her palm at him, her voice mollifying, her words appeasing. Saying she would call Buster but really saying, *Please don't hurt me.*

Then she'd been running towards a black and gray-topped buggy. It had tipped over in the street. She saw the horse on its side, with its spindly legs and big hoofs up in the air. The horse must be terrified and in pain. Its head was twisted, its large muzzle pointed skyward.

Lydia was inside of the buggy. Injured and trapped. In pain. Syra's heart was slamming, her breathing coming too fast. She had to get to Lydia. And the girl. The little girl was also in the buggy. Syra reached for her cell phone in her leggings pocket but she had nothing. No way to call for help. No one was around. Miles and miles of nothing but empty farmland. Lydia and the little girl were going to die because she couldn't help them.

"Syra," Jonas said. "Are you okay?" He stroked her hair.

She couldn't be alone. The dreams might return. Jonas could stop them from returning. She needed someone. She needed him.

"Can you stay with me?" she choked.

"Sure, sure," he said in his soothing sing-song.

Now she was safe. He lay her back down, and slid his protective body beside her in the twin bed. His skin on his arms was warm, almost hot. She felt fabric on her legs and took in that he must be wearing long johns. But his chest was bare.

"Thank you," she said, wrapping one arm around him, her hand on the muscle of his shoulder, pulling him as tight to her as she could get him.

* * *

SHE AWOKE with a jolt and instantly thought of the box. She needed to get Jonas out of the room as soon as possible.

She hadn't realized until she'd gotten him into bed with her how small the bed was. The box wouldn't be very far from the edge of it. There was a chance he could stand, look at the floor, and catch sight of it. She lay blinking at the bright light streaming in through the window, and her eyes traveled to the clock over the dresser on the opposite side of the room. Almost seven a.m.

She felt him shift and breathe in such a way that she could tell he was awake. Instinctively, she closed her eyes and tried to feign sleep as she feared her being awake would spark conversation. Or worse, he'd make a move on her.

Her body was throbbing with arousal, longing to roll

over and search out his mouth with hers, and to begin coaxing him to make love. His chest was perfect. Silky smooth skin, a light dusting of auburn hair. Thick, muscled arms. She was itching with temptation to grab that supremely squeezable ass and—

But her brain was too aware of the box below them.

His side of the bed depressed as he moved around, then sat up. She continued pretending to sleep, but couldn't stop her eyelids from lightly fluttering. Hopefully, he'd think she was dreaming.

It felt like he was sitting on the side of the bed, possibly looking down at her. No, *definitely* looking down at her. She could feel his gaze fixated on her. He was probably deciding whether to awaken her. Please, please don't let him awaken her.

The bed sagged and lightened on his side as he stood up. She heard the floorboards creaking as he walked towards the door, then shut it softly behind him.

Chapter Twenty-Nine

*R*elief surged through her as she read Liz's email. Her editor was horrified by Sam and Catrina. She too had once been cheated on by her live-in boyfriend and she remembered the devastation of it. For the first time, Syra was grateful that a woman understood the pain of betrayal because, once Liz knew the specifics of why Syra had taken off, her email "tone" softened.

"If you can get back by next week, that would be great as things will pick up, but I understand if it's too soon for you," Liz wrote. "And yes, I like the idea of a story on living in an Amish house. But your priority should be to recover."

Syra wrote back thanking her editor profusely, and saying she would definitely return by next week, as she needed to get back to reality and start the process of finding a new apartment. Then Syra closed out her email.

She was so thrilled with Liz's sympathetic response

that she almost forgot what had happened the night before—how Sam had lost his mind and attacked her in a cornfield. She still had a job, would still have money coming in that she needed for the move. For the moment, all was well.

Leaving Millie's office, Syra found the woman downstairs in her large kitchen. Millie offered to make tea for them and Syra accepted. She had a few things she wanted to grill Millie about, but wanted her interrogation to seem spontaneous.

"I had another question for you," Syra said, after they'd run out of small talk about the farmette. She knew it sounded nonsensical that she was filled with so many questions about Jonas and Lydia, but figured Millie could simply not answer them if she didn't want to. "Does anyone know what caused the buggy accident that killed Lydia?"

"That's a good question," Millie said, fingering the rim of her tea mug. "All I know is that the buggy tipped over on Pleasant View right by Elm Street. Not far from the Renno farm. Katie was the first person to come upon them."

"Katie? Katie Renno?"

The name was instantly familiar. The red-haired girl that Lydia had accused Jonas of staring at in church. Or was it a sing-along?

"Does—does she have curly red hair?"

"Why, yes. She does. The most beautiful hair." Then it appeared to dawn on Millie that there was no conceivable reason Syra should know this. "How do you…?"

"Oh!" Syra said, as if startled by the coincidence. "I

was in Thelma's the other day and admiring a woman's hair when someone called her Katie Renno."

"Noticed that with the *Kapp*, did you?"

Shit. Only then did Syra remember that one could hardly see an Amish woman's hair tucked under a *Kapp*.

"It kind of…" Syra floundered, swirling her hand around her face to indicate red curls that had escaped the covering.

Millie nodded, seeming to fully accept the explanation. "I can't imagine trying to fit all those curls under a *Kapp*." She *tsked* a little. "Between you and me, Katie is the last person Lydia would have wanted to find her."

"Oh?"

"My sister Ada told me that Lydia was always giving Katie the stink eye. No one quite knew why they had a rivalry going, other than they were the prettiest, most popular girls in Prairie. Amish aren't supposed to think about these things but, of course, they do."

"She found Lydia after the buggy accident?"

"That's what I heard. Katie saw the buggy turned over and couldn't do much on her own. So, she ran to her family's phone shed, where they kept a cell phone."

"Those are allowed?"

"Flip only." Millie waved dismissively, apparently as put off by the illogical Amish rules as Jonas was. "But she was able to call 911. Unfortunately, it all came too late for Lydia."

On the drive home, Syra couldn't banish the notion that it was more than coincidence that Katie Renno, the girl Lydia had been jealous of, happened to come across the buggy accident as Lydia lay dying. If it *was* coincidence, it sure was an unfortunate one. What must it have been like to be critically injured and your nemesis finds you, and is the person standing between you and death?

A dark thought occurred to her. Was there any way that this rivalry between the two "prettiest, most popular girls in Prairie" had continued long after Jonas was excommunicated? And was serious enough that when Katie found Lydia dying in her buggy that Katie had taken her sweet time calling for help?

Or even that Katie somehow *caused* the accident?

* * *

To GET to the letter that mentioned Katie Renno, Syra went through all of them, as she couldn't remember exactly which one it was. Her eyes skimmed the writing, once more drawn into Lydia's spunky personality and the girl's deepening feelings for Jonas. When Syra came to the correct letter, she put her finger on the relevant portion and drew an invisible underline.

I saw you looking at Katie Renno! I SAW you. You think you're being very sneaky but you're not. Yes, she is quite beautiful with her curly red hair. But she doesn't know you or care for you the way I do. Besides she has her eye on Simon Eicher, everyone knows this!! Except you, I guess!!

Lydia sounded definite about what she'd witnessed. But the very next letter, she did an about-face.

Sorry about that note. I admit I got jealous, it seemed like you were staring at her through the whole sing-along! If you say you weren't, then you weren't.

Lydia and Jonas must have had a talk, or exchanged a note, in between these two letters. He'd successfully defended himself. Perhaps he'd protested (as Sam used to say about Catrina) that he didn't even *like* Katie Renno.

Ten years later, Katie Renno is the one who happens upon Lydia dying in her buggy. What are the odds?

This new turn in the narrative reignited Syra's determination to dig into Jonas' and Lydia's relationship. And it gave her something she hadn't felt before—justification for doing so. While the community—or at least Millie and her sister Ada—seemed aware that Lydia and Katie Renno didn't like each other, Syra might be the only person in the world, besides Jonas, who knew the *real* reason Lydia didn't like Katie Renno. And how *much*.

This meant Syra had a *right* to read the letters. So she told herself, anyway.

She unfolded the first letter on top of the unread pile. The last one she'd read described how Lydia's stockpile of letters had been discovered by her nosy sister Gertie. Lydia had promised to do her sister's chores to avoid being ratted out. She'd then burned Jonas' letters and hinted they should run away together.

Jonas, would you ever think of going away?

Anxious to get to the next chapter, Syra's eyes traveled eagerly down the page.

Jonas,

I'm so sad that Mem put an end to our tutoring. I begged and pleaded but she says us girls don't need to read and do math beyond what is needed to work at the shop. She says I need to start focusing on my sewing and crocheting. Both things I despise! And she's pressing me to go on a date with Harley Yoder. When I told her I find him ugly with his crooked teeth and bad skin she said that was all the more reason I should give him a try, because I should not be concerned with such superficial things!

To avoid the torture of my going on a date with Harley, we need to get to the plan and fast! I miss you so much.

Lydia

Hmm. Syra began to have a clearer view of this "plan" Lydia kept referencing. In order to avoid dating Harley Yoder, whom the poor girl clearly wasn't attracted to, she and Jonas needed to start courting seriously. For whatever reason—likely their age difference—this hadn't happened yet.

One more letter couldn't hurt.

Jonas,

Thank Jesus things are starting to settle now. Mem hasn't mentioned Harley Yoder again. At first she wasn't too happy but when I made it clear that I would date who I want or I would not date at all, she gave in. After all, I'm 17 and need to start looking for a husband or I'll end up a spinster! The horror!!

Things went very smoothly after you put the word out, so thank you for that, my darling. Soon we'll have all the time in the world together with no one watching or caring what we do!

Lydia

Chapter Thirty

*T*hanks to a hand-painted sign that read, "Renno Farm: Apples, Eggs, Pumpkins" on Pleasant View Road, Syra had no problem finding the place.

Up the long dirt drive, she noted a dairy farm on the right, with many cows sprawled in the mud, staring at her with dark, doleful eyes. On the left, goats and ponies mingled in a large, sloping meadow. At the parking area on top of the hill was an open warehouse large as an airplane hangar.

Syra lingered at the meadow. Attached to the fence was a coin operated dispenser of corn kernels. She fed it a quarter and let a bold baby goat gobble the kernels out of her palm.

Barking filled the air. Nearby was a shed with several small outdoor runs housing Golden Retrievers hopping anxiously in their enclosures. It wasn't the first time she'd seen evidence of the puppy mills that dotted the area, but at least these dogs looked healthy.

Then she walked through the warehouse which was stacked with baskets of apples and other goods, including homemade soap, maple syrup, and artisanal wood signs with epigrams such as, *With God All Things Are Possible* and *Worry Ends Where Faith Begins.*

At the back of the warehouse was a small shop and a table covered with pies—cherry, pumpkin, pecan, shoo-fly. Syra felt as if she was gaining weight but there would be no shoo-fly pie back in Brooklyn, so she brought the pie to the counter and rummaged in her tote bag for her credit card. The Amish may symbolically live in a past century, but she had yet to run across any who didn't accept credit cards.

As a young Amish girl was ringing her up, a woman appeared from a back area. Syra's heartbeat went into double time as she noticed a few bright red corkscrew curls dangling provocatively around the woman's face.

And what a face. If the woman hadn't been Amish, she could have been a fashion model. Large brown eyes with extremely long lashes, a perfectly sculpted nose, full, sensuous lips, flawless porcelain skin. In her late twenties or early thirties. Syra's feminine intuition told her the woman's body—hidden under a plain mauve dress and long white smock—was something to behold as well. Hard to believe she must have half a dozen kids with that slender, elegant waistline.

If indeed this was Katie Renno, and not a sister or cousin, no wonder Lydia—no slouch herself in the looks department—had been jealous. Syra couldn't blame Jonas for the staring, as Syra was currently trying not to stare as well.

Wanting to buy more time, she put up her finger in a *hold on* gesture at the young girl, then roamed the shop, examining the Mason jars of foodstuffs, but keeping her ears alert for anything that would confirm the gorgeous redhead was Katie. But the girl and the redhead began speaking in Pennsylvania Dutch, effectively blocking her from eavesdropping.

Returning to the counter with a jar of pickled beets, the young Amish girl rang her up. Katie Renno—or the woman Syra strongly suspected was Katie—gave her a brief dispassionate glance before disappearing into the back area.

Chapter Thirty-One

"Speak English, Hannah," Jonas said. "Or I can't continue this conversation. I'm not as fluent as I used to be in that backwards language."

Syra froze with her mouth open, shoo-fly pie in her hands. The windows to Jonas' daudy house were wide open, and she'd been about to knock on the door. Now she heard the German-like dialect that was Pennsylvania Dutch coming from a woman, who then said, "I keep forgetting. Have you made any progress with her?"

Syra didn't know what to do. She didn't want to interrupt their conversation—but nor did she feel like getting caught in what would appear to be a major snooping session if someone looked out the window right then.

"No, she's not talking," Jonas replied. "I don't want to keep pressuring her. If I can save up enough, we can get her to a doctor in New York or Philadelphia. A real one, not one of those Amish quacks. But it's going to cost thousands. I probably need to return to woodworking. It paid better."

"But you need to keep looking, Jonas."

"The city girl is still there. She's leaving soon, though. I think. She keeps saying she's leaving, but never does."

Syra's mouth dropped even farther open. It was then she realized one hand was suspended in a knock gesture, several inches from the door. She could think of nothing to do but turn around and leave but was convinced one or both of them would see her as she retreated up the lawn to the main house.

She felt sick to her stomach with what Jonas had said. Of course, she knew he probably wanted her to leave so he could continue looking for the keepsake box, but the way he'd phrased it was so unlike the man who'd been showing her so much affection. Had it all been an act?

Just as she'd made up her mind to leave, the door opened. Standing before her was a female version of Jonas. Her hair was pulled back under a *Kapp*, but with her olive-green eyes, square jaw, and same-shaped lips, there was no mistaking this was Jonas' twin. When the woman smiled, Syra noted the Martin trait of a faint gap in the front teeth. All of it came together better on Jonas than on his twin, who could be described more as handsome than beautiful.

"Oh, hi!" Syra said, hoping her jovial tone would dispel any suspicions that she'd overheard part of their conversation. "Was bringing over a shoo-fly." She raised the pie as if Hannah couldn't see it.

"Of course," Hannah said, bowing her head slightly. "I was leaving anyway." She glanced back at Jonas, said something that sounded like *shen-nee-spera*, and left.

"Sorry, I—" Syra stammered. "She didn't have to leave because of me."

She thought it odd the woman hadn't introduced herself, but that seemed to be the sort of pleasantry that the Amish didn't indulge in.

"No, it's fine. Come on in." Jonas was pacing a little and appeared agitated. "That was my sister, Hannah."

"I could tell. She looks exactly like you."

Given how restless he looked on the heels of his conversation with his twin, Syra was second-guessing bringing a pie that had a sticker on it from Renno Farm. The plan had been to see what kind of reaction the farm's name had on him, but he seemed as if he was dealing with enough. Only, it was too late to walk out with the pie. Perhaps she could unseal it without him noticing the label.

But within a moment, he'd taken the pie from her hands and stood at the Formica kitchen counter, opening a drawer. "Might as well have a slice, eh?" he said. Then he went quiet. Syra knew he was looking at the pie—and had seen where it had come from.

"Jonas, I can, ah, I can leave," she said quietly.

"Why?"

"I don't know. You seem busy."

He turned. He had on light black sweatpants, a white t-shirt, and a black hoodie. She recognized the outfit as one the Amish boys wore while doing outdoor work around their farms. He'd removed his boots and was padding around in white socks.

"Went to the Renno place?" he asked. His tone was so neutral that Syra couldn't tell how he felt about that.

"Yeah. Was tooling around and saw it." Her intestines were twisted in a knot. She'd thought this would be her opportunity to quiz him, but instead it felt like she was the one under questioning.

"That's near where Lydia and Lala were found," he said, crossing his arms. "It was Katie Renno—she runs the farm—who came upon the overturned buggy."

"Oh. I—I didn't know."

"Millie didn't tell you?"

Her throat was so tightly constricted she could only shake her head. He stared at her for a moment too long and she felt he knew she was lying.

"Katie with the red hair," he said, in a sing-song, his look softening, his voice sounding far away. He let out a long sigh of… what was it? Resignation?

Then he turned his back to her. "How big a piece you want?"

"It's amazing how much Hannah looks like you," Syra said between bites of the gooey, decadent shoo-fly. "Though I guess that's not surprising given you're twins."

"You have any siblings?" Jonas asked. The pair sat at his small kitchen table, devouring their pie slices.

"Nope. All I ever heard my whole life was that my parents had trouble. They managed me and that was it."

"I might have seven but these days it feels like one," Jonas said. "Officially, none are supposed to be talking to me but I hear from them occasionally. Phineas runs a saw mill in Leola and has a bunch of kids. It fell on my next oldest brother, Ezra, to take over the old farm."

"Phineas. Ezra. Jonas. I have to say, Amish have some great names."

"You being sarcastic?"

"Not at all!"

"Syra's a pretty nice name."

She shrugged, feeling her cheeks flush warm.

"Actually, it's sort of… um…" She didn't finish her sentence, unable to confess she'd made up the name and her birth name was plain old Sarah Jane. To give yourself a jazzier name than the one you were born with seemed so *worldly*.

"Anyway," he went on, "of my sisters, Hannah's the one who keeps in touch. But she has to do it secretly because her husband doesn't approve."

"Hannah has Lala, right?"

"Right. She put in a good case with the bishop. Her husband, Levi, is Lydia's oldest brother. And Hannah and Lydia were always good friends. So that's where Lala is for now."

"This whole thing with Lala singing. You know, I've read of cases where that was psychosomatic." At his blank look, she added, "Where there wasn't anything neurologically wrong. Where the person was traumatized and—well, singing to avoid speaking."

"Hmm." He finished off his pie and peered up at her from under his shaggy bangs. "Avoiding speaking on purpose?"

"Yes. Like there was a major reason the person didn't want to speak." Finishing her slice, she leaned back in the chair, hoping she sounded as if she was offhandedly coming up with this theory. "You know more about the situation than I do, but could there be any reason Lala doesn't want to talk?"

He sat rubbing around his mouth, deep in thought. Then he said, "From what I understand, she was speaking alright after the accident. Not a lot, but doing it. When Hannah got control of her, she stopped." He sighed. "We thought it was the trauma of her mom dying and going to live in a new place. But…" He trailed off.

Syra remained silent. He seemed on the edge of telling her more, and she didn't want to say anything that might cause him to retreat into himself.

"See… Several months ago, I got a letter from Lydia. The first I'd had from her in a decade."

At the mention of Lydia writing him letters, heat swarmed Syra's neck and cheeks. She knew with some horror she was blushing. "Oh. What did she…?"

"Lydia said to come here. That she had something to tell me and Hannah."

"Okay," Syra said, the knot in her voice box making it come out a whisper. The fact that she was spending time each day reading his personal letters from Lydia felt glaringly apparent on her face.

"She wrote that she'd been keeping a secret from

us," Jonas continued. "A secret about our mother. She thought it was the time to tell it." He groaned and massaged his forehead, pushing his bangs up. "Remember when I told you my mother was sick? That actually happened last year. She's 71 and has dementia. Last year, she got pneumonia. We all thought that was the end. I was given permission to come and see her one last time. I drove from Ohio but by the time I arrived, she'd recovered. I was allowed to spend a little time with her and then left. She still lives at the old farm with my father, in the smaller house out back."

He paused, absently circling his thumbs, seeming as if he was trying to decide how much to reveal.

"In the Amish culture," he continued, "when a person is dying, they aren't supposed to die alone. Neighbors take turns watching them round the clock. Ma told Lydia something during the time Lydia was keeping watch in my mother's room. But before I could get back here and hear what it was, she was killed."

Things slowly fell into place for Syra. This is why Jonas and his sister were questioning Beulah about what Lydia had said in her final moments. The twins believed their mother had passed along some kind of secret to Lydia, who then passed it along to Beulah before dying.

Now the little girl was the only one who knew it.

"And your mother isn't saying?" she asked.

"No. She's nonverbal now. We think Lydia witnessed our mother's last time speaking."

"Why didn't Lydia tell you earlier?"

"Because she couldn't decide whether my mother knew there was another person in the room. Whether my mother was speaking to Lydia, or was speaking to herself. Lydia had been debating what to do. Finally, she decided she should tell us." Pause. "Maybe Hannah asking Lala what her mother said before she died caused her to stop speaking."

"I wonder why she wouldn't want to tell you."

Jonas stood up and took their plates to the sink. Then he returned and slowly sat back down, elbows on the table, twisting his big hands together.

"Lala is very close to her grandmother. My mother. Her name is Ruthie. They have a special relationship, even with my mother hardly speaking. Lala will sit with my mother, making up stories for her. Whatever Ma told Lydia, and if Lydia told it to Lala—Hannah and I believe it was something big. Something… *bad*." His expression was solemn, intense. "Maybe Lala doesn't want everyone to think poorly of her grandmother."

Syra couldn't curb a sudden smirk that happened against her will. She didn't want to doubt Jonas' story, but she couldn't imagine an Amish woman in the middle of miles of farmland doing anything so scandalous that she'd keep it a secret until her deathbed. And the two other people who'd heard about it would also keep it secret.

"I'll take your word your mother could have done something bad," she said. "But are you sure you and your sister want to know what it was?"

He steadily, almost challengingly, made eye contact with her, and his voice was unwavering. "Yes, we do."

Chapter Thirty-Two

Syra tried to sleep. She'd vowed not to read any more letters because her conflicting emotions about doing so had reappeared with a vengeance. Only yesterday, she'd felt entitled to keep reading because she had a vague sense that Katie Renno might have caused Lydia's death.

But now...

She stared out the two large windows that overlooked the red barn. The moonlight was so bright it was as if the house had floodlights placed all along its roof, like a prison. She could easily make out details of the yard—the barn's large five-pointed star hanging over the main door (an ornament she'd noted on many Lancaster homes), the white ranch fence, the tall rows of corn beyond.

Now she had another theory. Perhaps someone knew that Lydia was about to expose Ruthie Martin's deep, dark secret. And this person had taken it upon themselves to prevent the young mother from doing so by causing her buggy accident. Only, the perpetrator hadn't counted on Lydia having Beulah in the buggy with her —and passing along this secret to her daughter with her last breaths.

The theory was a bit of a stretch. How could someone know for certain that a buggy accident would kill Lydia and not merely injure her? And if the someone responsible for Lydia's death was Katie Renno, then what connection could she have to Ruthie Martin's big secret?

Before Syra had left Jonas' house in the afternoon, she'd hoped to steer the conversation back to Katie. To try to get a better sense of what his relationship with her had been, as it was clear there had been some kind of history. But she couldn't think of a smooth way to do it after he'd told her about his mother's secret.

As the letters were written a decade ago, when Lydia was a teen, there was no way they would contain Ruthie's secret—would they?

Perhaps there was a chance Lydia had known for years of whatever Ruthie was hiding, and the secret was buried in the letters. Perhaps the secret also had something to do with why Lydia and Jonas never got married.

These new possibilities freshly roiled Syra's conscience. She should tell Jonas about the box. But, at this point, it would be difficult. She'd had it long enough that most of its dirt had flaked off. How she'd explain she'd found it buried under the porch, yet it looked so clean? Could she dirty it back up?

Even more concerning, she was worried she'd gotten the sequence of the letters mixed-up. She presumed

Jonas had been the one to stack them. Given that he'd last read them a decade ago, would he recall their original order? What if he did, and Syra *had* mixed them up?

It felt impossible that it wouldn't be blatantly obvious that she'd had her nose buried in them. Her conscience refused to allow her to think she could hand the letters over without Jonas deducing this somehow.

Should she just admit she'd read them, then flee back to Brooklyn? What could he do to her? For sure, he'd never speak to her again—but did she even *want* him to?

She needed to move into the next phase of her life. And navigate moving into this phase while dealing with Sam, a man she now actively feared. She no longer had a best friend to lean on. And she wanted to diligently reapply herself to her job to make up for being away.

The last thing she needed was to be involved with a man who had even more drama than she herself did. Yet the idea of never seeing Jonas again gave her a stabbing sensation deep in her heart unlike any she'd ever felt, unlike even the pain of finding Sam and Catrina together.

She'd only known him for a couple of weeks but it seemed as if he'd always been there, was always right around the corner. As if her betrayal had been preordained, that it had to happen so she could find her way to Lancaster, find her way to Jonas.

She didn't know whether to trust this feeling, whether it was simply boomeranging her attachment—

from Sam to Jonas. Everyone would tell her this, as she would tell a friend in her own position.

Don't be stupid. You barely know him. You're rebounding. You don't NEED to go from one guy to another. In fact, it's pretty pathetic if you do.

But there was no harm in exploring. She wasn't going to change her life for him. But she did want to find out if there was something to this inkling, something true and solid. And she refused to apologize for that desire.

She needed to stay a bit longer.

Chapter Thirty-Three

Oh, Jonas. I don't know what to do. None of this is working for me. Is it for you? Having such restrictions on our time together. Somehow, I'd thought after the courting started, we'd have so many more opportunities. I thought we'd be watched less, but I feel like it's more. At least I don't have to worry about what Gertie will say. I can tell Mem that we couldn't help ourselves from writing to each other. She wants me to get married so she'll understand.

But yet it all seems so mixed up. Not at all like what I thought it would be. I feel as if I need total freedom. And then I feel sad, scared, and guilty for those feelings.

How do you feel? I can't wait to see you at church.

Lydia

Jonas,

This can't be true. What is this I'm hearing? You must know what I'm talking about. I know you tried to keep it from me. Didn't we talk about having more freedom? Being able to do what we wanted? Have you become too frightened? I can't write more. I'm too upset. Please talk to me. These rumors can't be true.

Jonas,

No, no. I'd thought we had agreed. Agreed we were going to live our own lives. Why did you say so to me if you meant to go in this other direction? I know you say it's for our good, that this will make things so easy, but will it? I loathe the very idea of it.

What about next year? If you're diligent at saving, there will be enough money. Mem and Datt still take mine from cleaning houses but perhaps I can start hiding a little bit. We can wait until then, can't we? I can wait for you, can you not wait for me? How can you feel the way you say you do if you can't wait?

Syra put down the latest letter, realizing she'd read three in a row. Three was her limit, a senseless arrangement she'd made with herself.

It definitely sounded as if the pair were struggling to decide whether to run away together or not. Millie had said that Lydia's parents wanted the teen to wait a year until she married Jonas, so that's what the last part of the letter must be referring to.

But it also sounded as if Jonas had another plan—some "other direction." One that Lydia wasn't in favor of. Was he trying to convince her to leave the Amish and she didn't want to?

But it sounded as if Lydia would have left too if given the chance. The letters were out of context and it was impossible to know exactly what was going on. Syra went back and reread key portions.

What is this I'm hearing? You must know what I'm talking about. I know you tried to keep it from me.

What could this be about? Had Jonas started courting Katie Renno behind Lydia's back? His reaction at seeing the Renno Farm sticker on the pie Syra bought seemed to indicate he used to have some sort of relationship with her.

And what exactly in these letters might cause Jonas to never gain custody of Beulah? So far, Syra hadn't read anything that wasn't typical of two young people trying to navigate dating, and doing it in an austere clan with a complex web of rules about every aspect of life.

She glanced outside. The sky was a lush lavender, signaling sunset. The day had completely slipped away from her. Returning the most recently read letters to the proper pile, she headed down the already dark hallway to her bedroom and pushed the box under the bed. Then she went downstairs, illuminating the windowless, pitch-black stairwell with the large claw-like flashlight.

She turned on the hanging lamp over the kitchen table, fed Buster, then arranged ingredients for dinner: a medley of various fresh greens simmered in olive oil, with a side of potatoes and yams bought that morning at a little outdoor stand. As was customary here, no one manned the goods and payment was expected to be deposited in a plastic container, on the honor system. She wondered how long it would take all of the goods to disappear if anyone tried that back in New York. Probably a hot second.

After dinner, she had the urge to visit Jonas, but could come up with no reason for a visit that seemed casual enough to be anything other than the real reason —that she liked him and wanted to be around him.

Nervous that he'd come unexpectedly to her door as he did last night, she made sure the doors were locked.

Then she went upstairs and slid out the keepsake box. The unread pile was frightfully thin—only a few notes left. She still had no idea what was in them that might prevent Jonas from getting custody of Beulah. It scared her to know that the answer could be contained in the last few letters. Her opinion of him may be completely altered if she kept reading.

But keep reading she did.

* * *

Jonas,

It's terrible that you aren't answering me, aren't writing to me. Can this be the same Jonas I care for so much? How can I know what is happening if you won't be honest with me?

Can we please meet at the gazebo on the river and talk? No one will see us there. I can go when Mem thinks I'm cleaning houses. I walk to and fro and can pretty much do whatever I want.

If you don't tell me exactly what is happening, I don't know what I'll do.

Jonas,

No, I don't agree with this solution. It's no solution at all. What happened to us being together IN GOD'S EYES? I told you then and I tell you now. None of this is making sense to me.

Jonas,

You are a terrible person!!! Anyone who could do what you did is not RIGHT WITH GOD. May Jesus have mercy on you!! Because I will not!! You led me along, made promises, said we would be together with JESUS as our only guide. Jesus who loves unconditionally. Instead, you LIED and BETRAYED. What you have done is UNFOR-GIVABLE.

Perhaps God will forgive you. We are supposed to forgive. But how can I? After what you've done? You did the worst possible thing imaginable that you could have done to me. What will everyone think if they know what you did? If they know WHO YOU REALLY ARE?

. . .

SYRA'S RIGHT HAND, the one that held the letter, was trembling slightly. The letter's vitriol, and the clear indication that Jonas had done something awful to Lydia, hit her as hard and unexpectedly as when Sam pushed her into the cornstalks.

The letters had gone from sweet and loving to mildly irritated to white hot rage. With what force Lydia had pressed on her pen—the black block letters had little globs of ink in their corners where the teen had forcefully crushed the felt-tip into the paper.

What... what could Jonas have done to her? This sounded like much more than courting Katie Renno behind Lydia's back—a theory that didn't make much sense anyway. If he'd wanted to be with Katie, then why run off with Lydia and get her pregnant?

Syra's hand wilted onto her lap. She stared out the window, doing what she always did—keeping her eyes on the front yard in case Jonas came to the door, though she wasn't confident she'd spot him in the dark.

He got Lydia pregnant. There was little doubt about that. He'd admitted Beulah was his child, which means that he'd—at the very least—had premarital sex with Lydia. And Beulah looked enough like him that it was almost certain he was the girl's father.

At some point, Jonas and Lydia had run off together. For a week. The letters contained no dates, so Syra couldn't tell when this had happened exactly. But what if it had happened *before* Lydia wrote this last letter? And this last letter was referring to *what had happened* when they'd run away together?

Syra's eyes traveled back to the start of the page. She slowly read through, her gut twisted and nauseous.

You led me along, made promises, said we would be together with JESUS as our only guide.

What would everyone think if they knew what you've done? If they knew WHO YOU REALLY ARE?

Syra's trembling increased. She gripped the letter so tightly that the paper crinkled, making it obvious that it had been recently read.

"Oh my God," she whispered. Buster, detecting distress in her voice, got up and wandered over to her. He sat at her knees, staring at her inquisitively.

The potential incident behind this letter began to bloom darkly in her imagination.

It would explain Lydia's accusation of a deep betrayal.

It would explain the last lines. *What would everyone think if they knew what you've done? If they knew WHO YOU REALLY ARE?*

It would also explain why, when the pair returned from their excursion, Lydia was pregnant, the pair stopped dating or even speaking, and they'd refused to tell anyone why they wouldn't marry.

And it would definitely explain why Jonas and Hannah were concerned about what Lydia had told her daughter in the moments before her death. It was the ugliest explanation Syra could come up with. But it was also the simplest explanation.

Perhaps it hadn't been that Jonas refused to marry Lydia so he could evade his responsibility.

But that Lydia had refused to marry her rapist.

Chapter Thirty-Four

*N*o, no. This couldn't be.

Couldn't be.

Not Jonas. Not Jonas.

Syra couldn't move from her chair. She kept staring into the middle of the bedroom, her mind cluttered with dark, despairing ideas. Then her gaze warily roved to the keepsake box, on the floor near her feet. There was one letter left. One.

The last letter could explain everything that came before it. It could say something that would turn her mind away from this most harrowing theory she was entertaining. Or could say something that would solidify it.

She knew one thing. She had to read it. Now.

She sat gnawing on the edge of her thumb, biting into it so hard that she gasped, then forced her hand from her own chomping maw. Before she could reach for the last piece of folded paper, her gut loosened.

She tossed the letter into the keepsake box and ran to the bathroom.

Her emotions had grabbed hold of her intestines and squeezed unmercifully. After spending a long time emptying her bowels, she took a shower, shivering as the barely lukewarm water pummeled her body. Millie apparently never got around to asking Jonas to fix the temperature issue.

She dressed and pulled her wet curls off her neck, then went to the bedroom and found the pullover sweater she'd purchased for cooler evenings. She had to read the last letter, but was putting it off. She couldn't stand the idea of it.

What kept going through her mind was Sam.

Sam, who'd thumped her hard with a flat palm, sending her tottering backwards into the cornstalks. Sam, who'd actually sat on her chest. Sam, who'd slept with her best friend.

Sam, the man she'd been with for five years. How had she not seen what he was really like? Had he showed his real self to her and she'd refused to see it? Or had she seen it but didn't recognize it?

Or had he hidden it so well that there had been no trace of it in those five years? No, there had been traces. There had been hints. Times he'd been rude to servers or airline stewards or pretty much anyone who didn't have as much power as he did. Times he'd spent money on clothes he couldn't afford, dressing for a job he no longer had. Times he'd told Syra he didn't like Catrina, while knowing she was Syra's best friend and he was working with her to start a new company. Not to mention fucking her.

All the small things Syra had noticed. Perhaps, if she were more honest with herself, they were more than *small* things. They were medium-sized things, ones that poked continually at her. But she'd managed to mostly bury her unease about them in favor of his better qualities. And even those cracks she'd noticed, that in her youthful naïveté she'd assumed would smooth out as he aged, hadn't added up to a violent Sam.

What will everyone think if they know what you did? If they know WHO YOU REALLY ARE?

She'd only known Jonas for a few weeks. Far less than she'd known Sam. He'd once gotten a young Amish girl pregnant, then left her. Yet Syra had allowed herself to be completely fooled. Why? Because Jonas had muscular biceps, kissable lips, a cute little gap in his front teeth. Because he'd driven the groundhogs to safety. Because he'd slept all night next to her, comforting her after nightmares, and hadn't tried to take advantage of the situation.

How else were you supposed to know someone? You took the evidence as it was presented to you, pieced it together, evaluated it, and made an educated guess as to whether someone was good or bad.

That first time with Jonas in his truck. How she'd inexplicably hidden a knife in her tote bag for the trip. Had an instinct about him led her to do that, an instinct which was subsequently suppressed under his cuteness and charm?

She would read the last letter. She had no choice.

But not right this second. She couldn't take any more. She placed the letters in the read pile on top of the one unread letter. Then the box went back under the bed.

Downstairs in the kitchen, she stood staring out of the many windows. It was dark outside, completely dark. Her theories about Jonas and Lydia, far from dissipating, began to burrow more determinedly into her imagination.

Jonas and Hannah weren't concerned that Beulah knew a secret about their mother. *They were concerned that Lydia had told her daughter how the girl had been conceived. That her father was a rapist.*

Had... had Jonas even somehow been the cause of Lydia's death?

I have to leave here, she thought frantically, turning from the windows. *I have to get back to Brooklyn. I can deal with Sam.*

Better the devil I know than the devil I don't.

SHE WAS ABOUT to turn the corner into the dark stairwell that led upstairs when she heard windowpanes rattling lightly in the kitchen, signaling that someone had stepped on the small back porch. She froze, wanted to dash into the hallway and disappear upstairs, but couldn't move. Then came the knock on the door. The knock that was too hard and loud for the visitor to be Millie.

She knew the knock, could feel it in her bones. It was Jonas.

Instinctually, she turned from the stairwell and blithely strode towards the door, heart spasming, but her expression arranged into a placid one.

"Hey, there," she said, opening the door.

"Hey there, yourself."

He was wearing a blue and black plaid flannel shirt, dark blue jeans, and his usual battered black boots. A part of her remembered that this was her favorite outfit on him, how alluring it made him look—handsome and rugged and outdoorsy.

The other part of her was chilly. His shaggy hair seemed unkempt, the faint gap in the teeth marred his features rather than enhanced them. Some part of her had closed off to him and was diligently working to roll back her attraction.

"I was wondering if you'd like to come over for dinner," he said, leaning one arm on the doorframe. "I picked up a bunch of groceries and could cook for us."

"That's nice but I already ate." She had on a wide, rigid smile, one she couldn't wrest into something more natural.

"Alright," he said, seeming abashed. "I could cook for myself then come back later."

"I—I don't… why?"

"Why?" His brows disappeared into his long bangs. "Because it's a bit dangerous you here alone with that ex of yours running around, don't you think?"

"Oh, I'm sure he's gone back to Brooklyn."

Ordinarily, she would have invited him in by now. He must be wondering why she hadn't.

"Is something wrong?" he asked.

"No," she laughed, airily. "Why?"

"I don't know. You seem kind of…"

"I don't feel well. To be honest, I've spent the past half an hour in the bathroom, if you know what I mean."

"Oh." He looked a little embarrassed, then a tentative grin crept across his face. "I see. I didn't mean to bother. I'm just concerned."

"Don't be. Sam's a coward. He wouldn't stick around after having a gun in his—" She stopped. "Um." She shook her head a little, trying to act as if she had just suffered a small bout of dementia.

"Gun?"

"Ha," she said, shoving a thumb knuckle into her mouth. She stared up at the dark starry sky beyond the porch.

"Is there something you're not telling me, Syra?"

"Dammit."

"Syra…" He forcefully strode closer to her and she had no choice but to move backwards into the kitchen. "Who has a gun? You?"

"Jonas… you've got to… to *promise*…"

"Promise what? Tell me what's going on."

"It—Oh, God. It was Beulah. Lala. She came out of nowhere and scared Sam off with a rifle."

He looked dumbfounded, said nothing.

"She saved me. Pointed the gun at Sam and ran him off. You should have seen her. It was incredible. But she asked me not to tell anyone."

Shit! Syra winced. It was a pronounced, theatrical cringe, complete with lower lip biting and eyes scrunched shut. She'd not only betrayed Beulah once but *twice*.

"She *asked* you? She can speak?"

Syra was so crushed with disappointment in herself that she staggered to the kitchen table, flopping into the nearest chair.

"That's why you mentioned all that stuff about her not speaking being psychosomatic," Jonas said. "You knew she could talk."

Gathering battle strength, Syra turned and faced him. She would defend Beulah, would fight for her.

"Jonas, she doesn't want to speak to you and your sister, okay? You two are asking her things she doesn't want to answer. Even if you think she knows something about your mother, it's really gruesome to put pressure on her. She's only a child!"

"You two had quite the talk."

"That's really none of your business," she snapped, a small rush of anger swirling within her. He'd conceived the girl—whether by force or consent she didn't know. (What was it Millie had said? *Not that girls are even taught what consent is.*) Then he'd abandoned her. Now he was back and tricking the girl into spending time with him.

And he only wanted to spend time with her to pry a secret out of her.

"Either be her father or don't be her father," Syra said, her tone biting and harsh.

Jonas crossed his big, bulky arms. Then he walked over to the table and settled himself into the chair across from her.

"I understand what you're saying, but there are things you don't know. I'm going to tell you something. Something Hannah and I have only told each other... and our mother."

His expression and body language were so charged with signs he was about to reveal something intensely personal that Syra's outrage on behalf of Beulah receded a little.

"Go ahead," she said. She didn't voice her next thought which was, *This better be good.*

"A long time ago, my mother was pregnant. Again. She'd spent most of her adulthood pregnant. As do most Amish women, whether or not they want to be. Whether or not they *should* be. My sister and I were very young, about four, so we don't remember anything about the pregnancy. Except for one thing. Around the time my mother gave birth, we were sent away. To our cousins' place. Amish women usually give birth at home, with a midwife."

He took a sharp inhale, then slipped the breath back out through his nostrils, seeming to corral determination within himself to continue.

"Hannah and I must have gotten curious or bored because we both remember sneaking up to our house, looking for our mother. We peeked through a window. And heard a baby crying."

When he fell oddly silent, Syra prodded him. "If she was pregnant, Jonas, that would make sense."

He slouched back in his chair, staring at the table. Or maybe her hands. Then his eyes turned up at her from under his heavy bangs.

"But we never saw a baby after that."

"I don't understand. It wasn't your brother? The one who had a heart condition?"

"No, Elam would have been about two. It took years for Hannah and I to share our memory with each other, and then when Hannah finally asked about it, our mother said the baby had been stillborn."

Syra couldn't fathom where all this was going. "Isn't —isn't that possible?"

"Syra, we heard the baby *crying*."

She rubbed two fingers round and round on the smooth Formica tabletop. She wasn't sure what to believe. Jonas could be making up a story about his mother when what he *really* wanted to know was if Lydia had told her daughter that she'd been conceived through rape.

"You and Hannah were four," Syra said, soothingly as possible. "Memories can be very unreliable. Even adult ones."

Syra tried to recall any memories she had that stretched back that far, to her toddlerhood. There were scattered ones: running naked in the waves at Far Rockaway; biting one of her little friends on the wrist and being scolded by her mother; realizing that her pet mouse had escaped its container. But had all of these snippets of memories really occurred at the tender age of four? Could they have happened at five or six?

At what age do experiences stop slipping like water out of your brain tissue and instead form deep-rooted canals of memories? How accurate are they?

"I was thinking that," Jonas continued. "Hannah

was thinking that. Separately. That this memory of a baby crying was wrong, imagined. That's why neither of us ever mentioned it to each other. But one day, we did. And we had the same memory. The *same* one. Both of us running through the cornfields from our cousins' house, then peeking through a window. We don't know how we got up to the window but we must have stood on something. And seeing our mother and hearing a baby crying. We're even pretty certain we saw the baby in her arms."

"Jonas." She struggled to keep her tone even. The man had grown up with birth all around him. Animal and human. But he was still a man and this meant he apparently still had pockets of ignorance. "It's possible the baby was alive for a few minutes, then died."

"That's not stillborn. Ma was very adamant. Stillborn. And if it were true that the baby was alive for a short while, there would have been a funeral. Amish custom would have dictated it. Hannah has asked a few trusted people about this and no one recalls a funeral for a Ruthie Martin baby."

"There was no funeral for a stillborn?"

"No. My mother said she and Da were too devastated and wanted to grieve on their own. That was the most she'd say about it. I know it's hard for you to understand, but that isn't the kind of thing Amish kids talk about with their parents. I was almost in my teens before I somehow realized babies weren't dropped from the sky. For Hannah to even ask our mother about such a thing took a lot of courage."

Syra understood. While intimate facts weren't as secretive between her and her parents as they were in the Amish community, she didn't, for instance, know all the details of her mom's miscarriages. How many or how far along her mom had been. She felt it was none of her business and if her mom wanted to share, she would.

"Over the years, Hannah and I began to wonder…"

"Wonder what?" Syra pressed when his trail off went on too long.

"We think this is what Lydia was going to tell us. What she learned from our mother." He stretched his legs under the table, pulling distractedly on his shirt sleeve. "There's no marker anywhere for this baby. No grave. At least that we've ever been told about."

"I'm confused," Syra said in a low tone, though what he was implying was slowly taking form within her. "I'm not sure what you…"

"Ma suffered from something her whole life. There were times she didn't get out of bed all day. And it got worse as she got older. She got very… *erratic* would be the right word. Sometimes she loved us more than anything. A minute later, she'd be boiling at us, mad as the dickens about nothing. Threatening to whip us bloody. She never did, but the threats were… scary. Hannah and I wonder if she… might have…"

His halting words, their implication, assembled into undeniable shape. And Syra looked directly at it.

"Killed the baby," she said.

* * *

SYRA WALKED with Jonas onto the porch.

"Are you sure you don't want me to stay?" he asked.

"No, it's fine."

She put her hand on his forearm. She couldn't help it. She didn't know if the story about his mother was true, but if not, he was doing a profoundly convincing job of appearing torn up about it.

"Jonas, if you don't mind my asking, why do you need to know what happened? If your mom had a psychotic break and hurt the baby, isn't that better left in the past?"

Staring off into the dark moonless night, he didn't speak for a while, then finally said, "Hannah and I want to know we're not crazy. That we heard what we heard."

"Can't you assume that?"

Buster began *arf*ing from the other side of the screen door, peeved that he wasn't getting to join their gathering on the porch.

"Let's take him out," Jonas said. "I could use a little distraction."

After retrieving the dog, the pair walked, Syra carrying a lantern, towards the daudy house.

"Your mom…" she began awkwardly. "How could she have… I mean, other people must have seen the baby, right?"

"Probably my father. The midwife for sure."

"Do you think they…"

"The midwife delivered all us kids. I know she and my mom were close. I always heard the story of Emma riding on a sled to get to the birth of me and Hannah, because there was a snowstorm that day. Would she have covered up for my mother—issued a death certificate? I don't see why not."

Syra slowed, shaking her head. This seemed inconceivable. And she wished she wasn't torn about whether he was telling the truth about it or not. But she knew women killed their children. She'd read enough news to know that.

"If the midwife filled out a death certificate, it must be filed somewhere. Have you looked?"

"I tried since I'm the one with computer access but do you have any idea how many Martins there are in Lancaster County? It was looking for a needle in a haystack, if you'll excuse the cliché. No, I never found anything. Maybe she didn't fill out any kind of certificate at all. My mother probably didn't even go to a doctor during her pregnancy, so there'd be no record of a baby."

"I'm not doubting what you saw but… there could be other explanations."

"See, Syra," he said, his head bowed, his big-booted steps keeping her slowed pace. "Then there's my brother Elam. We were always told his heart gave out when he was sleeping. Maybe that's what happened, but…"

Syra halted. The lantern hung down by her side.

"Oh my God…" she said. "You don't think…"

He stopped with her but didn't look at her.

"He was perfectly healthy his whole life. Running around. Working the farm. Riding his horse. One morning he doesn't wake up? He was small. Gentle. He would have been easy to… with a pillow or…"

The clouds had veiled the moon and the only light

was the pale, harsh light of the lantern still down at Syra's side but it was enough illumination to see Jonas' profile. It communicated torment.

"We only want to know what our mother might have told Lydia," he said. "Hannah thought Lala might open up to me, because she doesn't know me. And it's hard for her to get private time with Lala. She's got a husband and four rambunctious boys. If our mother *did* hurt anyone, we don't plan to call police. It's too late for that. But Elam. We owe it to him to know the truth. We feel we owe it to that baby, too. If there was one."

Syra's mind was a dizzying patchwork of thoughts. Could all of this be true? It seemed unfathomable, unspeakable. An Amish woman might have killed *two* of her children? And got away with it?

"If you suspected this, why would Lala be allowed to spend time with your mom?" She recalled how Jonas had said that Beulah was very close to her paternal grandmother.

"She was never alone with her. Lydia or Hannah was always with Lala if she went to see Ruthie. It's part of the reason Hannah has her now. She's like Lala's second mother. But we had no proof of anything. We couldn't ask the bishop to keep the girl from her own grandmother."

Syra began to comprehend the power a bishop had on his (it was always *his*) district, and what a dangerous thing this could be if the district got the wrong one.

In the dark, with Jonas' face lit with the lamplight glow, all that seemed real was his pain. His emotional pain over the loss of his younger brother—and possibly a newborn sibling. The implications of Lydia's last letter faded until they were barely detectable.

She took a few steps towards him, stood on tiptoe, and kissed him flush on the mouth. It didn't last long. But it was definitely more than a purely friendly kiss. He leaned into it, touching the side of her face. Everything he'd told her was the opposite of arousing, yet the urge to comfort him was so intense that pressing her lips to his seemed the only way to do it.

"Oh, man," she whispered. "What are we doing?"

He laughed softly. "I know. This hasn't exactly been the most romantic evening."

"No, no. It hasn't." She erupted into her nervous habit of laughing at inappropriate times. But the laugh came out so ragged and sour-sounding that she didn't feel the need to apologize for it—it obviously was a *this shit is so fucked up* laugh.

"Tell you what," Jonas said, holding her free hand. "What if I take you out tomorrow night? For a proper dinner. No Pennsylvania Dutch soggy green beans and apple sauce either. You like sushi?"

His hand felt so good to her. That wonderful slight sandpapery roughness to it that spoke of hard work, earth, and morality. His lips, on the other hand, were silken smooth, as she'd spent many nights fantasizing they would be.

"I do like sushi."

It came out of her mouth before she could rein it in. She was incapable of telling him she was planning to leave tomorrow. If the story about his mother was true —if it *was* true—then it would be cold-blooded as a snake to tell him she was leaving. Just when he'd confided in her. Just when he needed understanding and compassion.

The last letter she'd read. There was still a chance it was the angry but otherwise benign lashing-out of an emotionally-charged teen girl. Perhaps jealousy inflamed over Katie Renno. Perhaps Jonas—realizing Lydia was too young—had broken up with her, only for the pair to patch things up later.

"Then let's blow this place for a change and go somewhere nice," Jonas said. "Downtown has some happening spots, believe it or not."

She smiled but her gut was tightly, nauseatingly coiled. If there was any chance Jonas had fabricated a story about his mother committing double filicide, then the man standing before her had a nugget of pure evil within him that was darker and more twisted than Sam's. Or anyone's she'd ever knowingly encountered.

"Jonas, do me a favor." She interlocked her fingers with his. "Please don't push Lala. What happened to her was very traumatic. If there's anything to tell, she'll do it when she's ready."

"You're right. We only wanted to get to the bottom of it before anyone figures out I'm here and Hannah's husband stops Lala from coming to see me."

"*You're* her father. If you want to see her, you've got to go about it the right way. Hire a lawyer."

"Are lawyers free?" He grinned.

"Some are, yes. There are places that—" She bit off her words and tugged her fingers out of his. She didn't know if he should even be around Beulah. What that last letter might say about him. "I'm sorry, I'm exhausted."

"Me too. Dinner tomorrow?"

Her insides clenched, but were tingly with anticipation at the same time. If only she knew who he was, who he *really* was. Would Lydia's last letter to him tell her?

"Sure, dinner tomorrow."

Then, without thinking, she brushed his bangs out of his eyes.

* * *

INSTEAD OF RETURNING to the house, she crossed the street with Buster and ducked into the phone shed. She'd checked the time inside and it was only about ten p.m. but she worried it was too late. Still, she couldn't put it off until tomorrow.

"Did I wake you?" she asked when Millie picked up.

"Not at all. I'm a night owl. Everything okay? House getting too chilly? When winter comes, there will be propane heat but I haven't turned it on yet."

"No, no, it's fine. Though the water is still a bit cold."

"Bob Grady hasn't shown? That's my plumber. I'd thought Jonas called him but maybe he forgot. He seems pretty distracted lately."

Millie's voice had a teasing lilt to it, the implication being he was distracted with Syra.

"I haven't seen anyone."

"I'll call Bob myself then."

"Okay, but don't feel you have to rush. I might, ah, be leaving tomorrow."

"Oh! I'd started to forget you don't live here."

Buster, who was obediently sitting next to her, stood as they both heard the *clomp-clomp-clomp* of a horse approaching. She tightened her hold on the dog's leash so he couldn't dash off in front of a buggy. Within a few moments, the carriage passed, its large, red LED lights blinking steadily on its back.

"I have to get back to reality sometime," Syra said.

"Of course." A significant pause. "And Jonas? I'm sure he'll miss you. Miss having company out there, I mean."

Syra rested against the doorframe. She wished someone would put a chair in here, but supposed that would encourage the type of chatty telephone conversations that the Amish didn't approve of.

"Millie, I know it's nosy of me to keep asking questions about him. But…"

"You have something else?"

"Yes."

"I'll answer if I can."

"His mother. Ruthie. Did you ever hear anything about her being… emotionally unstable?"

An even more ballooned pause. Now Millie must *really* be wondering what Syra's deal was—why she didn't have these discussions with Jonas himself. A fellow city dweller may understand the expression *trust but verify*. But someone like Millie who'd lived all her life in the cornfields with unlocked doors?

"Is this what Jonas told you?" she asked, hesitantly.

"Yes, it is. I know you probably can't understand this, but I'm from Queens. We check things. Maybe that makes me paranoid, but it is what it is."

"I'm not a complete rube, you know. I watch the ID channel." She chuckled softly. "Yes, everyone knew Ruthie Martin had troubles. Nice woman, don't get me wrong. But there were many times she didn't come to church or dinners because word had it she didn't get out of bed. There was talk of her husband, Ben, bringing her to an Amish doctor who dealt with such things. It wouldn't be the way the English treat these problems, but I gather he tried."

Syra didn't dare ask what kind of treatment the poor woman had been subjected to. Given that she'd over-heard Jonas' remark about "Amish quacks," she could only imagine.

"The Amish are like everyone else," Millie continued. "And we—I mean *they*—have all the same problems."

Syra was feeling like a complete moron. The picture she'd had of the Amish—a solid, simple people who'd walled themselves off from the modern world and its pain and indignities—was bunk. A lack of cars and electricity and a fondness for grandfather clocks and suspenders didn't make them any more inured to difficulties, betrayals, and tragedies.

It was on the tip of her tongue to ask if Millie knew anything about Ruthie Martin having a stillborn child, but she couldn't bring herself to do it. It was probably only something Ruthie's close family, and her midwife, knew about.

More potent was the idea that Jonas had taken Syra into his confidence about something extremely sensitive. There was only so far her verification process could go before it trespassed into betrayal.

"Poor Ruthie," Millie suddenly added. "Lost the baby, then Elam. I'm sure that didn't help her state of mind."

"Right!" Syra blurted. "There—yes. There was a baby."

She hoped her delivery made it sound as if Jonas had shared this with her too, minus the part about Ruthie's potential involvement in the matter.

"It was only a few years after I'd left the church," Millie went on. "I was still trying to adjust, so I was very distracted. But my sisters mentioned it. Baby was stillborn. Ruthie and Ben didn't want any kind of funeral. Then a decade later, little Elam." Millie made dejected tongue clucking noises. "After that, no one saw too much of Ruthie."

"That must have been difficult for Jonas. And his siblings."

"Yes, but Amish can be a hard life, you know. Another woman lost three of her sons in different farm accidents. *Three*. Still, they went on farming."

Why so many young people decided to stay Amish was becoming a bit of a mystery to Syra. But she equated it to her continuing to live in one of the most chaotic, expensive cities in the world. It was simply the life she was born into. Even with the city's difficulties, she understood and could function within that world better than any other.

"Thank you for everything, Millie. You came through for me at a time when I really needed it. Once I get another phone, I'll text you. Let's keep in touch."

"You better. Come on down any time you like. If you need to get away."

Syra nodded into the phone, her heart full of emotion. No doubt she'd need to get away occasionally, back to this green and gold landscape, back to these simple people who may not be perfect but who still had a strange, magnetic pull on her.

As Syra headed with Buster back to the house, she was weighed down and wistful. This could be her last walk up the sloping driveway in the thick, surreal dark, with the stars above so clear and plentiful they were like billions of holes pinpricked in the dome of the sky.

Chapter Thirty-Five

*S*yra woke up early as usual. Her sleep had been surprisingly deep and uninterrupted for having so much on her mind. Submerged in her dreamless slumber, she hadn't thought of any of it.

Then it all began to trickle in...

Lydia, enraged at something Jonas had done to her.

Jonas, claiming his mother might have killed two of his siblings.

Beulah, holding so tightly to a secret, she was pretending she couldn't speak.

The light sifting through the windows was a pale, silvery-blue, the sky was bloated with dark-gray clouds so low that Syra felt she could leap up and touch them. Buster was at the side of the bed, staring expectantly at her for his morning walk.

"Come on, Bus," she mumbled, shaking off the remnants of sleep.

If she was leaving today, she needed to make the decision. Pack up her sparse things, clean out the refrigerator, return the rental car, head to the station. The idea of seeing Sam and Catrina made her sick to her stomach. And she had zero idea how she was supposed to carry on in the same apartment with Sam, even temporarily.

Perhaps she should ask Jonas to accompany her so she could gather up important things. Then she'd go stay with one of her friends. But who? New Yorkers of her economic status had small apartments. She could think of no one with a spare bedroom.

She had a couple people in mind who might lend her a couch but, once more, she was struck by the differences between Amish and "English." She'd lived in the city her entire life, yet she could think of only two or three girlfriends she could call on to put her up for a while. And she had no idea if they'd even agree. Now that Catrina and Sam were out of the picture, it was as if her entire support system had collapsed.

Meanwhile, from what she'd gleaned from Jonas' stories, the Amish regularly traveled from settlement to settlement, building homes big enough to accommodate not only multiple children, but cousins and aunts and uncles and friends and the barest of acquaintances.

The "English" certainly had more freedom, but Syra keenly felt her lack of a close-knit community. Then it hit her—the main difference between her world and the one Jonas had grown up in. And it had nothing to do with electricity, clothes, or modes of transportation.

While the pair of them had sat roasting marshmallows over the corn maze's fire pit, he'd told her that the Amish were taught that society took priority over the wishes of the individual. The individual's desires, actions, and behaviors mattered primarily in the context of how they impacted everyone.

Meanwhile, all Syra had ever known was the belief that what *she* wanted was of utmost importance, that her ultimate obligation was to *herself*. While this gave her a tremendous sense of freedom, freedom she'd utilized her entire life—choosing where to live, whom to date, what career to have—it also left her feeling solitary and bereft. When things with Sam and Catrina imploded, she had no one to rely on but herself.

And sometimes herself wasn't enough.

OUTSIDE, she walked Buster around the edges of the grounds, taking deep lungfuls of the fresh, crisp country air. How she would miss this air.

Yes, maybe she should talk to Jonas about helping her. Maybe he'd agree to drive her to the city. She'd first return Buster to Catrina. Then she'd gather clothes and documents from the apartment. Sam wouldn't dare do anything to her if Jonas was with her. Then, she'd check into a cheapish hotel she knew of in Park Slope.

But she had no idea if Jonas would agree to come with her.

Or… even if she should ask him. She was still conflicted about him.

The only thing that might give her closure one way or the other was the last letter in the pile.

She had to read it.

And she had to figure out the biggest dilemma—what to do with the keepsake box. Simply rebury it and forget about it? Rebury it and send Jonas an anonymous letter alerting him to where it was? She'd have to mail it from a different state so the postmark wouldn't tip him off. Even if she did that, wouldn't it be painfully obvious *she* was the one who'd found the box?

Back inside, she climbed up the narrow, windowless stairwell, heart thumping, stomach lurching. Her body was rebelling at the idea of reading the last letter. How much easier it would be to rebury the box and never know exactly what had happened between him and Lydia.

Anxiety attacked her so badly that tingles spiked within her, and tiny spasmodic jerks rippled down her fingers. She was steely-cold and a little dizzy, to the point where she braced herself against the wall for balance.

Inside the bedroom, she took a succession of quick, sharp breaths, trying to bolster herself. Then she jumped up and down several times, getting her blood pumping, pretending she was preparing for an athletic event—a marathon or bicycle race. Buster watched her with bewildered eyes. He must think she's insane. Before she could lose her determination, she dropped to the floor and stared under the bed.

The box wasn't there.

Her brain split in two—the refusal to believe what she was seeing; and the swift, hard punch of the box not being where she always saw it.

This couldn't be happening. It was impossible.

Wait. Wait! She'd been so upset by the last letter that

she must have left the box in the other bedroom where she did her reading. She rushed down the hallway and looked all around the second bedroom. Then she checked places where, logically, she knew the box couldn't be: under the bed, under the soft, square-patterned quilt spread on top of the bed, even inside the musty-smelling closet with sliding doors.

Is there any way she'd taken the box to another part of the house and wiped it clean from her mind? Once, she'd found her cell phone inside the refrigerator. Her mind could go completely blank if she was stressed. But misplacing an object as big as the keepsake box?

She raced to the bathroom, didn't see the box anywhere. Then she went back to the first bedroom and dropped to the floor again. This time, she wriggled underneath the bed, sweeping her arms in all directions, as if the box was there but had taken on the power to be invisible.

She pushed herself back out. Buster got under her feet and almost tripped her. "Buster, get out!" she scolded, pointing to the door. After giving her a startled, then saddened look, he slunk out of the room. She registered a sharp stab of guilt before a whorling tidal of panic billowed over it.

The box was gone. It was gone.

GONE.

Slowly, slowly, reality settled on her. The true, clear reality of her situation.

Someone had come inside the house. Someone had found the box. Someone had *taken* the box.

How, how? She'd slept on that bed all night, the box

right beneath her. Had someone really managed to get inside of the house, through the locked doors? She was positive she'd locked all three doors before going to bed. Then this person had slid underneath the bed, without waking her? And all without Buster making a sound?

Her mouth went dry and she could hardly focus her eyes.

Buster never barked when Jonas came over. It had to have been him. He'd come inside the house, found the box, and of course, knew Syra had read the letters. Everything he'd told her about his mother was bullshit. Just a way to redirect her suspicions until he could get upstairs and take the box. He must have seen it the night he'd slept over.

She hurtled out of the bedroom, scouring the hallway for Buster, but he was nowhere to be seen. "Buster!" she called, desperately trying to sound friendly enough to coax him back.

She had to leash him and get out of here. Get in the car. Go to the train station. She'd take her tote bag, wallet, and nothing else.

"Bus! Come on, boy!" She tried for a tone that would beckon a dog, but her throat muscles were stiffened with panic. She was only going to encourage him to stay away from her.

Buster wasn't in the kitchen. Why had she snapped at him like that? He was a sensitive dog and now he wasn't going to come to her. She'd open a can of his wet food. The popping sound of the aluminum lid being peeled back would hopefully do the trick.

She turned towards the cabinet where she kept his

food and caught sight of a face framed in the door's glass pane. A small scream climbed up her windpipe before she realized it was Jonas. His face was contorted, hardened. She instantly knew that he was not the same Jonas she'd been seeing all this time. He was a new, dangerous Jonas.

"Syra!" he bellowed, rattling the door handle. "Open up! NOW!"

Chapter Thirty-Six

*S*he stood with her stomach sliding between her legs, unable to move, unable to speak. Then she gasped as she saw that he had his axe held up high over his head. He was about to smash it through the door.

"Come out, NOW!" Jonas bellowed again. More than a bellow. A roar.

She fled out of the kitchen. The only place she could think to go was the mud room. She was so blind with fear that she knew she was going to trip and fall. Just like in a horror movie, she'd sprawl to the ground, and a man with an axe would soon be standing over her. But, somehow, she was out of the house and running down the side yard, towards one of the big cornfields.

She kept running until the tall stalks smacked her face. Squeezing her lids shut so the pointy edges wouldn't gouge her eyes out, she kept going until she was deep inside of them. Then she crouched down on the dirt-packed earth, heart slamming madly inside her chest, her breathing shallow and rapid-fire.

"Syra!" Jonas yelled out. He sounded rough and frantic. "Where are you?!"

She stuffed both hands over her mouth to smother her scratchy, hyperventilated breathing. What was to stop him from simply following her into the cornstalks? Would he hurt Buster?

"Syra!" he hollered, his voice moving closer to the cornfield. He must have seen the direction she'd run in. She stuffed one hand into her mouth and clamped down on it, staring wildly into the green stalks but they were so thick, she couldn't see more than a couple of rows ahead of her.

"Listen to me!" he yelled. "I saw a man go through the basement doors. I thought it was your ex! I grabbed my maul and came over to help. I was trying to get you out of the house because I thought he was coming up the basement stairs. I was a bit crazed. But it's Bob Grady, the plumber!"

Wow, the thought bulleted through her mind. *He's figured out a story. Millie must have told him the plumber was on the way.*

She got on her knees in the dirt and crawled in the direction she deduced would bring her farther away from the house. If she could come out the other end of the field, she could run. But to where? Would anyone around here help a strange, scared "English" woman? Would they slam doors in her face?

"Syra!" Jonas bellowed again. "I'm not going to hurt

you! What you read in those letters… it's… it's *complicated*!"

Oh my God. It was true. Absolutely true. There was no Bob Grady mix-up, no plumber misidentification. He'd come to the house to chop her to death because Syra knew he'd done something terrible to Lydia.

She stopped crawling, staring at a long wiggling worm she must have knocked out of its subterranean dwelling. Then the dirt around her started to shake as if it was alive, speckling with dark splotches. Rain.

"If you come out, I can explain everything!" he yelled.

She could tell he was closer, on the edge of the field. He was going to charge inside with his axe. Once he did that, his movements would be more confined. She could take that opportunity to run to the road. Could she call 911 from the shed? Could she lock it from the inside? Probably not.

Rain pelted the dirt around her. The drizzle gained strength and sluiced through the stalks, drenching her. Soon her knees and hands were sliding around in the sloppy earth.

It was silent except for the dull plunking sound of the rain hitting the ground and surrounding stalks. Could the weather have driven Jonas back into the house?

This was her chance. She only hoped she was pointed in the right direction. Standing, cautious not to slip in the mud, she began a run that was more like a slow-motion trot. The corn was planted in slightly higher rows than the rest of the ground, and between that and the sludge, the possibility of slipping was high.

Arms crooked out in front of her, she beat back the stalks, hearing them crunch and snap over the *whoosh* of the downpour. A blanket of soupy gray mist hung everywhere. Between that, the rain, and the stalks, she could hardly see a thing.

Eventually, she slapped her way to the end of the stalks. Wiping away rivulets of water from her eyes, she canvassed the area. The main road was right in front of her.

Across the street was the cornfield where Beulah had once disappeared. If she could get to it, she'd be out of Millie's property and farther away from Jonas, but still have a place to hide. When nightfall came, she could sneak out and run until she hit one of the main streets closer to downtown. There, she could go into a store and ask for help. Or perhaps the coast would be clear enough for her to use the phone shed.

The back of her mind was still spinning with the idea that Jonas might hurt Buster but there was nothing she could do about it right now.

She took a sharp breath, then dashed across the road. But as she'd envisioned in her worst imaginings, the mud on the soles of her flipflops acted as slippery as grease, and she went banging to the pavement.

Chapter Thirty-Seven

Fearful that a horse or car wouldn't see her in the opaque rain, she shoved off the pain stinging her bare knees and forearms, and pushed upright. She left her flipflops behind and ran barefoot across the street and into the next cornfield.

Her feet sank into the wet mud and she continued with a wide, waddling jog, smacking back the stalks with her forearms, eyes slit so the pointy leaves wouldn't jab her corneas.

Deep inside the field, she crouched down, panting. The rain began to let up and within ten or fifteen minutes stopped almost entirely, leaving behind a light mist. She was grateful for the whitish-gray fog, as it gave her even more cover.

"Syra!"

This time the voice was female. Millie? She listened hard, hoping the call came again. What if it *was* Millie? Should she run out?

"Syra! It's Hannah! Jonas' sister!"

The voice came from the nearby road. Though she doubted Hannah could hear her breathing, Sara instinctively plastered her hands over her mouth.

"Please come out. There are things—things you should know. I—I can't yell them out like this. Please trust us!"

Syra kept crouched, trying not to breathe too loudly. Then she heard a male voice. She identified the voice as belonging to Jonas, though she couldn't make out his words.

"Syra!" he finally shouted. "Hannah took the box. She got it into her head that you must be reading the letters. I agreed to distract you while she sneaked inside. There are things we could tell you if you'd only come out!"

Syra stayed in her same position, eyes darting back and forth as she took in what he'd said, wrestling with what to do with this new information.

"Tell them!" she spontaneously screamed. Then she smacked her hands back over her mouth. What the hell was she thinking? Why was she listening to them? They were conspiring together. Lying together.

"Can we do this inside?" Hannah wailed.

Syra heard more murmuring—Jonas talking to Hannah.

"Syra!" Hannah again. Something in her voice was desperate. Distorted and distressed. "Lydia—she—she died because of me!"

Syra immediately heard Jonas talking to his sister. His voice was firm and clipped, but she still couldn't tell what he was saying.

"It's that—well, you see—Syra!" Hannah continued. "It's that—those letters. They weren't written to Jonas. They were written to *me*!"

Syra's hands slowly fell from her mouth. Her brows furrowed in concentration. Had Hannah said what she'd thought she'd said? How stupid did they think she was?

"I know the letters were addressed to Jonas," Hannah went on in that same desperate-sounding tone. "My letters were addressed to her and I signed them as Jonas. But that was in case anyone grabbed one out of her hands. It would seem like I was passing notes back and forth for him and Lydia. The box. It says J. Martin. But that's my name. Johanna!"

"Tell me something in them," Syra called out. "Tell me who Lydia was jealous of!"

There was a long pause during which Syra cursed herself for falling for their trick. Her voice had probably allowed them to pinpoint her location, and soon they'd be trundling inside to get her, Jonas beating back the stalks with his axe.

"It was Katie!" Hannah called. "Katie Renno!"

Chapter Thirty-Eight

"*S*he was always so jealous of Katie," Hannah said, wiping her nose with a tissue she'd pulled from her smock pocket.

The three stood on the farmette's front porch. All were soaked. Syra, who had the least amount of clothes on, was shivering. But she refused to go inside the house with them until they explained more. Jonas could have simply supplied the answer to Syra's question.

No longer carrying the axe, Jonas had his hands shoved inside his sweatpants pockets. His long, thick hair was wet and sinuous around his face. He appeared a combination of mildly annoyed and expectant, his gaze continually shifting between his sister and his boots.

"There was nothing to be jealous about," Hannah said, despondently. "Katie and I were only friends. But because Katie never married, Lydia couldn't accept that. Amish women normally marry, you see. Even I did."

She murmured this, as if embarrassed, or possibly

disappointed with herself, and fiddled with the stick pin holding the top of her dress.

"But Katie was chosen to run the family farm. It's the most successful farm around here. She was the oldest, the most competent, and had no brothers. She didn't want any man telling her how to run things. So, she refused to marry, though she could have married anyone she wanted. It's caused a lot of judgment and gossip. The men can stay single with any number of excuses, but the women… if they don't have children, it's thought to be pitiable. But Katie is a very strong person and pays no attention."

The way she pronounced this gave Syra the impression that Hannah wished she were more like Katie.

"The day Lydia died," she continued, miserably, "Katie was at my farm, helping with the children. The two youngest were sick. Lydia came by unexpectedly and got angry. Said things to us that were completely untrue. Then she got in her buggy and raced off. Katie agreed to follow her as I couldn't leave the children. It was over by the Renno farm that Katie found the buggy with Lydia and Lala inside. It was a new horse, one Lydia wasn't used to driving, and she could be so impulsive."

Syra rubbed her goose-pimpled arms, trying to control her jaw, which was succumbing to tiny bursts of chattering. The temperature had dipped and being soaked to the bone clamped her with an icy hand. "Suh- so what are you telling me? You and Lydia were— involved? Romantically?"

"I—I guess I'm—" Hannah glanced self-consciously

at Jonas, as if hoping to get a sign from him about what to say. But she wasn't getting it. She turned her attention back to Syra. "Yes, that's what I'm telling you. But this is all… Amish life isn't what you're used to."

Her head slumped forward. Her translucent cap was askew, wet scraggles of dark hair escaping from it. She looked defeated.

"I assume you mean it's not allowed," Syra said. "Gay relationships."

"It's not even discussed," Hannah practically whispered. "As if it doesn't exist."

"But Jonas—" Syra looked at him, vigorously rubbing her arms to warm them. "—is Beulah ruh-really yours?"

"Syra, can we talk inside?" he asked. "I think we're all freezing."

Buster jumped up at the lower glass pane of the front door, erupting with a few *arf*s. Syra was startled but relieved he was safely inside. Then she examined Jonas and his sister. Really examined them, trying to make a judgment call about their story. Took in their sodden clothes and bedraggled appearances, their expressions sagging and somber with the weight of long-borne secrets.

"Alright. Let's go inside."

Chapter Thirty-Nine

*D*espite her continued and increasingly fierce shivering, Syra refused to go upstairs and change clothes. Jonas and Hannah were still under suspicion. She stood next to the kitchen door, ready to make a break for it if they came near her.

"Go on," she said. "Keep talking."

Hannah wiped her wide forehead with her hand. Syra once more was struck by how much she resembled Jonas, which made sense as they were twins. But it was their eyes that were strikingly exact replicas—the identical shade of muted olive-green, the precisely same size and shape.

"We talked about running away together," Hannah said, the words coming out with difficulty—she too was trying to control shivers—and with a degree of embarrassment. "I encouraged her more than I should have. I guess I thought she'd never really want to do it. That she understood it was all fantasy. But as Lydia grew older and her mother began pressing her to date, she grew more insistent."

Hannah's veined, workman-like hands, clasped in front of her apron, lifted to her top stick pin, then nervously caressed her throat.

"Lydia was younger than me," she said. "She had no idea of the realities of us trying to live with no money, no friends, hardly any education. Every time we'd talk more seriously about running away, I'd become over-whelmed with fear. As the older one, it would be up to me to keep us fed, clothed, and alive."

She glanced at Jonas, almost apologetically. But he was pointedly staring out the wall of windows, as if he knew what was coming.

"I told Jonas that Lydia liked him and he asked her on a date quickly, as I knew he would. All the boys liked Lydia."

A line from one of the letters came to Syra. *Things went very smoothly after you put the word out, so thank you for that, my darling.*

"We used Jonas as—as a cover. Because he was my brother. If Lydia was dating him, it would be perfectly normal that she and I were spending lots of time together."

"Did you know about this?" Syra asked him.

He kept staring out the windows, then slowly brought his focus to her. "Not at first. I thought she truly liked me. I liked her." He smiled wryly, then went back to staring at the gray mist shrouding the yard.

"I got engaged," Hannah continued. "To her

brother. Levi. It sounds terrible, but in my mind, it meant she and I could spend all the time in the world together. We'd be sisters-in-law. But instead, it lit her up like a firecracker. It was one thing to play at courting. It was another to get married and have children."

Syra realized that the *something* Lydia was raging about in the last letter must have been Hannah's engagement. To Lydia's own brother, of all people. Syra supposed that would have lit her fuse as well.

"She threatened to tell everyone what was happening between us," Hannah said. "I didn't believe she'd do it. Her parents were so strict, she would never risk it. But… she did tell one person."

Hannah glanced over at Jonas, who finally stopped gazing out the windows. He spread his palms open, saying, "That would be me."

"Why? Why tell you?"

"Because while she and Hannah were talking about running away, I was telling Lydia I wouldn't mind leaving," he said. "According to Amish tradition, the youngest son inherits the farm, and is the person to care for the aging parents. Once Elam died, that duty fell on me. Only you don't really *inherit* the farm, you have to buy it. Which meant I'd have to work with my father at the dairy farm for the rest of my life. What can I say? The thought of being stuck on that smelly farm for the rest of my days struck me with terror."

Hannah took over from him. "At the time, I was moving forward with plans to marry Levi. I kept telling Lydia this would only bring us closer."

"Then how—well, how did Beulah happen?" Syra asked. "I mean, I know how it *happened*, but…"

"It was Lydia's idea," Jonas said. "I was as close as she'd get to having a child with Hannah, which is what she really wanted. Then I'd refuse to marry her. This would get me banned. I'd be free from my obligation to take over the dairy farm and be my parents' caretaker. And Lydia would be free from having to marry. No one would push a good Amish boy on a woman with such…" He made a snorting sound. "…loose morals."

"You couldn't just leave?"

Jonas and Hannah shared a slightly incredulous look.

"Syra," Jonas said, patiently. "If I'd left on my own, they'd hound me. They'd track me down. They'd manage it, believe me. They'd hire a van and come do a kind of intervention. My mother would cry and plead. I knew a few people who'd tried to leave—they *always* came back. The Amish are *relentless* in getting you back. But if I was excommunicated? They'd leave me alone."

Syra was tempted to tell him that what he was describing—members of your community tracking you down and essentially forcing you to return to the fold—sounded like a cult. But she figured that wouldn't go over too well, nor was she certain he and Hannah knew what a cult was.

"In the church, we're taught that only bad parenting would cause a child to leave," Jonas said. "But if I was banned because of something I did, and my parents went along with it, then they were good parents. I wouldn't have to live with the guilt of leaving on my own and causing them shame."

"But you had to leave your daughter."

"Yes, I did. To be honest, it wasn't anything I thought much about until she lost her mother. I didn't think of her as *mine*. Do you understand? She belonged to Lydia and Hannah. I was a donor, that's all. A sperm donor."

At this, Hannah blushed, her plump cheeks mottled with a red so deep it was almost purple. She giggled a soft, almost noiseless, giggle.

"Well, I *was*," he said.

SYRA COULDN'T TAKE BEING CHILLED to her marrow any longer. She excused herself to go upstairs and change into dry clothes. She also popped into the bathroom to quickly rinse her muddy bare feet in the tub, noting that she'd also have to clean everywhere she'd walked.

When she returned, Jonas had a kettle boiling. He appeared to know where everything in the kitchen was and poured them all mugs of ginger tea. They sat at the kitchen table, silent and sipping.

"How did you know I had the box?" Syra asked, more into her mug than to Hannah.

"Jonas mentioned how you'd been to Katie's farm." Hannah shivered visibly. Syra shoved off her guilt that she was in warm clothes while Hannah and Jonas were still soaked. "Intuition—maybe woman's intuition, you might say—told me you went there to look at her. You'd only do that if you were reading the letters. I imagined you must like Jonas. Girls have always liked Jonas."

At this, Jonas passed his twin a withering glance that seemed to say, *Let's not go any further with that.*

"I knew if you were reading them, you'd be curious about Katie," she continued. "So, I thought the box must be in the house. It wouldn't take long to check the same places *I'd* hide something. When you went out with Jonas and the dog, I came in."

Let's take him out, Syra remembered Jonas saying to her about Buster. *I could use a little distraction.*

Syra was impressed with how smoothly he'd herded both her and the dog away from the house. Hannah must have been hidden in the darkness, watching. Once Syra turned down Jonas' invite to dinner, his twin simply waited until he got them out another way, then entered through the unlocked kitchen door. Fortunately for Hannah, Syra had also gone to the phone shed to call Millie, allowing her even more time to locate the box.

"Went straight to it, eh?" Syra said. "You should have been a detective."

"You'd left a lamp on in the bedroom, so that was the only room I checked. Then I did a little hiding in the mud room until I could escape." She grinned ruefully. "I was sure the dog would alert you to me, but he didn't."

Syra looked around the floor and found Buster snoozing nearby. *Useless*, she thought, shaking her head indulgently.

Returning her attention to Hannah, she said, "I

found box buried under the porch. Do you know how it got there?"

"About a year into our marriage, Levi came back from threshing wheat because he'd injured his foot. He caught Lydia and I holding hands. I did my best to come up with a good excuse, but he went through my things when I was out and found the box. He read everything and figured out the letters were meant for me and not Jonas. I assume he hid them to control me, in case he ever wanted to use them against me. Especially as the last letter… I trust you didn't read that one."

"How would you know that?"

"Because if you had, you wouldn't have run from Jonas."

Hannah slipped her hand into a pocket on her white smock and took out a small square. Syra recognized the shape and type of paper as identical to those in the keepsake box.

She watched as Hannah unfolded it, then read aloud in a soft, slightly shaky voice, "Hannah, it's time everyone knew the truth about us. No more lies. Jesus loves and forgives all. God is the Creator and Owner of all things! He made us the way we are and all love is beautiful love."

Hannah slid the note across the kitchen table. Syra picked it up and noted that the handwriting was the same as she'd been accustomed to on Lydia's letters.

"But the only person she ended up telling was Jonas," Hannah said, glancing at her brother with admiring but remorseful eyes.

"That's when the two of you ran away," Syra said to

him. "Millie said you and Lydia disappeared for a week."

"We did. She had an English friend, someone whose house she cleaned, who offered us a room. We went in there for a week." He grunted and shifted uncomfortably. "She came out pregnant."

Chapter Forty

Shortly after they finished their tea, Hannah explained that she had to leave. Her children were set to come home from school soon. Although Beulah wasn't speaking to anyone, the girl could obviously hear, so Hannah was still sending her to the one-room Amish schoolhouse.

At the door, Hannah held her hardworking hand out. "I trust, well, I trust that…"

"I won't tell anyone," Syra said. "Who would I tell? Besides, it sounds like your husband already knows, doesn't he?"

Hannah folded her sturdy hands demurely on her smock. "He thinks it was childish nonsense. I encouraged that view of it. After a suitable amount of time in which he believed I became fully enamored of married life, he allowed Lydia and I to visit again. But that didn't stop him from having the box where he could retrieve it should he want it."

"I hope you don't really believe Lydia died because of you. It sounds like a terrible, tragic accident."

"I shouldn't have allowed Katie over," Hannah said, her voice tremulous with regret. "I knew how jealous Lydia could get over her."

"But that isn't your fault."

"It's my fault that I didn't leave with her when we had the chance."

Then she hurried down the porch steps. Syra returned her attention to Jonas, who looked even more bedraggled than he had half an hour ago.

"You must be cold."

"I want to—" He ran one hand through his shaggy bangs, the other pulling the bottom of his flannel shirt. "I want to know if you believe us."

Syra considered. She remembered a portion of one of the letters that, at the time, hadn't made a lot of sense to her, but now made perfect sense.

Sadie is suspicious. She's the smart one. She keeps asking me 'Are you smiling because of Jonas?' Can you imagine?

The last line pointed to Lydia finding it *comical* that her sister would think Jonas was causing her to smile. If Lydia had been in love with him, there would have been no need to tack on that extra line. The teen had slipped up, probably one of several times she had.

And the "plan" that Lydia kept mentioning. That must have referred to her plan to date Jonas, which would allow her to spend lots of time with his twin sister. *And* get her off the hook with the persistent Harley Yoder. Unfortunately, neither Lydia nor Hannah took Jonas' feelings into account with their ruse.

Another portion of a letter came to Syra:

My English friend (I won't say her name here) gets books from the thrift store and gives them to me when she's done with them. I hide them (I won't say where here!). I know a lot more than Mem thinks I know.

She had the feeling this referred to the teen secretly reading about her body and sex. And very possibly learning when to have it for maximum chances of conception. Which came in handy when she and Jonas went into a bedroom for a week.

And, of course, there was the last letter. In handwriting that Syra knew pretty well. Its sentiments were unequivocal.

God made us the way we are and all love is beautiful love.

Yes, everything added up, clicked into place. There seemed no other explanation for everything.

"I do, Jonas. But why didn't you tell me? I'm not a bigot. I would have understood."

"For one, I had no idea you were reading those letters. And it's not my business to tell Hannah's story. The true story also meant admitting I'd abandoned my daughter on purpose. I wasn't ready to talk about that."

Now that the danger of being chopped to death had passed, Syra's own moral failing was squatting heavily within her.

"I'll apologize for reading them," she said, trying to articulate, not mumble as she was desperate to do. She owed him a strong, clear *mea culpa*. "There's no excuse for what I did. It serves me right that I misinterpreted everything."

"We needed the letters. Hannah can't tell everyone

who those letters were really for, she'd be banned. If Levi burns the last one, there's no proof that they weren't meant for me. The rest of them make me look like a fiend. You did us a favor."

Disappointment in herself, sore and pulsing like a fresh wound, deepened as she recalled that she'd only started on this misguided journey because she'd read Hannah's letter to her brother.

"Please, don't give me any credit." The impulse to confess her other sin welled up strongly within her. She decided to ride the wave before shame snuffed it out. "I not only read the letters in the box, but the one you had from Hannah in your desk drawer. I'm not normally like this, but after what happened with Sam and my friend, I stopped trusting. I thought snooping around was a short-cut to getting to know you. But it wasn't."

"We wanted the letters back, Syra. You got them back. The rest is a comedy of errors."

She burbled forth a jaded half-laugh—touched, humbled, and yet unable to fully accept that Jonas didn't hold her meddlesome prying against her.

"Look," he said, stepping closer. "I'm not perfect either. Agreeing to father a child I had no intention of raising isn't my finest moment."

"But you did it for your sister. And Lydia."

"I wish I could say that's true. I did it for myself, so I could leave. I hardly understood what Lydia was talking about. I wasn't brought up with any kind of sex educa-tion. When she told me she loved Hannah, I thought she meant she loved her—well, like *I* loved her. All I really understood is that she wanted my baby, and I wanted a way to leave. But I plan to do better for Lala. Getting those letters back is the first step."

Syra was reminded of an old movie she'd seen called *Gilda*. "Isn't it wonderful?" the title character, played by Rita Hayworth, had said to her paramour at the end. "Neither one of us has to apologize because we've both been such stinkers."

Everyone in this sordid little drama had done things they weren't proud of. Even Hannah was bowed down by her inability to break away from her conservative clan and live the life she wanted, be with the person she wanted to be with. And now it was too late.

"Everything you told me about your mother… was that true?"

"Yawp," he sighed. "Lala still isn't speaking to us. But we're not pushing. If my mother's secret dies with her, then that's something Hannah and I are prepared to accept."

He took another couple of steps closer. The energy between them pulsed, stimulating her insides in that familiar way.

"Did you really think I was going to hurt you?" he asked.

"I didn't know… I mean, yes. Yes, I did." Since she was on the honest track, she figured she should stay on it. "You're an imposing-looking man. You don't know what it's like to be low-grade frightened a lot of the time, but most women do. Besides, you were swinging your axe!"

"I understand," he said. Syra was impressed that he acknowledged her comments without trying to debate with her about them. "I've really got to change."

"It's not only you, Jonas. All of us have things we need to change."

"My *clothes*, Syra."

She erupted with embarrassed laughter. "Oh, right. And I should go get my flipflops from the road."

"But if you're still up for dinner tonight, the offer is open." Then he added, impishly, "I want to hear everything about me you'd like to change."

A smile tugged at her lips, a flutter in her belly dancing happily. In that moment, her attraction to him expanded in a new, more mature way. He wasn't only good-looking, intelligent, and funny... he was a decent person. She no longer had to wonder about him, have doubts poking at her. More than any of his other attributes, *this* is what made her feelings flourish and grow within like a flower spreading its petals in the sunshine.

"Sushi?" she asked.

"Sushi." He grinned, moving even closer to her, the fullness of him encompassing her immediate field of energy, taking up all of her space. She felt small and feminine this close to him, a feeling she didn't recall ever having with a man before, and she liked it.

Then he leaned down and kissed her.

Chapter Forty-One

"**W**ould you like to come in?" she asked, coming around the side of Jonas' truck. She knew what this would most likely mean, but that was good. More than good. It was what, all through dinner, she was making up her mind about, and her mind had decided.

Dinner had been delicious, downtown had been historical and charming, he had looked mouthwatering in a black button-down shirt and dark jeans, and their conversation had flowed fairly easily. They were still trying to get to know each other, and there were moments she wondered if they would make a good match or not, but that was fine. She was in no rush. But she was dedicated to exploring the possibility of a relationship, even if that meant taking a train to Lancaster every weekend after she settled into a new apartment.

Given she had to leave within the next day or two, and she wasn't sure when she'd get to return, there was one thing she wanted to know. Whether or not she and

Jonas harmonized in bed. By this point, they'd shared several kisses and that had gone extremely well, so she had high hopes.

"I *would* like to come in," he said, taking her hand. The gesture sent a scintillating thrill through her.

At the door, Buster was eagerly waiting.

"I should take him out first," she said.

"I tell you what. Why don't I take him for you and I can grab a few things from my place?"

She didn't ask him what things he wanted to grab, but figured it was sleepover things. A toothbrush. Floss, of course. And, hopefully, a condom. If not, there were certainly other ways they could explore each other.

During dinner, he'd elaborated on how little he'd known about sex growing up. Far from Syra's notion that he must have deduced the basics from being raised around animals, he said he'd hardly known a thing. It occurred to her that Lydia—who'd been reading about sex on the sly thanks to an "English" friend lending her books—had known more than Jonas.

"Sounds good," she said, grinning from ear to ear. Then she went up on tippy-toe and kissed him again.

IN THE BEDROOM, she changed into her sleepwear shorts and silky beige camisole. Both were casual and cheap, but sexy enough to let Jonas know she meant business. She had slipped the top down over her breasts when a shadow passed by the bedroom door. Her pulse skyrocketed.

Jonas couldn't have come back so quickly. Nor would he creep through the hallway without letting her know he'd returned. Her first thought was to get to the door and shut it. But there was no lock on it. Could she have imagined seeing what she saw? She'd had a couple glasses of wine at dinner.

She was torn between the desire to call out to try to confirm whether or not someone was really inside, and keeping quiet and getting herself in a defensive posture, ready to strike if the person entered the bedroom. Grabbing the claw-like flashlight off the dresser, she creeped towards the open door.

As she approached, heart slamming against her ribcage, a face suddenly appeared. A full scream ripped out of her throat. The face was childlike and lit by the glow of the flashlight, ghostly and terrifying.

"Why did you tell them?" the thing at the door said.

"Jesus fucking Christ!" she yelled, hand plastered on her chest. "You scared the shit out of me!"

She didn't care that she was cursing up a storm at a little Amish girl. The sneaky imp deserved it, gliding silently around the house and frightening Syra into a near heart attack.

"Why did you tell them I can talk? You promised."

Beulah was wearing her usual plain, formless, pale dress. Her hair was hanging long on either side of her wide-eyed, shimmeringly pale face. Shadows cast by the flashlight beam wavered along her cheeks.

"I'm sorry!" Syra cried. "I wasn't thinking!"

"Now I have to tell them," she said.

Taking several deep breaths to slow her rapidly

beating heart, Syra held up one placating hand. "Let's go downstairs. Jonas will be back soon. We can all talk then. Sorry for using every curse imaginable but you really did frighten me to death." She returned the flashlight to its spot on the dresser. "How—how do you know they know? I slipped up and mentioned it to Jonas, but he promised me they wouldn't push you."

"*Aenti* Hannah said, 'Lala, I know you can talk. Stop trying to fool me. Please tell me what your mem said before she went to heaven.'"

Hmm. Sounded more like Hannah was grasping at straws than that Jonas had repeated what Syra had told him.

"Listen. You don't have to tell them if you don't want to."

Syra paused, her mind starting to turn in the direction it had turned when she'd slid Hannah's letter out of its envelope. When she'd hidden the keepsake box under the bed. When, one by one, she'd opened each letter and read them. Her stomach was tingling with that same illicit combination of excitement and guilt.

"You could tell me first."

She could hardly believe that had come out of her mouth. But it had. The jittering all along the fibers of her body made her giddy in a way that was more potent than even the tingles she felt when Jonas kissed her. A deeply buried part of herself was drawn to others' secrets. She didn't know why, and only fleetingly surmised that everyone must be like this.

"If you tell me first," she continued, "then we can decide what to do."

Beulah's face, shadows pooling eerily under her eyes, making her look like she'd crawled out from a grave, seemed to soften, dispelling its resentment.

"But Jonas will be back any minute," Syra added, lowering her voice in case he'd already reentered the house. "Can you tell me quickly?"

Beulah remained silent for several seconds, then said, "No. We need to sit down."

"I UNDERSTAND, but I'm not going to deny I'm disappointed," Jonas said, unlatching Buster's leash and letting him shimmy into the kitchen.

His tone was amiable but even in the dark brightened only by the lamp in Syra's hand, she could see a touch of sadness in his eyes, as if he didn't quite believe her excuse of having an upset stomach. It didn't help that she'd already once claimed stomach trouble to prevent him from staying over. He must think she spent half her life on the toilet.

"I'm so, so sorry," she said, taking the leash from him, and contorting her mouth into a grimace. "I don't understand it. I felt fine when we left the restaurant."

"I feel bad," Jonas said. "The place has great reviews and I've eaten there before."

"No, no. Please don't blame yourself." She kept her hand clutched on her belly and made an *ugh* face, hoping her performance was convincing. "I don't know why I keep getting sick. Too much food, maybe."

"You sure you don't want me to stay anyway? I don't

mind if you spend most of the night in the bathroom." He grinned.

"I'd really prefer that things are a tad more romantic than that." Removing her hand from her belly, she placed it comfortingly on his bicep. "I want us to get to know each other. In *all* ways. I swear I do. But not like this."

She winced a little as if nausea was gathering momentum in her gut, and she should head to the bathroom before it was too late.

He nodded, still looking disappointed. They kissed and he turned, heading into the pitch-dark night.

She went upstairs to find Beulah.

BOTH THE KITCHEN and the sitting room attached to it had too many windows. With a lamp turned on, she worried Jonas might see inside and spot the girl. So she led Beulah to the bedroom's one chair, then went back downstairs. After making sure all the doors were locked, she steeped mint tea and carried the mugs upstairs.

Lowering herself onto the sleigh bed opposite Beulah, she watched the girl blow on her tea and take a tentative sip. It was only then Syra realized she'd handed the girl a mug that read, "I Love Intercourse."

She had the irrational urge to grab the mug out of the girl's hand. But that was absurd. Beulah wouldn't comprehend the double meaning of the town's (presumably) unintentionally ribald name.

The girl looked so young in the dim lamplight, her feet barely touching the floor. Syra was starting to feel genuinely nauseous, as if she'd manifested her own bilious stomach.

What she was about to do wasn't right. Why was she doing it?

Yet—as when she'd prepared to read the letters—threads in her mind lined up, touching end to end, twining around each other to create a justification. It was better she be the one to first hear the girl's secret. This way, if it was something that was going to hurt Jonas terribly, she could protect him from it.

Perhaps he didn't ever need to know that his mother had killed two of his siblings—if indeed that's what the girl was about to reveal.

"Start where you like, Lala," she said, slipping into a slight twang, as if a faux-Amish accent would put the girl at ease. "Only tell me what you feel comfortable telling."

This concession, a sly part of herself knew, was pointless. Once the girl got going, she wasn't going to stop until she'd said everything. It was hard enough for adults to keep secrets, let alone children.

Beulah took another sip of tea, and swayed her feet back and forth as if she was on a swing. Her feet were covered in her black plastic clogs. Syra had the awkward feeling the girl wasn't going to open up. That there might even be nothing to tell. Perhaps Beulah was insinuating she held a secret as a way of reaping attention.

Syra wondered if the girl had any idea about her mother's sexual orientation. She tried to remember being that young—how much had she understood about adults? About her own parents? Everything seemed murky. There were flashes of clarity within the murk—for instance, she remembered feeling as if her mother and father were preoccupied with each other, and that Syra had been only an afterthought. But mostly, the adult world had been a big, shadowy, mysterious blob that offered little decipherability. Now, as an adult herself, she didn't feel that much differently about it.

Maybe this was a terrible idea. There was still time to stop it. Time to let the little girl return to the woman who'd helped raise her, Hannah. Time to let the girl tell the correct person about Ruthie Martin's deep, dark secret, if there was one.

"Lala, you don't have to…"

"My Mamma didn't like Katie Renno," the girl said, making direct, somewhat unnerving eye contact. "She thought *Aenti* Hannah loved Katie. And my mem loved *Aenti* Hannah."

Syra didn't have regular contact with children. She had no concept that they were so forthright, so incisive. Or at least, *this* one was. By "love" did Beulah mean *romantic* love? Was that something she understood?

"Mamma told me we were going to *Aenti* Hannah's house because my cousins were sick and she needed help. We went to the barn and Mamma hitched up the horse. He was snorting and bucking a little. She'd bought him the week before and named him Thunder."

Beulah's little hands were around her double *entendre* mug. She looked like a large doll in the lamp-lit room, with her formless, pale dress, long, wavy hair, and wide, glassy eyes. Syra had noticed that the young girls in the area usually had their hair rolled on the sides and pinned back, though they didn't yet wear *Kapp*s. Beulah's hair was often hanging loose. A little rebel.

Syra felt a small, insistent tugging on her heart, an affinity for this Amish girl who'd already been through so much. And still so much that Syra—or anyone—had yet to hear.

But she was about to.

Chapter Forty-Two

*S*yra awoke with a start when Buster began *arf*ing. For several seconds, she was so groggy, she didn't think she could move. Buster would have to do his business on the floor. But then everything the girl had told her crashed in on her with hideous clarity and she jolted wide awake.

If it hadn't been for a small but loud dog with the urgent need to pee, she wouldn't have moved for hours, possibly days. Everything she'd learned was weighing on her physically, as if it was sitting on her. But the *arf*ing caused her to unfurl inch by inch from her fetal position.

Outside, she let the dog pee right on the front lawn, something she'd never done before. She was as disoriented as when she'd found Sam and Catrina in bed together. As if she couldn't find her way to the road and back, even though she could see it from where she was standing.

Back upstairs, she began listlessly packing important things into her tote bag but was leaving behind most everything she'd bought since her arrival. All she wanted was enough to get her on a train to Brooklyn—wallet, credit card, Buster's leash and carrier.

She worried she might lose her way to the car rental agency, but the alternative—staying in this house and having to see Jonas—drove her limbs to mechanically move from point to point so she could avoid that fate.

Outside, she plopped Buster on the Kia's passenger seat and swung her tote bag into the back. Her eyes kept roaming around the property. It was almost ten a.m., a brilliantly clear and warm day, and Jonas would be on the grounds doing chores. She had no idea what she'd tell him about her leaving without saying goodbye, but she'd come up with something. That is, if she ever spoke to him again.

She started the car and was backing up when Jonas suddenly appeared in her rearview mirror, leaving her no choice but to stop. Her stomach shriveled into a cold, queasy knot. She thought she might throw up in her own lap.

His expression was solemn and dark, and she knew something had happened, something beyond him seeing that she was driving away.

"Are you okay?" she managed to inquire through the half-rolled down window.

"It's my mother. Hannah came over early to tell me she's not doing well. They think today is probably the day. People have started gathering at the old farm."

Syra's mind went blank but her hands started to tremble on the wheel. Not wanting him to see this, she quickly dropped them to her lap. Her foot also began to shake and she worried she wouldn't be able to keep it firmly pressed on the brake, so she thrust the shift into neutral.

"I'm going to head over there," he said. "Bishop said I could come say goodbye. Wasn't that generous of him?"

"Jonas, I'm so sorry."

"It—it's actually fine," he sighed, though he didn't look or sound fine. "She's been suffering for a long time. I only hope she goes peacefully."

His eyes roved to Buster in the passenger seat and her tote bag in the back. "Where you headed?" he asked.

She stared straight out the window shield, taking in nothing but the solid, bright colors of the tableau before her. The extreme green of the lawn, the blank white of the farmette, the rusty red of the large barn.

"Were you leaving? Back to the city?" There was no mistaking the slight hurt in his tone.

"It's that, well, my…" She couldn't come up with a single reason why she would be taking off without saying goodbye to him. There was no inventing an emergency as Jonas knew she had no way for anyone to reach her. "I'm sorry," she blurted, squinting apologetically at him. "I felt I should go. I can't explain it. I was going to call you when I got a phone."

"Alright, Syra," he said with resignation. "Have a good trip back." He tapped his palm on the window, then turned and was walking away.

"Wait!" she cried. "Jonas!"

Before she knew what she was doing, she'd gotten

out of the car and chased after him. "Is there any way I can come with you?"

"With me?"

"Yes, to see your mom." She moved closer, touching his arm. "I want to support you."

"It'll be full of Amish and…"

"Please." She tightened her grip. "Would they let me inside?"

"I guess. As long as you're with me. I could say you're my girlfriend."

"Can you do that?"

His grayish-green eyes were boring into hers, trying to decipher what was happening. "It's not going to be pleasant. We could be there all day."

"We were going to spend the night together last night, weren't we?"

"Umm." He rubbed his beard. "I think so? To be honest, I've gotten so many mixed signals from you that I don't know what's going on."

"I'm sorry about that. But before my stomach acted up, it definitely seemed like we were going to spend the night together. That's a very intimate thing to do, isn't it? Having sex?"

"I suppose," he said, looking as if Syra had lost her mind.

"So why could we do that but not this? Why do we act like sex is so casual? It's not. It bonds people. It does. If we could do that, why can't we do this? Let me come and support you. Please."

Chapter Forty-Three

There were several black and gray buggies in the driveway, horses tied up to steel posts along a wood railing. Jonas parked his truck at the very bottom of the driveway, hiding it from disapproving Amish eyes. Syra hiked with him up the long driveway to the top of a hill where there was a white farmhouse that looked remarkably like the one Syra had been staying in.

"Let me go in for a minute," he said to her. "My father still won't acknowledge me and I need to make sure he's not in the daudy with my mother."

She couldn't fathom that at such a devastating time, a father would hold so stubbornly to such a harsh belief system. But she wasn't Amish, and couldn't wrap her head around much of what they did.

She nodded and stood on the porch, hearing voices inside the house. They were speaking their language. She felt blazingly self-conscious in her "real world" clothes of tight black leggings, the same navy cotton t-shirt she'd arrived in, and her new pullover sweater. But at least she wasn't wearing shorts.

Jonas, in dark blue jeans and a white long-sleeved shirt in a style somewhere between casual and dressy, fit in better with the typical Amish dress code, though it stopped short of the straw hat and suspenders.

Within a few minutes, he returned with his sister, Hannah, who was in a dark gray pinafore dress. Hannah's demeanor was outwardly calm but her olive-green eyes were unmistakably glistening.

Syra followed the siblings across the long back lawn, passing several Amish who were seated outside at a picnic table. Jonas held up his hand at them in a gesture of greeting and they did the same. Syra had no idea if the people—she now realized they were all men—were relatives or not.

At the edge of the property, as with Millie's, sat a smaller house, almost an identical of the main house. A man and woman came out and grimly greeted Jonas. No introductions were made before the pair walked off. The man had a slight resemblance to Jonas, so she imagined it might be one of his older brothers. Perhaps Ezra, who lived here. But she didn't know, and Jonas didn't clear anything up.

"You should have time with her," Hannah said. Jonas nodded and looked at Syra as if to ask her where she'd like to stand—in the house or out of it—but Syra quickly said, "Is it okay if I come in?"

"Um, sure," Jonas said. He and Hannah exchanged a look that seemed to say, *This is kind of odd, isn't it?* Then Hannah left.

* * *

RUTHIE MARTIN LAY on a simple wood-framed bed in a medium-sized, sparsely furnished room. A white quilt covered her body, but Syra could tell she was tiny. Her cheeks were caved in, her mouth was open, and her hands, clenched at her sides, were bony and gnarled. Jonas slowly walked to the head of the bed and looked down. He reached out to touch his mother's fist.

Syra was overwhelmed. She had never seen death up close, had never seen how the body shrinks and collapses into itself like a burned-out star. It didn't even seem as if the tiny woman was breathing. This is what all humans —if they were lucky enough to live this long—came to eventually, yet it seemed unfair, wrong, and perverse. How did plump little squalling babies end up like this?

"Jonas," Syra whispered. "I'll let you be alone with her."

He didn't respond. Syra walked out of the room, which was full of the peculiar, indescribable scent of decaying flesh. She sat on a small wooden bench that appeared to be placed there specifically for Ruthie's visitors.

A wall clock was ticking loudly, and she heard distant shouts from outside—children playing, blissfully unaware or unconcerned about death hovering nearby. At least twenty minutes later, Hannah appeared on the other side of the screen door.

"Everything okay?" she asked, voice hushed.

Syra was about to let her in when Jonas was back. At the door, he spoke to Hannah in their language. Syra felt oddly left out. Then Hannah disappeared. Jonas came and stood over her.

"It's Lala," he said. "She's talking to people now. Started this morning."

"That's great." Syra kept her voice extremely low. It was more than trying to be respectful. She had the unsettling sensation that Ruthie could still hear, despite no supporting evidence for this. According to Jonas, his mother had been nonverbal for several years and shown very little, if any, awareness of her surroundings.

"Yes, and she told Hannah she knows I'm her father. That's she's, quote unquote, 'not stupid.'"

Syra slipped into a small grin. The girl was definitely willful. Just like her mother.

"Hannah's taking her home, so I'm going to say goodbye and tell her that I'll see her soon. I didn't get to see my mother for the last ten years of her life and I'm sure as heck not going to make the same mistake with my daughter. Would you like to come? She's out back with some of her cousins."

"Oh, Jonas. I feel kind of out of place." She indicated her clothes. "Do you mind if I wait here?"

"Here?"

"I'll sit here." She tapped the plain wood bench underneath her as if he couldn't see it. "I'm sorry. I don't want to be stared at. Do you mind?"

He looked surprised but said, "No, that's fine. So long as *you're* fine. I mean…" He looked past her into Ruthie's bedroom. "I'm not sure how long…"

"I don't mind. I feel like such an oddball out there."

"I understand. Well…" He hesitated for so long, Syra thought he might change his mind and not leave. Then he said, "I'll be right back."

Syra waited about a minute after he left, then she stealthily got up and creeped to the door and peered outside. She saw the men in their straw hats sitting at the large picnic table. She saw a few children scampering in an area half-hidden behind the white house. She thought she spotted Beulah, her hair in two braids, toss a ball and run out of sight. She didn't see Jonas.

Then she turned and started to Ruthie Martin's death bed.

Chapter Forty-Four

*S*he stood on the right side of the bed and looked down at the woman. It was a very difficult sight to see. More difficult than she could remember anything being, looking directly on to that shrunken, dying face, seeing her bluish-gray skin, and her mouth in a small, toothless oval. To see how helpless she looked, how her humanity was rapidly disintegrating into leftover, lifeless flesh.

Syra watched carefully to see if the woman's chest rose and fell. After several moments of not seeing anything, it happened. The woman took a breath. The air caught in her throat, then she slowly let it out. Her white quilt had heart shapes stitched with light green thread. Inside each heart was a name. Syra began to recognize them—Phineas, Ezra, Jonas and Johanna. Elam.

Syra had the impression that Ruthie Martin's breathing was slowing, each breath coming later than the breath before it. That, very soon, she was going to stop breathing altogether. That she was closer to death than to life. Syra knew she should go find Jonas and Hannah and tell them to come quickly.

Instead, she touched Ruthie's gnarled hand, cool and smooth as alabaster. Then she put her hand on the headboard and leaned over. She had to be fast as she feared Jonas might return any moment.

"Ruthie," she said, quietly, in the direction of the old woman's ear, which was partly hidden under a long, silver-gray braid and an organdy *Kapp*. "It's Sarah Jane. Your daughter. I want you to know that I understand why you did it. It was the right thing to do. They've given me an amazing life. *You've* given me an amazing life. And don't worry. Your secret is safe with me."

She straightened up and watched and watched until Ruthie Martin's face went utterly still and her small, caved-in chest no longer rose or fell.

Chapter Forty-Five

On the ride back, Jonas was tense and silent. Syra knew he felt terrible that he'd missed his mother's passing by only a few minutes—and Ruthie Martin dying alone went against Amish beliefs.

"Jonas," she finally said, gently. "I know it's not Amish custom, but people often die once their loved ones leave the room. They wait for it."

She wasn't sure whether this sounded disrespectful. But she always remembered her mother saying that both of her parents had died when her mother had stepped out of their hospital rooms for only a brief time.

Syra's mother. She couldn't stop thinking of her like that and supposed she never would. Her mother, Devon Fragos. And her father, Marcus Fragos. They were her parents. They were the parents she appreciated so much more, realizing that her petty complaints about them were simply the reverberations of what the fabric of her being had always known—that someone else had given birth to her.

Now she knew why her mother had made the grating suggestion that Syra forgive Sam. Why Sam had said that her mother had sounded *eager* for him to come to Lancaster and retrieve her. Because her mother was on edge about Syra being in the area of her birth.

My Mamma was breathing hard and she said, 'Lala, in case I don't make it out of this, you need to tell Aenti Hannah what her mother said to me. Ruthie said she'd had a baby, a long time ago. And she gave the baby to some English who were staying next door for the summer. They were from New York. She didn't want any more babies. They needed the money. They prayed on it. God said the baby should go to a family who wanted one but hadn't been blessed with one. But she asked to name the little girl Sarah Jane after her mammi. And if anyone ever found the girl, to ask her to forgive, because she was weak and tired.'

It made all the sense in the world. Why Syra's birth certificate said Lancaster County General Hospital. Why her grandmother had once said to her, "We were so surprised when you came along. Your mother did a great job of hiding it from us!"

Her mother had once told her that she'd had so many miscarriages that she didn't want her family and friends getting excited for something that may not happen, and that she'd come to believe sharing the pregnancy news was jinxing it. So, Devon and Marcus had kept it secret from everyone until Sarah Jane was born. How exactly they'd kept it secret, Syra had never thought to inquire. It was one of the myriad bits of history that parents continually drop, all of it taken as gospel, none of it held up to scrutiny.

Once the plan had been set in motion, it would be

fairly easy to carry out. Amish women usually give birth at home with a midwife who fills out a birth certificate. It would have been simple enough to pay off the midwife to change the parents' names on the certificate. Ruthie Martin only needed to tell everyone she'd had a stillbirth and did not wish to hold a funeral.

Peering over at Jonas for a moment, Syra turned her attention to the empty stretch of dark road.

For the millionth time, she tried to imagine how it had fallen into place. Her parents must have been staying next door to the Martin clan for the summer. (Not the one weekend in Lancaster that her mother had always told her.) Somehow, they got to know the Amish husband and wife. Somehow, plans had been made for the couple to give their tenth child to the "English" pair in exchange for money.

Syra had done the math. Ruthie would have been about 43 when she'd given birth to her last child. The woman was already dealing with a two-year-old and four-year-old twins. Not to mention all her other children. She suffered from depression or another disorder. The childless, well-off New York couple next door must have seemed like a godsend. And, according to Lydia's version, God had blessed the transaction!

Whose idea had it been? Who approached who? Syra doubted that her parents casually asked the pregnant Amish woman if she'd like to sell her baby.

She imagined her mother, a sociable sort, had instigated a neighborly friendship, not with any designs on a baby, but simply because that was her mother's way. No going out to dinners or barbecuing together—they still lived in starkly different worlds—but greetings when they saw each other. Obligatory pleasantries that led to short, courteous chats that led to longer, more intricate chats.

The two women became closer. They talked about children, of course they did, given that some of Ruthie's children would have been in plain sight. Syra's mother would have told of her miscarriages. Ruthie would have smiled sympathetically, baby Elam on her hip, the twins, Jonas and Hannah, screeching exuberantly and running underfoot.

Then one of the women had put it out there, testing the waters. Probably as a joke.

Well, you're welcome to one of mine. (Haha)

Or…

I'll take one off your hands. (Haha)

But the "joke" took root. And then, one day, maybe when they were both hanging laundry outside to dry, or when Syra's mother had come over to buy fresh eggs or a bottle of unpasteurized cow's milk, it had been voiced.

Her mother would have put on her most ingratiating smile and said something like, *I know you weren't serious. Naturally, you weren't serious. But if you ever* were *serious…*

Ruthie would have been silent for a long time, contemplatively rubbing her protruding stomach. Eventually, she would have said something like, *That depends.* Or, *How serious would you like me to be?*

Or, *God works in mysterious ways.*

* * *

"WILL THEY LET you go to the funeral?" Syra asked. Jonas had pulled into the driveway, and they sat with the engine off.

"Hannah is going to talk to the bishop, but probably."

"What if he says no?"

"Then I won't go. I have to respect her choice to stay Amish, with the rules that it has. And I have to accept that I made a decision long ago that came with a certain price."

They grew quiet. Syra began to feel supremely uncomfortable with him, in the dark, intimate confines of the truck, his body turned towards her, one knee on the seat between them. She thought of a memory that, last night, had suddenly blasted past layers of forget, emerging from her subconscious. When she was eight years old, she'd had a retainer. A night retainer that had closed up a small gap in her front teeth.

"Syra," Jonas said, gently. She could tell by the tone of his voice that he was going to bring up their relationship, and she stiffened in apprehension. "I'm feeling things have changed and I don't know what's going on." He pulled one of her hands towards him. "Just tell me if I did something wrong."

"No, no. Nothing."

The words nearly choked her, the muscles in her throat coiled up tight. The slightly coarse texture of his skin, which she used to luxuriate in the feeling of, felt icky. She pulled her hand from his, practically ripping it away. "I don't think this is the right time," she said. "We both have a lot going on."

315

His sad, dejected gaze slinked past her towards the glove compartment. She hated that she was hurting him but had no idea how to stop doing so.

Today, with all of the distractions of Ruthie dying, she'd managed to mostly wall off one of the most distressing parts of her discovery—that she'd had erotic contact with her brother. She was eternally grateful that the contact had stopped before it went any further, thanks to Beulah interrupting things, but it had gone far enough. Waves of revulsion had pummeled her until she'd literally pictured shoving those feelings into a metal box and locking it.

"Syra?" Jonas asked.

"I need to return to Brooklyn tomorrow," she said in a monotone. "I'd meant to go yesterday but…"

"Sure, I understand." He sounded so forlorn that she was sickened with herself. "At least can I kiss you goodbye?"

"No!"

It was as if he'd jolted her with an electric prod. Jamming her hand into the door handle, she got the door open, and jumped to the ground as if trying to escape a madman. Hurrying around the other side of the vehicle, she saw Jonas had exited already. He blocked her path.

"What's going on? I don't understand."

"I've got to walk Buster!" she practically shrieked.

He got in her way again, holding her back with one arm. "Is this about your ex? Just tell me."

"What?" she asked, breathless and dazed.

"Your ex. What's his name…"

"What about him?"

"Are you—I don't know. Still in love with him or something?"

"Yes!" she screeched. "Yes, okay? We're back together."

The look on his face. She'd never forget it. She'd cut him in a way she had never cut a man. She would have preferred being the victim of this kind of cut than the perpetrator.

"You don't care that he slept with your friend," he said.

"It's not that I don't care. It's just that—he *explained*, and... I don't know! I need to give him another chance."

"When did all this happen? When we got back from dinner, you seemed friendly enough."

"It—before that. I called him."

"I thought you didn't remember his number."

"It came to me. So we talked. But I'd already agreed to go out with you and was confused. When we got back, I—I faked a stomachache. I needed to figure things out."

"And you figured them out."

"Yes."

His expression was skeptical, but his stance was mounting an increasing defense against her, subtly stiffening. "At dinner, you didn't act like you were with him. We kissed on the street. That didn't feel like the kiss of someone who'd already reconciled with her ex."

She winced, as if she'd bit into the sourest of

lemons. She couldn't help it. Good god, would he please not remind her of any of that?

"I was confused!"

"You know what I think? I think you used me."

"Used you? How exactly did I use you?"

"To make your ex jealous. Like Lydia used me for a baby. And my ex, Kelly. She only wanted a nice Amish boy to impress her religious parents. When she realized that wasn't me, she dumped me."

Syra shook her head, sternly. She couldn't have him believe this. The opposite was true. Everything she felt for him was so genuine that, in the light of her new understanding of their true relationship, her feelings had turned repugnant, unnatural.

"That isn't true at *all*, Jonas. I didn't *use* you." She chopped her hands at him, emphasizing every word. "I did like you. But I've been with Sam for five years. I've *got* to give it one more shot."

"Don't you think five years is enough time? Wouldn't you know by now if he was the one for you?"

Her mouth popped open to argue but she had nothing to say to that. Of course, he was right. Five years had been more than enough time. But Jonas had inadvertently handed her a lifeline and she was clinging to it. She needed to buy time, to sort all of this out in her head, to figure out what, if anything, to tell him.

Last night, she'd gone over and over everything. The basics: Lydia had said the New York couple had been staying next door to Ruthie and Ben Martin for the summer. Syra had been born in mid-August.

Jonas had said he and Hannah were four years old

when they spied the baby through a window. Syra was four years younger than he was.

Syra had hazel eyes. Not the twins' shade of muted green, but close enough.

And the thing that had surged through layers of her subconscious—the retainer closing up the small gap in her front teeth. That, most of all, had convinced her of her origins.

But there was still a chance all of this was coincidental. She'd once seen a documentary on doppelgangers, people who looked astonishingly alike but weren't related. Often, they had an uncannily long list of things in common—spouses with the same names, the same types of jobs, the same preferences in cars, clothes, or hobbies.

As she recalled, according to some sort of doppelganger expert, *all of us* have at least one dead ringer out there. The explanation was jaw-droppingly simple: Coincidence. Perhaps there was another Sarah Jane out there who had all of these attributes in common with Syra.

And then there was how much Jonas was even entitled to know about his mother. Whatever Syra told him, he'd share with Hannah. Pretty soon the whole community would know. Didn't Syra owe it to Ruthie to keep the woman's secret not only because she'd promised to do so, but as a thank you?

If Ruthie had given her up, Syra didn't fault her. The poor woman had been a baby machine for long enough. And Syra was glad she hadn't been raised in this environment, forced to leave school at 14 for gender-assigned menial labor, then expected to marry at a young age, her world confined to cooking, cleaning, and birthing babies. None of it aligned with her spirit and desires.

And there was Jonas himself. She didn't want to reveal what would be a catastrophic shock to him on a day when he'd suffered enough. Especially if whatever she confided wasn't the unmitigated truth.

Buster began barking from inside the house. Their voices had roused him. "Please," she said to Jonas. "I need to go walk the dog. Can—can we talk later?" She didn't want to talk later but needed an escape.

"Doesn't seem there's anything else to say," he returned. Without another word, he stalked down the long, sloping side yard towards his house.

She watched his broad silhouette vanish into the impenetrable dark and had the strong impulse to chase after him. The almost unstoppable urge to squeeze her arms around him, to comfort him.

But she didn't.

Chapter Forty-Six

She undressed, putting on her sleep shorts and one long-sleeved shirt. The weather was cooling, and the house seemed to tightly cling to every cold molecule.

This was her last night here. She was dead certain about that. She'd be up at the first flush of dawn, out the door, and would wait at the station for the first train to Penn Station.

Having to return to Sam and Catrina was a trivial thing. If Catrina had angry words for her stealing of Buster, fine, she'd take them and apologize.

She'd keep Sam calm and assure him that she wasn't going to bad mouth him to friends and family. Yes, she'd driven him away, she saw that now. Everything was her fault. She'd spout whatever bullshit she needed to so she could grab some belongings and head to a hotel, putting everything on her credit card, and dealing with the debt later.

None of that drama came close to *this* drama in her life. And it was *this* drama that took up her head space, kicking Sam and Catrina so thoroughly out of it that she didn't give one damn what the pair of them did for the rest of their sad, little lives.

In bed, she lay with the lamp on a dim setting, staring up at the ceiling. She didn't expect that she'd be able to sleep. Perhaps, if she was lucky, she'd drift off at some point and snatch a couple hours' worth.

How could she get her mother to tell her the truth? She'd have to catch her by surprise. Ask her mom to come to Brooklyn to help her move. They could go out to lunch and Syra could bring it up and watch her mother's face. No matter what her mom said, her expression would reveal the truth.

Perhaps her father was a better bet. He'd always been willing to admit various faults. She remembered years ago he'd decided to stop drinking alcohol. He'd been a moderate drinker as far as Syra could tell, but he'd said he felt like he was turning into an alcoholic, so he'd quit. Would he be willing to admit he'd paid for a baby that had been dangled before him and his wife?

She tossed around, legs under the quilt, legs over the quilt. Buster, on his favorite spot on the braided oval rug, kept lifting his head to look at her—she felt he was almost glaring at her, willing her to please stop tossing around so he could sleep.

DNA. How could she get DNA? She'd read that saliva was the best method of DNA testing, but how on earth would she get saliva from anyone? But thanks to

Catrina, of all people, she knew another method could be done.

Catrina had had a difficult childhood, with parents in a toxic relationship who repeatedly separated, then reunited. Because of this, Catrina had always had some doubt as to whether or not her father was her biological father. When Catrina's paternal grandfather died, she and her sister had walked into the funeral home, opened his casket and plucked out several strands of his hair by the roots with a pair of tweezers.

Catrina sent the hairs to a company that tested such things and received DNA confirmation that her father— via her paternal grandfather—was indeed her biological parent.

Syra would never forget Catrina telling this story. It was shortly after they'd met through mutual friends. Syra had gasped through the whole tale, not certain if Catrina, who'd had a few drinks, was bullshitting or highly embellishing. But throughout the years of their friendship, Catrina had always stuck to the story of her and her sister walking into the funeral home and stealing the hairs off their dead grandfather's head.

Syra figured getting hair from Ruthie would be too risky. The woman was likely already in a funeral home or coffin, or at the very least being watched over by members of the community.

She was supremely irritated with herself that she hadn't attempted to take hair when she'd been alone with the dying lady, but she'd been focused on telling her what she'd come to tell her. Then she'd gotten out of the room quickly, wanting to beat Jonas' return. Nor did she happen to have tweezers on her.

Wait. Could she get hair from Jonas? He had plenty of it.

Her mind began to twist and turn, meandering down various routes to retrieving a few strands of Jonas' shaggy locks. Did he use a hairbrush? He must. Where would he keep it? Could she sneak into his house? No doubt he didn't lock his door.

Or should she knock, ask to have a talk? Apologize for everything? During their talk, she could excuse herself to use the bathroom and search for a brush, but what if he kept it in the bedroom?

What if he wanted to kiss her? Should she allow that for the sake of trying to scrounge up DNA? Was it so *terrible* to kiss your brother if you didn't grow up with him? Syra grasped at the hair on her own scalp and yanked sharply, as if to pull that perverse thought out of her skull.

Then she bolted upright. The little girl. Beulah. She'd been right here. In the bedroom. Syra's eyes shot to the lone wooden chair that Beulah had sat in when she'd told her story.

Lala, Syra had said, *that's your grandmother's personal business. No one needs to know about it. Can you keep a secret? Do you promise?*

Yes, the girl had said, quietly, her feet dangling in their blocky black shoes right above the bumpy linoleum floor. *I can keep a secret.*

Syra threw the quilt back and got out of bed. She turned the two lamps to their brightest settings, grabbed the claw-like yellow and black flashlight, and dropped to the floor by the chair.

Inch by inch, she smoothed her fingers along the floor, the harsh beam staring down hard onto it. Two fingers of her left hand traced along carefully, searching for forensic evidence of the girl's presence. Beulah. Her niece. Maybe.

With as much hair as the girl had, with how her locks had been hanging down long and wavy out of their braids, there must be a strand laying around. There had to be. Several times, excitement jittered through her as the beam picked up what appeared to be a strand of hair. But when her fingers pushed it, it didn't move. A scratch on the floor.

Buster watched her, curiously following the movements of her fingers. Worried his clumsy paws would knock a strand to the side where she wouldn't find it, she called him out of the room, shut the door, and went back to searching.

* * *

THE LIGHT SHONE ON A LONG, pin-thin slash of dark color. Her fingers traced it, expecting it to be yet another scratch. But this time the thing moved. A hair. Again and again, she tried to lift it with her fingers, pinching it, but it wouldn't rise off the floor until she was able to grasp it between two fingernails.

Shining the flashlight directly on it, she saw it was not the curly texture of the hairs on her own head, but longer and straighter. It *had* to be a strand of Beulah's hair. With how fastidious the Amish were, there was no way this would be left over from the Yoder family.

Her stomach did a massive flip. A big part of her wanted to drop the hair. To never know. The other part of her was shaking with anticipation. Now she'd know. She'd know for certain.

Chapter Forty-Seven

*D*ownstairs, Buster started barking. He'd only bark if someone was approaching the house. He probably wouldn't bark if it was Jonas, but the dog could be in an irritated mood, being denied sleep, then booted out of the bedroom. Could it be Millie? It wasn't that late, not quite eleven p.m.

Syra's main priority was to not lose the hair, as she didn't know if she'd find another one. She had to get it somewhere safe but couldn't figure out how to do so in the bedroom. Anywhere she could think to put it—her tote bag, inside a dresser drawer—seemed like a gaping hole through which the hair would easily disappear forever. She needed to find a sealable plastic bag or container.

The kitchen. There had to be something suitable in a drawer or cabinet. And she'd figure out what was stirring up Buster.

Flashlight in one hand, strand of hair squeezed tightly in the fingers of her other, she moved through the pitch-dark hallway, then inched down the stairwell. With both hands occupied, she couldn't hold the railing. As soon as she got to the bottom, she no longer heard Buster barking.

"Bus?" she called. "Buster!"

Nothing. Fear brushed along the surface of her skin. Determined not to lose the strand of hair, she decided to look for something to secure it before searching for the dog.

Placing the flashlight on top of the kitchen counter, she opened different drawers. The third drawer contained dozens of plastic containers, the bottoms and their lids separated into mismatched piles. This wasn't going to be easy. She'd have to dig through the containers with one hand.

"Syra."

She screamed and jumped at the same time, whirling around to face the voice. She couldn't tell if the strand of hair was still pinched between her fingers, but she had the awful, despairing sense that her hand had opened and the strand had slipped away from her grasp.

The shadow in the middle of the room stepped closer and she recognized it.

Sam.

As he closed in on her, she was nailed to the spot. She remembered that when she'd come inside the house from the driveway, she'd locked that one door, but not the other two. She'd been upset and distracted by her exchange with Jonas, and had simply forgotten about it.

"I'm coming back tomorrow," she said, ludicrously, as if they'd been having a casual conversation about her schedule. "I'll give Buster to Catrina and we can figure out the apartment."

She already knew he cared nothing about any of that. A person doesn't travel to a different state and break into a house late at night to discuss such mundane matters.

"Too late," he said. The only illumination came from the flashlight, so his face had the same flat, eerie look that Beulah's had the night she'd sneaked upstairs. "You know who called me?" he continued. "Your mother. She had a few things to say. Know who else she called? *My* mother. And who else? Catrina."

Syra's gut was icy and twisting. She had no idea if he was telling the truth but he probably was. She wouldn't put it past her mother to get a few things off her chest with some outrage calls.

"I—I know nothing about that," she stammered. "But Sam, people were going to find out. Didn't you plan to tell your mother?"

"That's up to *me*. You tell *me* to keep my mouth shut, then you go tell your mother everything? And tell her *your* version? Why can't you keep your mouth under control, Syra?"

He continued to walk towards her. There was no more time to gauge what he was planning or how she could talk her way out of it. She turned the claw-like flashlight so the beam went directly into his eyes. He threw one arm up in a blocking motion.

"Shit," he spat.

The magnet holder full of knives was on the other side of the sink. She didn't think she'd be able to get to it without Sam getting to her first. Her goal was the kitchen door. Syra slid sideways, the endless kitchen counter at her back.

He waved his arm as if to brush away the flashlight's beam, then increased his pace towards her. The harsh beam directly in his eyes wasn't stopping him. She flicked the flashlight's lever and the room plunged into complete darkness.

"What the fuck!" he yelled.

She switched the flashlight into her other hand, flattened her palm on the counter and used it to guide her to the door. When she hit the end of the counter, she thrust her arm towards where she knew the door was located. He had left the inside wooden door open, so the blind groping of her hand landed on the handle of the screen door. She pushed it open and fled.

The moon sent enough silver light cascading down on the lawn that she could see where she was headed but it was a cloudy night and still very dark. Her mind was making a series of lightning-quick calculations about which way to run. To Jonas' little house? To the street? Into one of the cornfields? Into the barn?

Each one of these potential destinations came with its own set of rapid computations about whether it offered the best chance of survival.

She dashed in the direction of Jonas' house. While on the surface that might be the best bet—she knew Jonas was home, she knew he kept his doors unlocked—it was also a risky proposition because that side of the yard was dangerously dark.

Her ankle buckled sharply, and she tumbled to the

lawn, the flashlight knocked from her hand. She knew from the hard, round shape of the thing underfoot that she'd stepped on a walnut.

"Syra!" Sam called. "I just want to talk!"

Hands out in front of her, she crawled along the grass, trying to regain a sense of equilibrium. She pulled herself upright, but her ankle was aflame with pain, and she had to stagger with her right leg dragging behind her.

"Help!" she yelled but her voice didn't sound loud enough for what might travel all the way to Jonas.

Then she heard barking and growling, along with Sam's muffled cursing. Somewhere in the dark, it sounded as if Buster was attacking Sam. He must have earlier let the pug out of the house, which is why the dog had gone quiet.

Limping along, a sprawling dark mass rose before Syra. It came into focus as the corrugated tin roof and stacked piles of wood logs where Jonas spent much of his time. She limped around it and crouched down, trying to quiet her raspy breathing but unable to do so.

"Get the fuck off me!" she heard Sam shout. "Buster! Down! Fucking shit dog!"

She knew that her theory was true—little Buster was attacking him. *Good dog*. But she worried Sam might have a weapon and would hurt him. She limped to the side of the woodpile and peered around it, but she couldn't see either of them.

It was then her left hand knocked into something long, thin, and solid. It fell to the side. She turned and stared at it. The thing had been leaning against the woodpile, but now lay on the ground, its blade awash in gleaming moonlight.

The axe.

With both hands, she picked it up. It was heavier than expected. She had no idea how to hold it properly or if she could swing it with any degree of accuracy. But it felt good. For the first time, a sense of power, of rightness, coursed through her.

"Sam!" she called.

More growling from the dog, and more cursing from Sam. Then silence.

"Sam!" she tried again, tightening her grip on the axe, one hand directly under the blade, the other firm on the wooden handle.

"Where are you?" he shouted. "Stop playing these stupid games!"

"I told my mother how you fucked my best friend. Disgusting piece of trash! And I'm going to tell all your idiotic, moronic, shitty friends, too! And I'm going to plaster it all over social media! And tell anyone on the street who wants a good story!"

"You don't want to do that!" His tone was threatening not requesting.

"Why the hell not? You're the asshole here, not me!"

She heard nothing, and bent her knees in a readying stance. She sensed him. She knew him. He was stealthily moving closer to the woodpile. Finally, he said, in a pitch close to normal, "How come you never know when to shut up, Syra?"

Yes, he was directly behind the woodpile. She relaxed her knees, bounced a little, dug her bare feet deep into the soft, dewy grass. The pain in her ankle was gone.

"No, I don't know when to shut up," she said. "And I never will! Not with you!"

"You're a fool, Syra."

"I sure am. Over here!"

She stepped out from behind the woodpile. He was about thirty feet from her. Not far at all. Wearing dark clothes, blending with the night. But the moon had cooperated and emerged from the clouds, sending its beneficent light down to the yard.

A rush of wild, animal adrenaline propelled her, and she headed towards him with confident, determined strides.

Chapter Forty-Eight

*H*e collapsed like a string puppet. Crumpled like she'd crumpled in those thick, crackly cornstalks when he'd thumped her with his hard, cruel palm. He screamed, too. Screamed loudly and agonizingly.

She hadn't expected him to scream like that. When he did, she knew what she'd done was real and irreversible. But now he was only a stick figure on the ground. Lifeless as Ruthie Martin had been after she'd let out that last breath and failed to draw a new one.

She heard something, a rustle like boots crunching through leaves, and a kind of grunt. A man was standing behind her. He too stared at the stick figure on the ground. The man must have said something, but what, she didn't know. She also saw a little dog, running this way, then that way, and finally running up to her and sitting, panting. Its wrinkled folds of silver fur reflected the white moonlight.

"Jesus Christ in heaven," the man said.

He knelt down and was doing something to the stick figure. Holding its wrist in his hand. Then he bent farther and put his face up to the stick figure's face. "Syra, what—what—you killed him. God in heaven. You killed him."

She recognized the soft, twangy accent, and realized the man was Jonas.

Babbling sounds poured out of her mouth. Linguistic oddities that were close to language but not language. She slapped her free hand over her mouth to dam up this stream of warble.

Jonas came over and pried the axe out of her other hand. He had to peel her steel-clawed fingers back from the handle.

"Oh my God!" she howled into the night, up to the glowing moon.

"Syra, quiet, quiet," Jonas said, forcefully. He pulled her into him and she tearlessly wailed into his chest. She was shaking, adrenaline surging through every fiber. What had happened? How had it gotten to this point? Could she take it back?

"Syra," Jonas said. "Did you *want* to kill him?"

"I don't—I don't—" She tugged at his shirt with both hands, as if he was a mountain she was desperately trying to scale as a storm lashed around her. "Is—is he —definitely—"

"Yes, he's dead, he's definitely dead."

"I don't—I don't know what happened! I can't remember!"

"Syra." His voice was low, straining with a forced

patience. "You called him to you. I heard it. I saw it. You *called* him. You were… taunting him."

"I don't—why? Why? No. No!"

He pushed her away, pulled her up by her shoulders. Thrust his face right up into hers. "Listen to me. You have to listen. Shut up and listen!"

She was going into shock. She was shaking so badly that it seemed as if she was having a seizure.

"Listen!" Jonas barked. "He's got a phone. They'll trace it right here. And there's whatever car he hired. There's no escaping this. There's no getting rid of him."

She could only shake and wail uncontrollably. Still without any tears. Just a mob of horrible, inhuman howls streaming from her wide-open mouth. *Oh my god, oh my god, oh my god.*

"Syra! Stop! Goddamn it, shut up and listen to me!" He shook her harder. She wanted him to slap her. That might make her stop wailing, stop howling. But he didn't.

"Now listen. This will go a lot smoother if you leave it to me. He's your ex-boyfriend and he came here once before and assaulted you. Lala knows that. She saw him hurt you before. She can testify to that."

"I think—I don't—" She shook her head, clutched at his shirt, used his body as a brace or she would fall. How had it gotten to this point? Her life would never be the same. Never. The one life she had. She'd thrown it away.

"He came here again," Jonas said. "He chased you across the yard. I heard you screaming. I came out and he had you on the ground. He was trying to kill you. I grabbed the maul. I swung it at him."

"No, no…"

"Yes, I did. Syra, listen. Damn it, listen to me! I'm Amish, hear me? Or close enough. They know me. The police. They know my family. They know my people. It will go better, so much better if you let me handle it."

"I don't know why I did it. I don't know why. It just happened. Something took control of me."

"If you ever say that again, you're finished. I saw you. I heard you. You called him to you. You weren't defending yourself. You provoked him."

"But why? Why did I do it?"

"Because he's a piece of shit, that's why."

He pushed her away. Then he began bending and straightening, bending and straightening. She realized he was wiping down the handle of the axe with his shirt sleeve.

"I saw him on top of you," he continued, not looking at her. "He'd been here before. This time, he wasn't going to stop. He was furious you'd left him and were dating me. Are you listening? You need to remember all this."

Snot was oozing from her nose into her lips. She wiped it with the back of one arm and tried to stop her trembling but couldn't. Her teeth were chattering, clanking violently.

"My whole family saw you today," Jonas said. "They know you're my girlfriend." She watched as he deliberately put his palms and fingers all over the axe handle. "You were getting the dog and coming to my place when he found you in the yard. You yelled for help. I thought I saw a weapon. A knife at your throat. He's from the city, I assumed he'd have a weapon. It was so dark. I grabbed the maul. I defended your life."

Her spent lungs could no longer produce the dramatic assortment of sounds she'd been making. And through it all, her eyes had remained bone dry.

"Hair," she said, quietly, hoarsely.

"What?"

"Hair. He was already in the house. They'll find hair. Or fingerprints. Or footprints. They'll know he was in there. I'll have to say he found me in the house, not the yard."

They stared at each other.

"You weren't back with him, were you?" Jonas said. "That was a lie."

She said nothing.

"Because you love me. You were scared. Frightened of your feelings. Or was it because you were trying to protect me? You thought he'd come after me? You thought a good ex-Amish boy wouldn't fight for himself."

Now she smelled it. In the air. Metallic, tangy. Foreign and familiar at the same time. Faint, but she knew what it was. Blood.

He dropped the axe and encircled her with his big arms. She buckled, resting on his chest until her shaking subsided. Her pulse started to slow. Her uncontrollable trembling eased into a mild shudder that could have been caused by nothing more than the cool night air. Everything around her went from hazy and lost in the dark to ultra-crisp, defined in a way she'd never seen before, as if she'd swallowed a psychedelic.

She turned a little and peeked at the shadowy stick figure heaped on the ground. In the dark, the figure was nearly indistinguishable from the logs scattered nearby.

There was a way out of this. She could still have a life. There was so much truth in this alternate version Jonas was handing her. It was *almost* true, a mere degree or two away from the truth. It's what *would* have happened if she hadn't been a step ahead of Sam. It's what *would* have happened if she hadn't had enough of him, if he hadn't used up every ounce of her patience.

She didn't understand it now, her mind still too shattered with shock. But she'd understand it later. Later, it would be painfully clear, the not-so-subtle threat that Jonas would report to the police what he'd witnessed: That he'd seen Syra lure Sam to her.

You provoked him.

That Jonas knew, and he wholly understood, that Syra had slaughtered her ex-fiancé not because she was *forced* to but because she *wanted* to.

"I'll call the police if you're ready," Jonas said, his twang low and husky, his broad, muscular body barricading her from the world's dangers. The dangers that weren't him. "If you're ready to let me do the talking."

He was willing to take this fall. But for a woman. Not a sister. He could never love a sister enough to risk his own freedom, probably not even Hannah. After all, he'd left Hannah to venture into the world. But for a woman he loved, he'd take this fall. So Syra must remain a woman to him. Nothing more, nothing less.

And wasn't this where she belonged? Here, among this green and gold farmland, and these impeccably white farmhouses. Here, with these intractable people in their defiantly simple clothes and customs.

After her birth, she'd only been in this area for a few hours, or perhaps a few days. But it had been long enough for its sights, sounds, and smells to imprint on her cellularly, to brand her synapses with *home*. Before her birth, she'd lived inside an Amish woman for nine months. Heard nothing but an Amish woman's voice, consumed what she consumed, and was built out of her cells. Didn't that make her one of them?

If, one day, Beulah told her father what she knew about Ruthie Martin's secret, that was okay. Jonas didn't know anyone named Sarah Jane.

And he never would.

"Yes," she said, taking his hand into hers. "Call them. I'm ready."

Also by C.G. Twiles

Visit CGTwiles.com or Books2Read.com/CGTwiles
for all retailers. Please request at your local library.

About C.G. Twiles' most recent psychological
thriller, *The Perfect Face:*

"An out of this world thriller." —Liz Alterman,
author of *The Perfect Neighborhood*

Looks can be deceiving

Reporter Maddie is ecstatic to be on a picturesque Greek
island for her summer holiday. But then she meets a beautiful
12-year-old girl, Ruby, traveling with a woman claiming to be
her mother.

Soon, Maddie suspects the girl is being trafficked to a nearby
private island, one owned by the brilliant and reclusive
billionaire Dexter Hunt. To help the girl, she joins forces with
a local man and a rival reporter.

Maddie may have checked into the billionaire's notorious
island—but can she ever leave?

Other psychological thrillers by C.G. Twiles.

The Little Girl in the Window: A Psychological Thriller

At 14, Romy accidentally killed the town's beloved prom

queen, Misty. Years later, when a crisis forces her to return to the scene of the crime, a little girl with eerily blue eyes begins appearing in her window, taunting her. Who is she? And how does she seem to know Romy's darkest secret?

Brooklyn Gothic: A Modern Gothic Romantic Thriller

A young, idealistic reporter working in a Brooklyn Gothic mansion begins to suspect that her new boss—and lover—is keeping dark secrets. For fans of the Brontes, Daphne du Maurier, Darcy Coates, and Ruth Ware.

The Neighbors in Apartment 3D: A Domestic Suspense Novel

Cintra's compulsive lying has torn her family apart. But when she notices a chilling sign taped to her neighbors' door — "I'm being held" written in childish handwriting — she's determined to help the kidnapped boy, regardless of who believes her… —BookBub

The Last Star Standing: A Psychological Thriller

A forgotten talent show winner has a second chance at success. But first, she'll have to kill the runner-up.

How far will Piper go to save her family and reclaim her former glory?

The Ghost Wife: A short tale of suspense

Tabitha wants one thing for the holidays: For her family to face reality. And the reality is… she's dead.

So why are they acting like she's still alive?

Neighbors and Other Dangers: A Psychological Thriller Box Set

Three heart-pounding, up-all-night psychological thrillers in one economical box set: *The Neighbors in Apartment 3D, The Last Star Standing, and The Little Girl in the Window.*

About the Author

C.G. Twiles is the pseudonym for a longtime writer and reporter who has written for some of the world's largest magazines and newspapers.

She enjoys traveling, animals, old houses, ancient history, and cemeteries. She lives in Brooklyn.

Please find her on social media, she'd love to connect!

facebook.com/cgtwiles

instagram.com/cgtwiles

goodreads.com/cgtwiles

bookbub.com/profile/c-g-twiles

Acknowledgments

As always, profound thanks to my readers, especially those who take the time to write thoughtful reviews. You're the reason I write books.

This book couldn't have been written without Polly Kahl, who allowed me to bunk at her beautiful home in Berks County and drove me to all the Amish hangouts (Green Dragon!) and watched *Witness* with me again. So much gratitude to the Amish couple who hosted me and let me pick their brains. I'll never forget your hospitality and openness—as well as for Jonas the Amish kitten (@JonastheAmishKitten), who became an Instagram sensation and made my Amish journey so much more delightful (thank you to Anna and Greg for giving him such a fabulous home).

I remain eternally in debt to my emotional and technical support team: Megan Easley-Walsh, Liz Alterman, Christina McDonald, Finola Austin, Priya Malhotra, Judy Dutton, my mom, and everyone at Wide for the Win, Vellum Help, and JS Designs.